SEEK

Being the First Part of The Suffering of Solomon

By N. B. Goldzer

Martin Sisters Publishing

Published by
Martin Sisters Publishing, LLC
www. martinsisterspublishing. com
Copyright © 2013 Noah Goldzer
Martin Sisters Publishing, LLC, Kentucky.
ISBN: 978-1-62553-061-5
Editor: Tiffany Nichols
Printed in the United States of America
Martin Sisters Publishing, LLC

For my first readers, Connie and Dawn
My first generation, Alek & Genia
And my first hero, Mom

Prologue

June 8ᵗʰ, 2025, 1800 hours

Your mother picked you up thirty minutes ago. Another two days with you, my girls. To come: another five without. You know, some things about children are timeless. Others…not so much. Amidst dancing on the sofa to MTV and coloring the dog's nails, Rebecca turned to me with sternness and asked, "Daddy, what did you do to make you go to jail?" Samantha, you immediately turned off the screaming blond tweenagers and sat on the couch next to her. Now I had an audience. I'd thought about it so long, of what I would say when the question finally popped. I tried to remember all the speeches I had practiced, but my mind shot a blank. Rebecca, you actually had to tug on my vest just to remind me where the question had come from.

As a journalist, my instinct is to always write and speak the truth. Henry Anatole Grunwald, who was editor-in-chief of *Time Magazine* when Daddy was just a starry-eyed kid weeding through Grandpa's recycled magazines in Long Island, once said that Journalism can never be silent. "It must speak, and speak immediately while the echoes of wonder, the claims of triumph and the signs of horror are still in the air." Grunwald was the man who wrote *Time*'s editorial calling for Nixon to resign, though it was my own Alma Mater, *The Washington Post* and Woodward and Bernstein who broke the story. They were all my heroes. I'd seen the stiffness and defeat in Nixon's face throughout those taped interviews with David Frost only a few years before Tricky Dick's death. That was a strange time to get into that kind of thing, especially for a kid. Without context—the kind of context that comes from living through Watergate, through any scandal or atrocity—it's hard to give those names meaning. I could see him sweating, but I didn't understand why. The only memories I have of Richard Nixon are of his concession speech, his strained admission of guilt on those tapes, and his death, spoken of quickly by local newscasters on the five o'clock report before they switched to the more pressing matters of weather and traffic.

I tried first with the truth, with context, which you now know quite well. As a newsman I am a failure. I can no longer be taken on by serious organizations, those who remain from the newspaper days and still bother to keep reporters on retainer. My debts, and debts on loans to my debts, have piled up since prison, not to mention alimony and child support. If I thought about not telling the truth, this would be the context of why. But it's not the context of the truth and so, despite a feeling of obligation to embellish in front of you, I decided to go the Grunwald Route. I thought about flat out lying, don't get me wrong. "Daddy was innocent" or "sometimes bad things happen to good people" are both as often true as they are bullshit, but I didn't say those things. I told you, my Rebecca, a little twinkle in your eye, that Daddy stood up for what he believed in, and what he believed in was against the law. I hope you'll remember this talk one day.

Samantha, you were more suspicious of me with every weekend and snapped back something like, "Then why was it against the law?"

I sat down and told you the best I could just how it had happened, why, and that I wasn't proud but that it wasn't something that I should try to hide either. I wasn't about to get overly detailed with a twelve-year-old and a nine-year-old. Forgive me for that, but trust me when I say now that no important details were withheld due to your youth. And certainly by now, through your own initiative or this log you've learned all that I know about these events in my life. In our lives. I've held nothing back. When story time was over, and I'd felt satisfied giving my plea to the Hello Kitty jury, I took a deep breath and prepared for judgment.

Rebecca, you just shrugged, said, "Okay daddy," and ran after the dog. Samantha, I'll never forget your scoff. You turned back and went for the remote. I walked to the kitchen for a beer. Tomorrow you'll have woken up in your beds, breakfast will be waiting for you, your driver will take you to school where you're popular or unpopular and probably can't remember anymore anyway. Your stepfather will have driven you home on his way from the links. And you will not have spent one minute of the day thinking of me, your father, who will spend his entirety thinking of you.

I'll put in a couple blog entries. There are a few sites to edit and a *Law and Order* marathon on Wednesday, but there won't be a moment of that time in which I won't think, *What if it never happened?* And would I do it again? How strong are my principles? All that I lost and how little I gained—debt, my record, my daughters. Should I have just let it go? I honestly don't know. Maybe, when you're old enough, when I'm old enough, or if I haven't explained by then, if I'm too sick, or dead, if the obituary isn't kind or too short or covered by flashing ads for singles dating on the side of your newsfeed dashboards, maybe this will be able to tell you what dignity really is and how much trouble it can really get you in. Maybe by then it'll be too late. I hope this finds an answer and reaches you in time.

Seek Solomon

June 15ᵗʰ, 2025, 1630 hours

Came home to find another delinquency payment taped to my door. They used to find their way under the windshield wipers of my car, but then the IRS took my car, so they've had to settle for the door. Maybe when they take that, they'll have to wait till I come home and stick them to my forehead. And what happens when they take that?

At this rate, I'm falling deeper into debt than I was in prison. I popped open the fridge and threw the notice in when I saw it contained no beer. The cable still worked, if you can call PBS cable. They were airing a special on Joe Louis, one of those one-hour spots where they remind us of someone we're too lazy or introverted to remember. I was surprised to find out that Joe, the Brown Bomber (gotta love old school racism), also had his run-ins with these paper-cut leeches. So I started taking notes. Here's what I came up with:

A fighter all his life, Louis was one of the longest reigning champions since they put down liquor and picked up gloves, defending his belt (and his honor) twenty-five times. This was at a time when gambling had all but eaten the sport alive. When the war came—that's

World War II—he donated money to the cause, fought to entertain the troops, and eventually enlisted. There's very little in the production about his time in the war. Maybe it's hush-hush, maybe boring, lost to history. But it ends strong.

When he'd come out of the war, after being called a nigger and letting the army squander his prizes, the IRS came for him too. And what did he do? He fought, that's what. After giving the Nazis whatfor, he got right back in the ring and fought some more, winning prize after prize, an American war hero, just to pay off the buzzards who squandered his winnings in the first place. He died young and broke, and I may have kicked the TV over near the end of the program. Guess I can save money on that too. Now you know why there was no more MTV at Daddy's house.

Seek Solomon

June 20th, 2025, 2200 hours

Opened my inbox today and came across something extraordinary. Amid the motley of digital crap sent to me by the IRS and West African princes was an email from my old friend Hiri at the Post. I haven't been able to publish under my own name since going under, so every now and then, when he gets wind of something worthwhile, Hiri sends it my way, lets me ghostwrite it, and publishes it as his own, passing me the commission. I think he feels as if he owes me a livelihood, and maybe he's right, but I'd never hold it against him if he didn't.

I opened a new tab and ran a wiki search for San Magnus but came up with nothing. Well, not nothing. There were some sites in Italian with pictures of old churches in Tuscany and a medieval portrait of a sour-looking friar that had been sewn together like a Picasso reject, but "San Magnus Island" came up empty. Looked up the coordinates on Google Earth but again, nothing but blue. It's simply not there. Hiroto has never steered me wrong before—not in twenty years, not in prison, not in the war, not ever. We all have our share of flaky sources, "stepping stones" we call them, not sturdy enough to stand on but enough to get you where you're goin'. Hiroto's no stepping stone, and this has the potential to be real history, real truth, Grunwald stuff that's more than conspiracy, more than just a wild goose chase, chock-full of cheap tricks to get a few dozen nerds' rocks off in blogspace. I was a real journalist once, and Internet willing, I will be again.

I had already heard of Dr. Metzger, "the Butcher of Belzec," and his Wikipedia search proved far more promising. Born in 1902 to Otmar and Maria Metzger, Gerhardt Konig Metzger was a popular physician in his hometown of Hohenberg, Austria. He earned double doctorates from the Universities of Vienna and Frankfurt, where he studied "Racial Hygiene." When the Nazis came to power, they approached him as a spokesperson for the science behind their views on Aryan superiority. He rose quickly in their ranks, married Mathilda Kirsch, a lesser-known German actress (with a much smaller wiki page) who starred in a few propaganda films and never bore him any children. Then, when Hitler began his mass extermination, Herr Metzger was assigned to the death camp at Belzec in southern Poland.

The image search for Belzec isn't pretty. If they weren't in black and white, I'd have vomited all over my view-screen. Aside from the mass graves and mutilations are evidence photos of his personal experiments. They're simply ghoulish. Wiki says he experimented with blood and organ transfusion, using healthy organs from Jewish prisoners to perform transplants for German soldiers. The result could have been a theoretically unstoppable army, though I can't imagine it was too popular with the racial purists he worked for.

The image search for Metzger himself doesn't reveal quite as much. A typical proto-man—dark hair, dark eyes, maybe six feet tall, complete with dark bushy eyebrows and one of those long mustaches like you see in old French detective serials. There was one thing, explained by Wiki, that made him stand out: a long scar running from the side of his cheek down his neck and disappearing behind the brown of his Wehrmacht uniform. He'd apparently been sliced in his first week as camp physician by a prisoner. The placid, tempered expression in the picture spoke for his resolve in whatever happened to that poor man, woman, or child.

There's a second link to a group called the Vorkämpfer (the

9

Pioneers). Run by Metzger, it was a collection of doctors like him, sort of like a clinic club from various camps, bent on exploiting the morally empty tactics of Hitler's Germany to further the science of genetics, which was just then coming to fruition. There were none of the gruesome lampshades made of human skin—no, these guys were testing the limits of what a person could endure, sticking them with diseases and then racing to slow the illness, timing their life spans. There might have been a second breakout of the bubonic plague if Belzec had been a work camp.

It didn't last very long. By '45, the Russians came rolling in from the East, handkerchiefs in hand, burning and raping what was left of Poland as the Nazis ran back to Germany. This is sixty-nine and seventy-three years respectively before you were born. I don't know as much about my grandparents' (your great-grandparents you never got to know) story as I should, or would like to. What I remember from what little they'd say whenever I'd poke and prod, was that they were the only Shlomowitzs' to make it out of Poland alive. Who knows how big our family might have been?

When the Nazis had cleared out, Metzger wasn't among the captured or killed. He wasn't found in Belzec, later in Berlin, or later still at his summer home in Austria. He wasn't found at all. He's been missing, assumed dead, for eighty years. My money is on dead. Also missing from Poland was the royal casket, a four-hundred-year-old coffin filled with the valuables of thirteen Polish Royals, and another eighty pieces of gold, silver, art, and jewelry. I would call them priceless for literary effect if they hadn't been estimated at six billion U.S. God, Hiroto, I don't know how you came up with this, but you'd better be right. The hunt for war criminals went on for decades, but Metzger was never found. Neither were Jung, Vogel, or Ebersbach, Ph.D, M.D, D.M.D, all colleagues of Metzger, all Vorkämpfer.

According to Hiroto's message, Metzger became another one of those psychos like Mengele, Rudel, Eichmann, who fled to South America, only he was never caught. They're all dead now. There's hardly a soul alive who remembers the horrors of Auschwitz, Treblinka, or Belzec. My own grandparents were at Dachau, in the heart of the Nazi hate machine. One of the few things they'd say about Dachau was that there my grandfather had met Georges Charpak, who, before he died fifteen years ago (two years before my bubbie and five years after my zayde), won the Nobel prize for physics. Electric currents and ionizing radiation and other things an English major has no business talking about.

They had a great reverence for their American liberators, my grandparents, hence my parents' citizenship, mine, and now yours. It's why your name is Solomon instead of Shlomowitz, and why your eyes are hazel instead of blue, like my grandmother's. It was she who rocked you in her arms the night after you were born, Samantha, the night of that awful hurricane. You remember her smell, I know, from that day before I went away. Your mother brought you over when I was packing, and your grandfather tried to give me bubbie's old roll-top desk. You said it smelled like soup and musk and it reminded you of a hospital.

America, for the most part, has forgotten the Nazi, that most dastardly foe of modern history whose destruction fueled American ascension to the tumultuous and waning status of world superpower. Aside from Godwin's Law, a couple of late-night documentaries, and the last teeth-grinding old Jews who themselves had not yet been born to see the horrors "we shall never forget," we have indeed forgotten. The vomit in my throat at the sight of Belzec's image search attests for that. It is a shame, and I have no idea how long it will be, if ever, when you, the fourth generation, develop some concept of anti-Semitism, concentration camps, genocide... These things have no bearing in your lives, no context, no relevance to Twitter or nail polish, soccer games and sleepovers. It's like it happened in another world, to other people, not to the woman you once spit up on and picture whenever it's chicken soup night. Not to your own flesh and blood less than a century ago.

And so I'm going to do the stupid thing, if just for a chance to give peace to those few and myself, to remind the many who've forgotten, and to put a couple more lines at the bottom of Herr Metzger's Wiki page, under headline: aftermath. If that were all, this would be worth it. These men...they haven't escaped history. They haven't escaped me. Uncovering the truth, finding out how long and where and how Metzger and the others were able to avoid capture, is incentive enough to find them, never mind the six billion other incentives. It's about time for another foolhardy manhunt.

According to Hiroto, San Magnus lies about seventy-five miles off the coast of Argentina and was only ever mentioned once, on a map from the 1910s. Seems to be one of those tiny blips, inconsequential and remote, that the Spanish and Portuguese named in a hurry as they rushed over to carve up the continent. But I can't find a single source that even says they landed there. There are no ports or drawings of the island itself, nothing visual to indicate it's really there at all. But Saint Magnus himself, the lucky long-dead martyr they picked out of a big metal hat, was Albertus Magnus, patron saint of medicine. If that isn't an uncanny coincidence, then let me come back empty-handed. Or let me come ashore on the tropical retreat of the good doctor and his cadre of murderers and warmongers.

It's entirely ridiculous, but I want so hard to believe it could be anything more than desperate conspiracy theories camouflaged as a convenient history lesson. And if it's true—and Hiroto has never been wrong before—it might be my second chance to do something great, to expose real evil, and to lay to rest the thousands of dead left unavenged. Standing on the shore with a shovel in my hand, an unmarked Nazi grave, and a hundred pounds of gold at my feet, the IRS won't be able to take enough. I'll chuckle and think about Max Schmeling, Hitler's invincible warrior, knocked out in the first round by Joe Louis just before the war broke out. Schmeling, who paid for Joe's burial fees. That's the least Metzger can do for me.

I spent the night packing, choosing carefully. Getting there comes secondary to not being seen getting there. One does not simply row into Mordor... I can't imagine there will be too much trouble on arrival, though. Hiroto's message says he'll be waiting in a small hostel off the Boulevard Caprico in a town called Mar de Sur, about four hundred miles south of Buenos Aries. San Magnus, he says, is someplace east of that little hamlet in that great blue abyss, the Atlantic.

If he's right about the bodies, I'm bringing synthesizers and a camera. If he's right about the treasure, maybe I should bring a couple of duffle bags... I want to comb every inch of that island. I'm deactivating the heat, the electricity and maybe your mother will look after the dog until I come back. Maybe I'll use the extra cash to buy a few drinks on the beaches of Argentina. It's about time I had myself a tropical vacation.

Girls, I'll see you next weekend. Wish Daddy a good trip.

Seek Solomon

June 24ᵗʰ 2025, 0930 hours

If it weren't for the cold keeping my gag reflex down, I'd erupt like Mt. Puyehue. It's absolutely freezing here. My tablet says the temperature is forty-five inland, forty on the coast, and thirty-two here in this shabby motor-powered skiff. It's half painted, patched with duct tape on the bow side (at least I think that's the bow side), and it reeks of shark guts and dogfish. It's one of those old boats, still has sails because the motor is as decrepit as the fishmonger we rented it from. Despite all that, my new companion assures me that he'll reach San Magnus without getting us stranded halfway there. It almost makes me miss Afghan sand.

My plane landed two days ago in Ezeiza International, the same airport where the Peronists stepped off their flight from Spain and began firing indiscriminately into the crowd. I wasn't even a fetus when it probably never hit the news in the States. I decided to take the highway down the coast rather than another little plane, just a few rolls of cheap adhesive from being this dinghy's winged stepsister. Whenever I travel I like to take the bus. Anonymity gives me time to think and to write, and the enclosure makes me feel like I'm still in the culture, even if the other passengers are clearly Canadians, Swedes, or well-to-do Argentinian men with connections in Canada or Sweden.

The bus ride itself was twice as rough as the Atlantic but smelled half as bad. A company called Omnilineas ran twenty-year-old buses with those fuzzy gray seats and the ten-inch TV screens playing your choice; either the virtual tour of all the places we were driving by, or the local soap opera, which was twice as culturally educating. My eyes were on any eyes that were on me. The whole way down—and ever since—I'd been mindful of any possible leaks in information. Could someone have been watching us like we used to watch them? Nothing arose, so I took out my touch pen and drew a little digital sketch of the man sitting three seats in front of me.

He was dark-skinned; his face was wide and his forehead narrow. He rode his armrest a llama's saddle, tense and tight. And I thought to myself that maybe one day, after I'd retired and you had all grown up and gone off to college, I'd come back here and do a piece on that man and the life he's living now in our twenty-first century. The idea didn't stick too long in my head before I fought it, rationalizing, *What good is a piece on people caught in the past written for people living in the future?* The historian in me was assured of the noble goal but the rest of me... I couldn't quite justify the context. And then I thought, *Well, if he was Jewish and a Holocaust survivor, you wouldn't hesitate,* and as it turns out I'm a hypocrite. But I'd be more than happy to let the internal debate languish on for years at a time while sipping drinks on the beaches of tropical South America.

Which, I'm certain, was part of the appeal to our good Dr. Metzger and his team of fun-in-the-sun-loving jackboot, lab-rats I'm now dead set on uncovering. After the bus stopped in Mar Del Plata, I took another, and then a cab to Mar Del Sur, just in time for an early happy hour at the San Telmo, a dusty little bar with those little swinging saloon doors I used to see in the movies. You'll see them in the history books. Hiri's message said he'd be staying upstairs and that he'd meet me in the bar that night. He never showed. I hung around for a while, got laughed at when I asked for tequila, and ordered a less amusing Rolling Rock Red instead. After a couple of hours, with the sun fading over the other side of the continent, a man in a cowboy hat sat down next to me.

He asked, or rather stated, "You're an American?"

So was he. And then the bad news. "Mr. Ota," he said, had already left for the island, "couldn't wait," and would "meet me on the other side." The man told me he'd left for the island two days ago and that "Mr. Ota" had asked him to meet me at the bar instead. That certainly

14

did sound like Hiri, and I said so. Damn well if he was going to let a real journalist get there first, that little hacker. I think at that point, maybe after a few more beers, I tried talking the man into taking us out that night. I got a little impetuous, and he tried calming me down, saying we'd freeze to death if we left at dark.

Freeze—*ha*. It's freezing now, and I've got the sun in my eyes. He introduced himself with another round, saying as he tried to hide his Texan accent that he was Chuck Polanski, Hiri's South American connection, the man who had confirmed Hiri's story in the first place. He's a pretty big guy, maybe six-foot-four, bald, goatee, stands out quite a bit from your average five-foot-five Argentinian, and built well too. Too well to be a paper boy. I remember thinking he talked like he was a former something-or-other, probably a Marine stationed in the region who liked cheap liquor and small women too much to go home. His eloquent Spanish spoke for that, though it may have been less than I imagine. In fact, it could have been Portuguese after the fourth round.

I do remember grilling him pretty hard over his credentials, what he knew about Hiroto, the island, and me, to see if he could be trusted. Many a reporter has been bribed by a few well-timed drinks. But I also remember being satisfied with his answers. His Hiroto sounded like my Hiroto, despite the fact that he called him by his surname—which no one does—and he even knew the names of the man's mother and sister, who are undoubtedly glad to be rid of him for however long this adventure of ours will last. So we celebrated our future discovery for a while, which he assured me would be on the island. That was when he claimed something fascinating. Some of the older locals nearby, he said, had been child workers on the island, and one or two of them apparently remembered a tall man with glasses and a scar on his neck, a man fitting Metzger's description.

In the morning, with a massive hangover, I'd asked him if I could re-canvas the men he had talked to about construction on San Magnus. He suggested that if we wanted to meet up with Hiri, we'd best leave first thing. I agreed but, determined not to be suckered, ran into his hotel room and spewed into his toilet. The issue was closed. Mr. Polanski and I took a cab further inland, to a quaint little place called

San Jose de Balcarce. The town looked old but new-old, like it had been one of the first places around to experiment with cement and plaster in five hundred years. De Balcarce held a certain attractive contradiction, resembling those Gothic Spanish cathedrals you find around Madrid but built like your average suburban shopping mall. As we headed into a social club, the Vista de Balcarce, Chuck assured me he'd do the talking. I assured him that my Spanish hadn't improved since high school and that he'd have to. He translated as we sat with a man in the back smoking a home-rolled cigarette. He looked an awful lot like the man on the bus I'd spotted the morning prior.

He greeted us warmly enough and had obviously talked to this hard-to-miss statue of American curiosity before. Mr. Polanski said his name was Santino. I started in with the questions.

"How old were you when you went to the island?"

Chuck translated, telling me that he was nine when he worked with his father putting down foundation for a villa on the island, that his father had put down a similar foundation in that very club.

"Fundación cemento?" I asked.

"Si," he confirmed, running off on a tangent about how they were the only buildings that had withstood some storm from fifty years ago but that they were hot as all hell in the summertime. Lucky for us it was winter.

"How many others were there on San Magnus?"

Mr. Polanski asked him, and the man immediately sunk in his chair and began to tear. He tried to roll another slip of flax, but his hand shook so hard he spilled the tobacco all over himself. I looked him in the face and reached out to calm his hand, took the grinds and, remembering the way my father had done it, rolled them myself. The old man wiped his eyes as he watched me, sat up, nodded, and answered. I passed him back his cigarette and listened, his response coming from the American twang to my right. He said there had been at least a hundred others working on the island, from all over the country. He'd met an older girl from down south in Patagonia; she brought them water and wet towels to wipe their heads. He said that when they were done working, his father would put him on a boat to head back to the mainland with some other children.. One day the boats stopped coming. Santino never saw his father again.

"Y ninguna de las mujeres." And none of the women or girls either.

As we were paying our respects and leaving, he muttered sharply, "San Magnus," and took a long, solemn drag. Satisfied, we returned to our hotel and laid plans for early the next morning. Surely by now Hiri had found out all the juicy material and was simply waiting for a decent writer to come along and make a story out of it. We laughed that he'd be sitting on a trunk full of golden trinkets in the lobby of some abandoned villa resort, sipping on nineteenth-century French chardonnay, discussing firewalls and encryption algorithms with the toucans. Assuming there wouldn't be a live power source left on the island, he suggested I use what little juice I had left in the tablet as best I could. My Kindle has more battery life than the energizer bunny, but I keep it on eighteen hours a day and it's an ancient model. Reception would also be nonexistent, which is why we hadn't gotten a call from the front desk claiming a crazy-sounding Asian man was on the line, rambling on about the El Dorado of the Carpathian Mountains.

And so here we are, in this Datsun of a floating devise, as Fitzgerald wrote, "beat[ing] on, boats against the current, borne back ceaselessly into the past." A few more nautical miles and we'll have washed up onto a time machine, a place hardly touched or seen by any man not speaking German, or now XML, in nearly a century. Awaiting? Tragedy. Horror maybe. A retreat for some of the worst monsters I've ever hunted, far too old for capture, but never too late for exposure. I shake a little more in this rocky dinghy, thinking of all the skeletons we're going to find, literal and otherwise. There could be streets filled with bodies there—and who knows whose—washed in from the shore or floating all around. The anticipation kills me. I think I might need to vomit again.

Seek Solomon

June 24th, 2025 1045 hours

San Magnus has one of the most beautiful beaches I've ever seen. Postcard beautiful. It's winter, and cold, but even the poles prove unable to bathe these sands in gray. It's white-gold, not like the pale yellow grains of the Sistan Basin back overseas or the nickel-colored beaches we have on Long Island or in Jersey. It's by far the prettiest piece of property ever occupied by the Third Reich, and likely the last.

We pulled our skiff ashore on the north side of the island, having found the docks sunken and being slowly eaten away by the brightly colored orange coral. Up the beach you can see the outline of what must be the villa. There's a tower to the south...a lighthouse maybe? Looks more like the guard tower of a prison or a death camp.

I plan on turning this off until we make our first big discovery. We're not likely to find any three-prong outlets on the island. But I do want my first impressions to be recorded, and they are that San Magnus, last great secret of the Evil Nazi Empire, pleasure paradise of the fugitives of the modern world, is a truly gorgeous place, from the beach at least. And this is its first, possibly gravest terrible reality, that this place of hidden corruption could be so lovely, and that had it not been for Metzger, I would never have found it. Could it have been like any other resort, just as pleasant to the eye had the Swastika not washed up ashore? Would there be a resort built on it without them? Then again, would there be that tall watchful tower to gaze over it?

Under different circumstances I might have liked to take you here, lie out till my pasty skin tanned brown, and watch you running along the beach, building little sandcastles. Let you bury me in the sand. Do you remember the summer we took the car to Florida, to Disney World, Minnie and Mickey Mouse, and the old woman stuck with tubes, dying in that hospital bed in Fort Lauderdale? I'm tempted to say this vacation would be just as melancholy. All in the shadow of that tower. We're going to unpack the supplies from the boat and move out as soon as Chuck finishes tying her ashore. I wouldn't be surprised if Hiri was sitting up in that place watching us like ants in the sand right now. Haha, ants in the sand. If I have time, I'll draw out a sketch of the island with the touch pen and document where we find what. Well, here we go, my next great manhu

ERROR REPORT 5061

Please restart your device.

Act I:

The Pursuit of Happiness

Chapter I

Stephen Solomon awoke to the sound of thunder and a thousand thuds crashing above him. The pain in the back of his skull throbbed to the fast-paced beating in his chest, but massaging the flaky spot with his fingers revealed the blood to be dry. *How long have I been out?* He put his other hand on the floor and achingly pushed himself up. Looking around, Seek couldn't find a hint of the beautiful golden sand he'd sunk his feet into upon coming ashore on the island. Still dazed, he made out what looked like a gigantic clock standing before him, its hands frozen and stoic. On his feet, Seek turned around, facing another ten-foot tall, unwavering timepiece. Through its fuzzy glass he gazed toward the beach, bathed in a heavy downpour, as the sun was slowly consumed by a storm invading from the West. His fingernails rattled against the glass, and when he squinted to make out the street below, he was shaken as lightning crashed in the hills behind him.

It was the shake, or the chill that followed, raising the little hairs on his neck and chin that drew his attention to the protrusion, an abnormality, like an oblong iron splinter in his throat—a metallic Adam's apple just a centimeter shy of his actual one. It too was dried and scabbed over. Seek wiped down a thick wall of dust from the glass pane on the west-facing clock. The force of the sneeze that followed sent a flame down his throat and nicked the object. In the dripping, clear mirror reflection he saw it, a small medical tablet-shaped object in a clump of varicose veins wrapped around his jugular.

"Jesus," he whispered, each syllable a match struck against his voice box. "What the hell is this?"

"It's your new friend," screeched a voice from the corner of the room. Seek turned quickly but saw no one. The clock tower was barren, filled only with boroughs of cobwebs and a few of his belongings scattered about. "Here," the voice said again. Solomon flipped his coat and hat off the floor. Under the dry heap of his jacket he found his glasses, which he clamped back to his ears. As he picked up his CU Lions baseball cap, a small hands-free cell receiver fell from the brim.

"Find it? Put it in your ear."

Solomon picked it up hesitantly, spotted a small stool near the door and squatted over it, arching forward and tapping his feet on the mold-ridden wooden planks of the clock tower. "Who are you?"

"Have some patience, Mr. Solomon," snapped the voice, a high-pitched spit riding static into his ear, a sound more robotic than man.

"You're hiding your voice?"

"And much more. I've hidden something in your neck. I see you're sitting. Good."

As the voice rattled on, another somber chill ran over Solomon's skin, and he darted up to gaze wildly though the clock windowpane. *He can see me.*

"Sit back down, Mr. Solomon," the bluetooth barked. Solomon did as he was told and listened, scanning the island in a frantic panic all the while. "Yes, I can see you. No, you can't see me. I hope it doesn't hurt too much, my little pill. It's insurance, a quaint device I've come across in my travels, a sort of shock collar for really big dogs. On your side is the fuse, pinned to a one-sixteenth gram of polymer-bonded explosive. That's RDX embedded with a little thermocole and just a pinch of dioctyl phthalate. It's all just a little complicated. And it's all just a millimeter from your jugular vein."

Seek ran his index finger around the protrusion.

"On my side is the remote. That's not complicated. One button, one explosion. Try to take it out on your own, it goes boom. Try to disable it, it goes boom. Disobey, refuse, try to escape, that little plug will explode and take your throat out with it! You'll be dead in under sixty seconds. Do you understand?"

Solomon nodded.

"Good," replied the voice. "You're here for a story, Mr. Solomon, and if you do what I say, I'll let you leave with one. Simple. And this is what I want. To the east of you, in the cliffs overlooking the ocean, is the Kapitalzukunft, and in the bottom of the Kapitalzukunft is the vault of the Kapitalzukunft. I want what's in that vault. You are going to get it for me."

"The Kapital…zukunft?" Seek asked.

"Surely you came to San Magnus knowing full well of its…teutonic travelers. They had it built in the rock face, so it's impenetrable to anything short of a hydrogen bomb. Kapitalzukunft. It means Future Capital, or Capital of the Future. You're going in there."

"What is it you want in there?"

"Don't play stupid, Mr. Solomon. You know damned well what's sitting in that vault. I suggest you not waste any more of your own time. That implant may not be time sensitive but the island's inhabitants are, meaning you only have an hour left of light in the storm, and I wouldn't be in that clock tower when it's gone."

Seek started to panic, running to the windowpane to see nature's hourglass slipping away behind her bushy red clouds.

"Across the plaza is a small townhouse with a large red blotch on the door. Go there and find your friend Mr. Polanski. He's tied up in the basement. Don't take too long, or you'll have to spend the night. The clock is ticking. Press 'send' when there's two of you."

The wireless clicked as it went silent. Seek quickly threw it in his pocket, pulled his cap over his head, grabbed his coat, and bolted for the door. As he turned he noticed a shiny black reflection on the floor, his Kindle tablet computer, a great big crack down the center of its screen. It was still on. He scooped it up and woke it from hibernation, skipping over steps in rapid succession as he descended the tower staircase. The tablet's small battery image flashed low. He turned it off and tossed it into his pocket with the hands-free.

As he raced down the winding staircase, Seek kicked up a whirlpool of dust, whipping up from the gray slab steps. If it weren't for the adrenaline, he'd have walked right over the body at the bottom of the stairs. Instead, he tripped across its boots, falling face-to-face with a pair of bare, skeletal eye-sockets. The gash in the back of his head screamed with another crash of thunder echoing from outside. Lying on the ground at the bottom of the stairs, he looked the body over, skinless, bloodless, toting a black ragged field blouse and trousers.

23

It wore a small golden swastika on a patch where its heart had once been.

Seek kicked through the door and fell over himself into a small puddle along the sides of the walk between the clock tower and the turquoise cobblestone street. Drenched and staggering to his feet, he made for the center of the plaza and jumped onto its corroded fountain. He held tightly around its small copper boy statue holding its torch high, staring up into the night's sky. Rain poured down Solomon's face and clinked against his glasses like so many coins tossed into the fountain. Past the clock tower in the distance lay the fortress the voice had spoken of, the Kapitalzukunft, invincible cradle of the Nazi Intelligentsia. Seek was breathing heavily and spoke softly, if only to hear something familiar. "It's real. It's all real."

He looked down to itch the throbbing blue protrusion in his neck and saw something shining back at him from the murky brown water at his boots. He sunk his hand in, scraping the sides of the fountain and came up with a small, minted trinket, a silver Reichsmark. Solomon closed his fist tightly on it, repeated, "It's real," and slipped the coin into his adjacent empty pocket. His wallet, with his ID, was missing. "That's how," he scoffed, gazing at the tower overlooking San Magnus Island. "That was definitely not Hiroto."

Solomon scanned the houses in the villa for a painted mark. They all looked the same, built in royal fashion but in a royal hurry, red ceramic shingles cracked and lining the ground in front of them. If they had been painted, the color would have peeled in droves following what could have been a hundred Argentinian summers. *How long has this been here?* There! A red swab over the doorframe of the center house, its windows boarded, fortified, and out of place. He shook the handle violently, but his wet hands slipped. It wouldn't budge. On the ground before him lay a small wicker rug. "You've got to be kidding me," he spat, kicking it aside and grabbing the key.

The house sulked in black. The dying light from outside could hardly seep through the cracks of its windows, blocked with the remains of furniture and varied strips of wood. Solomon wiped his glasses free of the rain and ran his hands along the wall in search of a

24

switch. Finding it dead, he continued along until he stumbled into the kitchen. He ran his hands over a countertop until he felt a circular metal design. Seek quickly found the gas burner that flickered to life with a flip of his wrist. With the flame he could make out an old icebox in the corner and ebony or onyx handles on the sink and drawers.

He looked around for a tool or a rolling pin before settling on the long-nosed rusted sink faucet. He grabbed it by the head and tugged it over and over again. *Come on, come on.* He could see the orange sunlight pulling away behind the wooden bars of the kitchen window. "Come on!" Seek jumped and lay on the counter, driving his foot through the base of the faucet, breaking it off in his hand. A third shooting pain drove up from his heel. He dropped back onto the floor, grabbed an old dishtowel from a dusty black cabinet handle, stuck it into the broken end of the faucet, and pushed himself up against the oven to run the towel over the burner.

With a controlled fire above his head, Seek made his way through the open living room and down the back staircase that led to the basement. He slid down slowly, fearful of another body at the bottom and hoping heartily that it would not be Chuck's. The narrow gap opened as he stepped onto cold, dank cement, water still dripping from his jacket. With the torch light out in front, he could make out vines creeping through the ceiling panels, spilling patches of dirt on the floor. And then the smell. Sweat. Seek held his flame bearer tightly, spotting the outline of a man in the corner, curled and wiggling. Chuck had been tied up, hands behind his back, tape over his mouth. As Solomon circled over to him and moved to pull the tape off, he saw Chuck's eyes, dark and petrified as the flame burned in their reflection. Chuck motioned down with his head, down to his chest or neck. Solomon couldn't know. Holding the torch closer, he ran his finger over his friend's neck, down to the bright blue veins wrapped around what looked like a pill in his throat.

Chapter II

Solomon ripped the tape off his companion's mouth and quickly replaced it with his hand.

"Shhh, don't talk yet," he whispered, taking the hands-free out of his pocket and holding it up between them. Solomon pressed the call button. "We're both here." Chuck remained silent, but his pale expression spoke volumes. They stared at each other for a moment, the burning dishtowel displaying each to the other's horror. That moment seemed to last forever, in the darkness, hiding from some unknown force, under the floorboards of a long-dead stranger's house. A drip fell from a protruding root to a puddle on the south wall; a tropical winter breeze shook the creaking wooden braces upstairs; but not a mouse, not a monkey or an iguana or a termite scurried by. This was a truly dead place.

Static came through over the wireless, followed by the high-pitched digital voice from before.

"Good. Very good, but you're not done yet. Not even close. Mr. Polanski, I'd introduce myself but you're running out of time. Mr. Solomon, there are two more members of your team you'll need to collect."

"What team?" Seek gritted through his teeth.

"The team you'll need to get into the vault of the Kapitalzukunft. The closest one to you now is Ms. Ferreira. She's in the cellar of the butcher's shop on Karl Braun's Street, the road running southward. The further one is Mr. King. He's on the north outskirts of town, in a water tower on the east side of Hermann Oberth's. Like the townhouse, the butcher's shop and the water-tower have red painted blotches on their hatches. Any building you find with that mark should be safe for the night so long as you remain quiet. In any other place, run or turn invisible." *Click.*

27

Seek helped Chuck to his feet, and together they hobbled up the stairs.

"What's going on, Solomon?!"

"Keep it down. I don't know. You see this thing in your neck?" Seek grazed it with his finger.

"It's been hurting like all hell since I woke up." They pushed together through the doorframe and out to the street. Seek looked around and closed the door. He pulled the key from his pocket to show Chuck, locked the door, and then dropped the key to the dripping cobblestone, pushing the rug over with his feet. "It's a bomb, a tiny, evil fucking bomb, and we need to go find that woman or they'll explode."

"Jesus," Chuck said, holding up Seek's makeshift torch so the limping man could wrap his arm around Chuck's shoulder. "What's wrong with your leg?"

"I hurt it making the torch," Solomon whispered between bursts of thunder.

They stumbled down the block, lucky to find the rain dissipating as the night raged on but drenched from head to toe all the same and now blown back by heavy gusts carrying a foul odor. The shaking post at the corner read *Karl Braun*.

"And there are people living here?" Chuck shouted into his compatriot's ear.

"There are things living here at least," Solomon answered. "We can talk more when we get to the butcher's. Save your breath!"

The sun had passed away behind the Argentinian coast, leaving only streaks of orange and red beneath the clouds to cover its retreat. Chuck's torch hand shook wildly, the flame at its tip fighting for life in the harsh thrashing winds. They looked around at the cross between Karl Braun and Hans Geiger to the west. Their eyes darted across broken windows and shattered doorframes, desperately looking for that superfluously important crimson mark. Hobbling down the former street, the pair tripped and toppled to the street over another skeletal frame draped in uniform at their boots. Its head had been crushed with great force, teeth crammed into the tarmac between the stones themselves. On its hip sat a holster. Seek rolled as Chuck set him down in favor of the the firearm he pulled from the cadaver's belt, an old rusted Luger of greater years than both men combined. Chuck shoved it into his pocket and lifted Solomon to his feet.

"Stop. What was that?" The twosome spun around in the direction of the sound. Darkness. Solomon wiped down his glasses but could see nothing. Battling the winds and the last spits of rain spray, their torch light could not pierce more than a few meters in front of them. From the shade both men could feel the void staring back at them. Their steps slowly traced backward against the row of crippled buildings, hands against their cracked and splintered walls. When Chuck pushed Seek behind him, giving the smaller man time to feel his way around, Solomon's fingers slipped into a groove, an indent in the woodwork at their backs. The men turned, and Chuck spotted a wooden ham hanging lopsidedly from the roof overhang. Seek's eyes were dead set on the human scratch marks in the hard oak threshold his fingers now pressed into. Their eyes met in the middle at a painted ruddy stain between them. Chuck stuck Seek in the corner under the sign, propping him up and kicked aside the wicker mat at their feet.

"What kind of place is this?" he said, turning the key and helping his friend into the shop. They fell back against the inside of the door, soaked and exhausted. Chuck muddled with the key, desperately trying to lock it behind them. Their breath weighed heavy in the clogged dry air of the decayed old butchery. Looking around, the men spotted the shop's most intriguing features. Like the townhouse they had fled, the long, glass windows of the shop—once a quaint but effective display of imported juicy-cut wild boar and Austrian-style smoked sausage— now lay in jagged pieces on the floor. The gap was filled in by splintered boards with crooked rusty nails and broken-down coffee tables propped up against them. Along the butcher's walls still swung the hooks of the trade, like sharp-toed bats hanging upside-down from the ceiling.

It took a moment or two for the stench to hit them straight on, filling the calm vacated as their adrenaline raced to catch its breath. Chuck wiped the torch in front of them trying to drive back the stink, but Seek had already turned and coughed up his early-morning meal behind the cashier's counter. He stood there for a moment, balanced over the countertop, and stared down at his sick. "Chuck, hand me the faucet."

"The what?"

"The faucet! The torch!"

Dazed, Mr. Polanski gave his weapon a second glance and saw that it was indeed the long head of a shower or sink spigot. He handed it over to Seek, who prodded it down into his spew. Solomon pulled his head back in suspicion at the sight and put a finger in his mouth, feeling the inside of his cheeks and the length of his tongue, but he felt nothing. He reached back further, tempting his gag and quickly pulled out. The firelight seconded his caution as a watery drip of blood trickled down his index finger away from the flame.

"What is it?" Chuck asked, breathing through his hand. Seek looked back at the man sitting up against the door.

"Nothing. Come on. Help me to the cellar."

The men slowly dragged their muddy boots across the creaking hardwood floorboards, desperate for silence. After so many decades, the store's supplies had been either pilfered or squandered and let off the horrid stench now rife in their nostrils. Behind a bathroom more foul than the blackened Black Forest ham, stood a solemn metal door, and beside it a drop hatch into the basement. They pried open the breach in the floor and scooted down on their butts, Chuck pushing the light out in front of them.

The stench in the hold proved twice as pungent as that above, and Seek and Chuck reared their heads just to fight for air. The walls in the slaughter basement, like the previous hovel, were riddled with the protrusion of native vegetation, roots and vines looking for new homes in the abandoned villa. In the center of the expanse hung rows upon rows of the metallic flying rodents, some empty, some sporting the remains of decayed ancient wholesale. Hooks driven through empty eye sockets filled with the glazed bodies of flies and mosquitoes in that room where even the decomposers were dead.

As their palms graced the width of the room, searching desperately for the woman in the voice's last message, Solomon and

Polanski came to the corner, where a certain lone catch held an oversized piece of meat, a human frame still holding a little muscle to its bones. Chuck held up the torch to spot where the short noose wrapped around the rusted end of the claw. A white, stained smock dangled from his neck, and a solitary wooden stool lay slantwise on the floor under his feet. And by the stool lay a wide-eyed, dirtied, and stomach-turned Liliana Ferreira.

Chuck dropped Seek before her and held up the torch illuminating the area around them. "Ms. Ferreira?" asked the journalist, putting the emphasis over the *i* instead of the *e*. She nodded emphatically, staring at the two men. In the shadow of the flame she could see the outline of a pistol in the taller one's pocket. Seek freed her in the same way he had freed Chuck, untying the knot that had kept her wrists together. Chuck bent down to give them more light, but with her hands free Liliana quickly snatched the pistol from his pocket, fell backwards against the wall, and held it on them.

Her hand shaking the clip inside the butt of the gun, she ripped the tape off her mouth and shouted, "Who are you? Who are you?!?" Shocked, Chuck dropped the torch and a shot rang out, deafening the three. In the dark they clamored. Seek found a pair of legs and pulled them toward him. Chuck dived, jabbing his hand on something sharp in the gloom of the slaughter room.

"Stop. Stop! We're here to help you!" a voice shouted, grabbing for the Luger. Seek proved more capable on the ground, rolling over on top of Liliana, wrestling the gun from her and chucking it hard into the echoing basement hall. He lay on top of her, pinning her arms with his knees and covering her mouth with his hands. "We are not going to hurt you, lady. We're trying to help you!"

Liliana broke a hand free and reached for the torch beside them, waving it frantically, trying to burn a hole in her attacker's face and get him off of her. In a rage he moaned, smacked the torch aside, and slapped her hard across the face, knocking her back against the cold, hard cement. He tried to grab it, but was too late. Solomon watched in anguish as the torch rolled along into the dark and extinguished in a shallow slop grate. Exhausted, Seek fell backward against the wall beside the unconscious woman.

He breathed heavily, coughing hard before finding the strength to ask, "Chuck, are you shot?"

The response came back through the dark. "Fuck, no, but one of these fucking hooks just stuck me." From upstairs came a creak and a rattle. The men froze in silence. Chuck, clutching his hand in pain, slid toward the wall and felt Seek reach for him.

"You locked the door, right?" Solomon asked.

"Yes, it's locked. It's definitely locked."

Silence again. Another creak. Not from above but from the street behind them. "It's the sign. Just the sign. Okay. Stay here. I need to find King."

"Who?"

Seek had already started limping out before Chuck could protest, which he dared not do loudly. Crawling up the stairs, Seek slid open the trap door and popped his head out. He could spot no bodies, living or otherwise, so he crept out and back toward the counter. Exhausted again, he fell on his knees in front of the door, resting his hands over the hardwood. At eye level with the keyhole, the persistent journalist pressed his face to the slot, the rims of his frames clanking with the iron gap, and gazed out. He could see his breath moisten the metal in the gears, the gray twilight, bathed in water, reflecting off the cobblestone, and the decrepit, broken granary across the street.

And then a foot, bare and dark, nails long and unfiled, grappled a pair of fist-sized cobbles. A massive leg, also bare, dripping, and muscular, followed and the figure came into full view. Two of them. Three. He gazed for just a moment at the behemoths, downpour flowing from their long locks. Crouched, they walked the streets of the storm-struck ghost village, hunched forward to touch the ground with their hands and feet, lumbering casually like a pack of wolves stalking a downtown metropolis. Falling back, Solomon dragged himself on his ass toward the slaughter room and the safety of its stank, rotten darkness.

Chapter III

Without looking, Solomon backtracked down the wrong hallway and fell flat into a storage closet, tin cans and utensils free falling onto his head and legs. From among them he scooped up a deep clay bowl, reached around in the dark and filled it with pot holders and a half-empty box of cooking oil. Hearing the rattling and desperate to stop it, he ran his fingers along the floor for the box of matches that had bounced off his ankle. As he reached out in front of him, he heard another rattle on the door to the shop. A scratching sound. Sharp nails pushing into the finger-shaped groove he had rested his hand against only minutes earlier. The doorknob jiggled. In the dark, Solomon scraped his fingernails over the hardwood boards until a single little match caught under his middle finger. He lodged the twig under his cheek and crawled back around to the basement stairs with the bowl in front of him.

Closing the keep behind him, he sat on the third step, popped the cap off the cooking oil, and poured it onto the pot holders. "Seek. Seek, is that you?" echoed from the other end of the room. Solomon spat the match out of his mouth, spread his legs, and made a small rhetorical prayer. He struck the match on the fourth stair between his feet, bringing to life an infant flame which he quickly tossed into the bowl for a roaring fire. Chuck spotted his compatriot from the far wall and moved to help him over. "What do we do now?" he asked.

"We can't go out. The people… The things are out there. We'll have to stay the night."

Solomon's makeshift campfire helped to keep away the stench of the slaughter basement, and the survivors gathered around it to warm their faces. Burning mildew and seventy-year-old cooking oil smelled to them like rose potpourri compared to the odorous decay of the cellar. With a chance to breathe, they let down their guard. Solomon noticed his friend massaging his wounded palm in the shadow behind him. He handed Polanski an unlit potholder from his pocket.

"Okay, Chuck. Who are you, and what have you gotten me into?"

Wrapping the cloth around his hand, Chuck followed a scoff with a deep exhale. "Hiroto. Do you think...?"

Solomon sighed and put his head in his hands. "He's certainly not bathing himself with jewels in that fortress. The Kapital...zukunft? And who is that voice?"

"Who is that girl?" Chuck responded with the gun in his lap, motioning back toward Ms. Ferreira, who lay peacefully unconscious against the back wall.

"I don't know that either, but my guess is she's in the same boat we are. She just got startled is all. I couldn't say I wouldn't have shot at you myself." The men chuckled to themselves. Then, quiet. Chuck took the chance to run his hands over his neck and the bump in his throat. He stared at the same bump in Solomon's throat.

"Well, there's one way to make sure."

Chuck grabbed the bowl and walked back to the corner where Ms. Ferreira lay on the ground. Seek propped her up against the wall and brushed the blood and dirt off her face. "God, I've never hit a woman before." Chuck tilted her head to the side and ran his finger down her neck. There, in the pit of her throat, sat a familiar blue-coated lump.

"I guess you're right."

They plopped back against the wall, Solomon on one side of the unconscious stranger, Polanski on the other. "She's just knocked out, right? I didn't...?"

"No," Chuck scoffed. "I can see her breathing."

"All right, good. I think we should let her sleep. Any nightmare she could have would be better than this."

Seek took the wireless out of his pocket. It was indeed just a phone, like any other bluetooth receiver, nothing inherently special about it except for the fact that it worked, had battery life, and would only receive or send to one signal. "There's a PAN on this island somewhere."

"A what?"

"A personal area network. Or I guess it could be a radio set and the receiver is programmed to a frequency. Either way he's got a power source someplace on this island. That's how he can talk to us. And his...detonator. It has to run on batteries or something. None of this stuff would work without electricity."

"But the villa's all out. There isn't a lightbulb with power in this whole place."

"Somewhere there is," concluded Solomon. He stared at the dancing sparks from his portable fire as they rose and disappeared into the musky dark of the basement. Suddenly he felt a building sensation in his gut and a bellowing cough let up into the night. Seek struggled to breathe as Chuck crossed over the concussed woman to help him. Seek held him back with his outstretched hand and spit out a murky mass of blood onto the concrete. "God," he whispered. "What is this?" He summoned up a saliva salvo and spat, but no more blood came up. "It's not in my mouth."

"You all right?"

"Yeah. Peachy." He paused. "I saw them when I was up there," he said, changing the subject.

"What are they?"

"Hell if I know, and I do mean hell. Maybe seven feet tall. Their arms are as long as their legs. And they have claws, Chuck. Claws."

"Claws? What has claws? People don't have claws. I don't have claws. Why do they have claws?"

"I don't know," Seek admitted, laying his head back against the wall. "So let's focus on what we do know. Number one, we can't leave. Number two, it's insane for us to stay. Tomorrow, I'll click the receiver again and tell the voice we found trigger-finger here. Then we'll have to find the other one."

"That one better not shoot at me too."

Solomon let his eyes roll up toward the ceiling and studied the fungus and vines crawling through from the outer dark. They looked as if they were coming for him, stretching down from above to grab him, choke him, strangle the little remaining life out of his puny, wounded, violated body. His finger itched the Kindle in his pocket, as his eyes fell back further into the black.

Several hours later, light crept through the holes of their basement harbor and shone into Chuck's eyes. He yawned and took stake of their situation, looking over to his left at Seek, still asleep. Dropping his hand to shield his eyes from the sunlight, Chuck found himself staring directly down the chamber of his salvaged little pea-shooter, a 7.65 millimeter Luger Pistole Parabellum 1908, the standard sidearm of the Nazi Germany war machine. Chuck knew its history; he knew that pistol had put many a victim—Jew, gypsy, intellectual, dissenter, young and old, plucked from their beds in middle of the night—into shallow mass graves across East, West, and Central Europe. Behind the gun stood Ms. Liliana Ferreira, five-feet-two-inches tall, no more than one hundred pounds, a stranger and the third member of their team.

"Who are you?"

Seek's eyes slowly opened, and he hit his head on the back wall when his eyes met the sight before him. Liliana kept the barrel pointed straight ahead, steady, staring at the lump in Chuck's throat and spoke to Solomon. "If you move, I put a bullet in him. Now who are you two? Where are we? What is this?" At the last question she pointed with her free hand to the RDX capsule in her throat.

Chuck thought to reach out his hand, and as he did Liliana stood forward and stomped it down on the cement floor, pointing the Luger that much closer to its target. Solomon spoke up through Chuck's squeals of pain. "Ms. Ferreira? My name is Stephen Solomon. I'm a journalist from the states. I used to write for *The Washington Post*. You're pointing that gun at my friend. His name is Charles Polanski. He's an American too and a source for a very good friend of mine, Hiroto Ota, also of the *Post*. I came upon him just the same way we came upon you, tied up in a house a couple blocks from here. We're on an island about seventy miles from the coast of Argentina, and we're all prisoners. All of us."

Liliana let out a long, slow breath. She ran her free hand along the curve in her throat. Solomon continued. "That little painkiller in your neck is a real killer. There's a man on the island, a voice on this little headset I have here." He took it out of his pocket slowly, drawing her ire for a moment before he held up the small harmless device. "He's planted those little things in our necks and claims he can explode them on a whim. But he won't... If we do what he wants." Solomon paused. "I had to knock you out last night."

Liliana turned the gun to point at him. Seek held out his hands as if to block his face from a traveling bullet.

"There are things. Great big...*things* out there. I didn't want them to hear you screaming. I'm sorry."

Liliana looked back and forth between them but kept the Luger trained on Solomon. "What is it he wants?"

Chuck interceded. "Why don't we ask him ourselves?"

Seek nodded. "If—if you'll just put down that gun, I'll get on the wireless and ask him myself. Will you put it down? Please?"

A pause. She hesitated at first, looking at the two men who had attacked her while she'd remained restrained late the night before. Ms. Ferreira looked around them at the intruding vegetation, the rotten petrified hogs, and the lone, decayed butcher hanging by a hook in the slaughter room of his own shop. She gagged at the sight of him, a gag that turned into a hard cough. Bending forward, gun still pointed in Seek's direction, she spat a dark red rosebud into the sewer drain where the torch had fallen. "Oh God," she whispered.

"That's been happening a lot too," said Solomon.

Chapter IV

Liliana Ferreira sat calmly at a rickety bocote wood table on the second-floor balcony of the butcher's shop. She had put the Luger away but only as far as her front pocket. Chuck had been fighting unsuccessfully with the bathroom sink, his good grip around the nozzles and an empty bucket under his elbow. Solomon sat with his feet up on an old, tattered sofa that he'd dragged over to the archway overlooking the street. It was lined with small brass Iron Cross buttons and accompanying embroidery. He put down a recently emptied can of salt-pork, wiping the disgust from his lips.

With the daylight the storm had ceased, and the picturesque view with which Chuck and Solomon had been greeted upon arrival to San Magnus returned. The winter sun glancing off the ceramic rooftops of the resort villa, shimmering in the shards of glass and peeled the color from the bones littering her cobblestone walkways.

"Are you ready?" Solomon asked. Liliana nodded. He bit his lip and clicked on the device. Hollering, Chuck came out to the balcony from the bathroom and sat across from Liliana, the pot-holder bandage wrapped around his hand. A familiar static came over the hands-free, and Solomon pressed the speakerphone button and dropped the headset on the table.

"Are you enjoying your sunbathing, Mr. Solomon?"

Liliana's eyes darted around the block.

"He can see us, but we don't know how."

"That's correct, Ms. Ferreira. I can see you, but you don't know how. I couldn't see you as you hid in the basement last night. Hog-tied, trapped in a muddy cellar with a convicted criminal. Ms. Ferreira, I do hope he didn't take too many luxuries with you..." Liliana looked down into her lap. Solomon moved to grab the bluetooth, but the voice cut in. "Now, there is still one more member of your team to collect, and there are hardly enough hours in a winter day to waste lounging in the villa."

"We're not going to budge until you give us more information. Those things last night, those monsters in the street, what are they? Where are they?" demanded Solomon. The hands-free went quiet. Chuck looked over at Solomon with questioning eyes, Liliana with a worrying face.

"Need I remind you, Mr. Solomon, that I hold your pitiful, worthless life in my hands? Would your children miss you, Mr. Solomon? Would your ex-wife miss you, or rather, would your few remaining readers miss you if a geyser spewed from that neck and you bled to death, here and now, relaxing on a mezzanine in the tropics while people's lives were at stake?"

Solomon grabbed the receiver off the table. "How the hell do you know about my family?"

"Oh, I know a lot about you, Mr. Solomon. I have your wallet, remember?" Seek dropped his head down and sunk in his seat. "And a lot about you as well, Ms. Ferreria, former candidate for the chair of the anthropology department at São Paulo, soon to be its only tenured professor ever to be...'untenured'. And you, Mr. Polanski, ex-US Army, ex-US Marine, ex-gun-for-hire, armed patsy for the EU and NAU oil interests running amok in democratic Bolivia. What goes for Solomon goes for all of you. I have one button for the lot. I press it and San Magnus's population drops a percentile. Do your jobs, do I as say, and I'll let you go. I'll let you all go."

Liliana chimed in. "What it is you want?"

A pause.

"I want you to move north and free Mr. King from his water tower. He's been in there for a couple days now. Find him, and I'll give you another task. Complete that, and I'll give you another. You have seven hours of daylight remaining. I suggest you use them well. You should be safe enough in those hours to move about freely, but don't waste time. There are a number of reasons not to stay too long on San Magnus island." Click.

Chuck locked the door as they left. As they headed north,

Solomon pointed out to Liliana the corpse his partner had taken the pistol from and the clock tower he himself had awoken in. Chuck ran his hand through the grime-rich water in the fountain, massaging it back and forth. Liliana motioned him to let her see. "It's all right. I'll be fine," he replied sharply, rolling his palm back up in the bandage.

"Big soldier man," she said, rolling her *r* like an extension of the *d*.

Chuck looked away, walked to the outskirt of the plaza, and stopped in his tracks to stare up at the ridgeline to the east and the great concrete fortress, the Kapitalzukunft, burrowed like a mole's home within. Apposed to the green and brown foliage shedding over the hilltops around it, the fortress bore a stark gray-teal color, like a castle sucked into a collapsed plateau. What Solomon had first assumed was a lighthouse, the great hexahedron tower stood too far inland to prove an effective nautical construction. It seemed to him far more adept at keeping watch over the island than the seas.

"That's the tower you thought Hiroto was in?" the Texan asked.

Solomon felt the insult like a pang in his gut. "Yeah. But maybe there's someone looking down from there after all."

In the light of day, gazing at the rows of quaint villa houses and away at the silhouettes of swaying palm trees dotting the shoreline, Solomon found a peace that had all but been driven from his mind the night before. "It's amazing what a difference a day makes, isn't it?"

With Chuck pulling up the rear, Liliana answered. "In South America, you are never more than a sleepwalk from the jungle."

Solomon feigned a smile as they rounded the crossroads of the north plaza and headed back in the direction of the sunken docks. "This is my first vacation, you know."

"And how are you enjoying it so far, Mr. Solomon?"

Seek arched his neck and ran his hand over the pill in his throat. "Whatever happened to just a chocolate on your pillow?"

"Hey," they heard boom from the Texan up ahead of them. Chuck knelt at another finely dressed cadaver, this one hanging from a broken first-floor window of what appeared to be an infirmary. Rifling through its pockets, he pulled out another Luger, stashing this one in his belt, and an accompanying ammo clip, which he handed to Liliana.

"Do you know how to use one of these?"

The professor shrugged. "The bullet comes out of the pointy end."

"Yes, that's right," Chuck replied. Along Hermann Oberth north he showed them the basics of handling a pistol, though he had to admit first, "This thing is a hundred years old and rustier than I am. But the principles are the same." He explained the function of a double-action, that it was old but not old enough to require cocking. He displayed how to react to the strange way the gun's toggle kicked when it recoiled, how to expel and replace a clip, and most importantly according to Chuck, how to use it like a club by grasping the barrel when it misfired. "You know, it's funny. Back in the States these guns would be worth a lot of money."

"Yeah," Solomon replied.

On the outskirts of the village they came across the tower, or rather a large, lopsided, tin cylinder hanging from a ladder and some broken boards. As Liliana and Chuck ran over to it, spotting the red blotch on its exterior, Solomon walked across the street to a large, engraved wooden sign, chipped and faded. He ran his fingers along the grooves of its lettering and stepped back. "Die Villa Roma." "Die indeed, Herr Metzger," he said under his breath.

"Seek, come quick." In the bottom of the can, curled into a ball, was a shivering, pale and thin man with a long, shaggy goatee. Chuck crawled out of the gap with the man over his shoulder and propped him up against the tower's disheveled scaffolding.

Holding her palm over his forehead, Liliana sighed. "He has a fever."

"Mr. King. Mr. King, can you hear me?" pleaded Solomon, but the man just shook more fiercely. Seek reached out to grab him when static broke free from his back pocket.

"I see you're all getting acquainted. That's good. Now you need to turn the power back on," it screeched, muffled through his pants fabric.

"The power?" barked Solomon, rifling through and holding it out in front of him. "You know so much about us. You know none of us are electricians."

42

"Mr. King is."

Liliana turned and snatched the com from Solomon's hand. "This man is almost dead, you monster!" she poured through an accent thick with rage. Seek and Chuck backed away from her slowly.

"You have Mr. Solomon to thank for that, Ms. Ferreira. If he hadn't spent so much time mucking around with you last night, he could have gotten to Mr. King before the morning sun. And now another day and night will be lost and your lives irrevocably shortened!"

"This man is not going to survive," she barked.

A discernible sigh came over the device. "Then you will do what you can to make sure he does...Dr. Ferreira." Click.

Liliana threw the blue-tooth back to Solomon. "You've got some big balls...ma'am," said Chuck.

"We need to get him back to the hospital we passed. Agreed?"

The men nodded. Solomon picked up one of the lengthy wooden boards from the dilapidated water tower and walked to the "Die Villa Roma" sign across the street. "Give me a hand would you, big guy?"

The stroll back to the center of town took twice as long. "It's damn lucky he's so small," Chuck spouted, dropping the sign in front of the infirmary with the feverish man atop it before collapsing onto the cobblestone.

"This place doesn't have a red mark."

"We're not staying the night." Liliana took out her pistol and went pilfering for supplies. The lobby was empty, but down the hall she found a medical closet with a box of hermetically sealed morphine. She pushed the box into the hallway, tossing in a few things—a package of Penicillin, shears and needles, bandages—and tread into the bathroom to look for tampons.

Chuck and Solomon heaved King off the street and into the hospital, his limbs over their shoulders. With all his might, Solomon sprawled the shaking man's legs out on a sofa in the waiting area. Before either had a chance to wipe down their foreheads, there came a scream from the back of the building. Solomon ran toward the shriek, Chuck following closely behind him. When they got to the door at the end of the hall, Chuck pushed him aside, drew his Luger, and yanked

43

the door open. Liliana spun around with her gun in his face.

"Jesus fuck, lady! You have to stop doing that." He exhaled and put the pistol away. Liliana lowered her arm and stepped back, pushing through the men and into the hallway. A body lay, more preserved than any they had yet seen, draped in a white lab coat, on its knees with its head resting in the bowl of the sink. A knife stood tall, stuck into the floor beside the toilet plunger.

No one said a word. After a moment, Liliana regained her composure, stuck her pistol in her pocket, and pushed back through the gap she'd made between the two men, who stood watching as she reached over the body for the medicine cabinet to grab a box of Ohne Binde sitting on the bottom shelf.

"A little privacy," she said.

Solomon and Chuck proceeded back to the lobby, where they put up their feet and watched helplessly as beads of sweat dropped from the hallucinating, scrawny man on the sofa cushions.

Solomon had himself a short nap and was awoken soon after by the sound of arguing.

"He might not make it through the night. The exposure was bad, but the fever is worse," Liliana snapped.

"He can't spend the night here," replied Polanski. "What if we relocate you to the butcher's shop?"

"I am not spending another night in that dungeon."

"Forget the butcher's," impeded Solomon as if he'd been awake the whole time. "The basement, where I found you," he said, looking to Chuck. "That's a safe spot, and there was some food in the pantry. Is that fair?"

Chuck nodded, and then Liliana. "The voice said this was our team, the four of us. I don't know what that means, or how or why you got trapped here with us, but we need to work together. There's no one else who can save this man. That's on us. I'm not a doctor, but apparently...you are?"

Liliana nodded again.

"Okay," Solomon continued, "then we'll move him back to the house, and Chuck and I will scout supplies, look for a power source, a

44

radio or something, and stay out of your hair while you do your magic."

Solomon's democracy moved into action. They carried a table and a chair into the basement of the fortified townhouse across from the plaza, found an intact oil lantern from a house across the street, and enough foul but edible German rations in the pantry to make them wish they'd never heard of herring. With enough daylight to scout, Chuck and Solomon walked back to the sunken docks and toured the beach, but no boat could be found, including their own. More success was found on the south side of the Villa Roma, and they returned to the cellar with a pail of water drained from a storm grate, two cartons of matches, two more clips for their Lugers, some wool blankets, and a map of San Magnus Island Solomon had pilfered from the doctor's office. Solomon paid special attention to the label above its key, where the initials *H.E.* had been written in faded black ink.

"Did you find a radio? A phone?" Liliana asked, meeting them at the bottom of the steps.

"No, nothing works. We need the electric guy. How's he doing?"

Mr. King's shaking had slowed, but in the gloom of the basement he looked paler, wetter, as if he perspired more quickly in the cool air.

"What if he dies?" Chuck asked, dunking a towel in the water bucket and handing it to Liliana.

"Well—" Solomon sighed. "He won't have to worry about this anymore." He pointed to the ever familiar lump in the man's neck.

"That's not what I mean, Seek. You have to think about us. What do we do if he dies? What's the plan?"

Solomon sighed again. "Has he said anything?"

Liliana put the washcloth on his temple. "'Beth 'r fuck."

"Birther fuck?"

The three sat waiting impatiently, as if expecting the feverish man to snap out of his pyrexia and come to their rescue. In the meantime they filled each other in on their individual pieces of their puzzling predicament. Ms. Ferreira was indeed a doctor and professor at São Paulo, a university she insisted was "the best in South America," as little as that meant to Seek Solomon, who casually slipped into the conversation his degree from Columbia, despite lacking the prefix of *doctor* that accompanied Ferreira. Chuck, while keeping rather quiet, admitted himself to be a discharged marine and, when pressed by the persistent journalist, also conceded that he had last worked as a mercenary in Bolivia during that country's conflict for the sovereignty of its natural gas deposits. He assured both Ms. Ferreira and Mr. Solomon, however, that he had not fired a shot in all that time.

"So these dead men in the streets and the houses—they were Nazi's?" asked Ferreira.

"Looks that way," said Solomon. "Hiroto said this was a sanctuary for a big group of them and their families after the war. I'll bet half the bodies we've found so far are on a war criminals list at The Hague."

"And this man, this voice... Is he a Nazi?" she continued.

"I doubt it," Chuck interceded. "That was eighty years ago, and it looks like they've all been dead for fifty, maybe more."

"Yeah. Besides, he wants what's in the vault, and he doesn't have the keys. He's here to rob the place."

Solomon made no mention of the Polish Royal Casket.

"He wants us to turn the power back on. For once I agree with him. See here?" Solomon pointed to a spot on the map he'd found marked *Villa Vienna* to the south. "It says kraftwerk. I'm no linguist, but that sounds like craft works, doesn't it?"

"Sure it does, but I've no idea how fix a century-old Nazi generator," Chuck replied.

"I guess we know why he's here," emphasized Liliana, wiping the sweat off her patient's face.

"I wonder why we're here," posed Chuck.

"It was all a trap, a set up, the whole thing," muttered Solomon.

"Looks that way," Chuck replied, "but how could he have known we were coming? And who the hell is he?"

Solomon shrugged. They sat silently for some time before Liliana worked up the courage and spoke.

"There's a small tribe that lived along the rivers of the Amazon between Peru and Brazil. They were called the Matsés. I wrote on them for my graduate thesis. Their lands were being poached and deforested and they were starving." She exhaled deeply.

Seek and Chuck got comfortable.

"It took some time to build trust, but eventually they told me the story of Quechimutu, the old man who lived in a cave under the waterfall upriver from their villages. But to the Matsés, all things are spirits—people, trees, rivers—and the old man was the spirit of the river, the spirit of life, the flowing of the circle. One day the loggers filled the river with their tree trunks and blocked the waterfall, so the old man came out of his cave and cursed the Matsés for letting their river be taken so easily. His curse became real; their women miscarried and the children fell ill. Their medicine was derived from the trees blocking the river, which dried up. I was told to leave when the attacks began."

"Attacks?"

"The Matsés believed the old man had ordered them to fight back or the river would never run again."

Solomon looked at Chuck, whose attention had turned wholly to cleaning and stripping his Luger.

"And what happened to the Matsés?" asked Solomon.

Liliana dipped the washcloth in water and rinsed it before placing it back on the sickly man's head. "The military moved in. I'm one of a half-dozen people versed in their language now."

Solomon sat back in his chair and blew a sigh from his mouth. As he did, he felt a cough strike up from his gut. He stood up quickly and ran to the corner. Bending forward and holding onto the wall at the crux, his whole body shook as he expelled another chunk of blood from his throat.

Chapter V

In the morning, Chuck found himself the third of the party to cough up blood and did so with some anguish upon emerging from their underground retreat. "I don't know if I can take much more of this yin-yang, night-and-day shit," he spat, relieving himself in the side street behind their fortified townhouse.

Solomon, squatting over a dented German stahlhelm just around the corner, replied, "Why couldn't we have come in summer?"

On their return to the house, they found another surprise waiting for them. Mr. King, the fourth and final member of their party, pried out of a tin can like the salted fish they'd force fed him, had recovered and was very, very awake.

"Uhhh, King. Yes, that's right. How did you know that? Cledwyn King actually, or just King, or just Cled. It doesn't really matter. What matters is you've gotten me out of boghole, so thank you raz, but shush your noise when I say I'd rather have a cwch with my parole officer back in Cardiff," he rattled on in his rampaging Celtic accent, like an enthusiastic tidal wave just swept ashore from Britannia. "Oh, bore da, boys," he passed along to Chuck and Seek as they stepped into the living room of the loudest villa on San Magnus island. "Sut mae? Hope you had a pleasant piss and all. I was just discussing with this lovely angel the details of this little situation and, well, might I pry from you some information regarding what the heavenly fuck is going on around here? And why I've found myself with this cheap piece of trash in my neck?"

"Cardiff," Chuck replied. "You're Welsh?"

"Well now, there's an intelligent fella! Large, a Darren and munting at that, ey, what kind of scrut you be? Now don't tell me. I know it. You're an American by the smell if it. I do hope you're not the brains of this grotty-like shandy van. It's certainly not a wonder as to how you were bamboozled into the getaway from hell."

Chuck's smirk dropped quickly and he bit his lip. Solomon, holding out his hand between the two men, intervened. "The man in charge gave you your little friend there. Do you know what it is?"

"Yeah. This lovely dark-skinned maven told me all about it."

"For the fifth time, my name is Dr. Ferreira. Doctor."

"You're a doctor, I'm a doctor. We're all doctors. That's why we've come here—the golf and mojitos. It's all right, boys. I've had worse tiffs in a Mexican flat with a much bigger deposit in a much less comfortable re-cept-acle of my body before, so forgive me if the jewelry doesn't spark a panic."

"You don't seem so worried about your situation, friend," Chuck posed, still dead-faced.

"That jewelry is a bomb. You know, like, go boom?" Solomon interceded.

"Yes, right, do what we say or you die. Very familiar—cliché really—but at least this one lets me walk straight. Is there anything else I should worry about 'round here or just the food and this piece of bling? I'd really like to have a potch down the gully for a pisser myself if you're onto me. Bein' honest, I feel like I've gotten real drunk and swallowed my ankle bracelet."

"This is our electrician?" Chuck scoffed.

"Electrician? God, no," King snapped back. "No, I'm a thief. A pickpocket. A scammer, grifter, hustler, bunko artist, a swindler. I like a good fight every now and again, and forgery and fraud can be fun, but my real love, my true gift, is vaults, cases, doors, alarms, locks, and bigger vaults. And from the sound of it, we've got ourselves a mega lush porker to crack, eh?"

"I have no idea what he just said," admitted Dr. Ferreira.

Solomon did his best to fill in their new companion with what he knew about where they were, how they'd each heard about the island, how they'd been ambushed, where they'd found King, how they knew where he was, why they had to stash out at night, and a short history lesson on Dr. Gerhart Konig Metzger and his party of escaped Nazi fugitives. Seek left out the part about the six billion dollars' worth of Polish Royal jewels tucked away in the fortress they were going to break into.

King, not one to take a lecture sitting down, was up on his feet and pacing. He had picked up a dusty little globe-shaped paperweight and rolled it up and down over his hands until scooping it down to the floor and balancing his weight on it at the end of Solomon's story.

"Don't you just hate those fucking Nazis?" King replied. "Always going around mucking up people's vacation spots. I hear Warsaw was quite nice in the spring."

"How were you able to get over that fever so fast?" Chuck cut in. Liliana raised her eyebrows and tilted her head, letting him know that she hadn't had a clue herself.

"What? A fever? Mate, as you so astutely pointed out, I'm Welsh. When you've suffered the bloody English and their cooking for a hundred generations, all you need is a few hours' sleep and a swill in the bosh and you'll be safe and sorted! We beat the bubonic plague for piss sake. Now, am I going to assign you all names based on sexual attraction or are we gonna have ourselves a proper introduction? You're not gonna like yours, big man."

Solomon introduced himself and the others by name, extending his hand for a shake. Cautious, Liliana let King press his lips to the back of her own hand, and Chuck, though reluctantly, nodded his head a discernible inch.

"And what about our last guest at the party? Mr. Bling Bling?"

Solomon took the hands-free from a medic bag he had taken from the infirmary and wiggled it in the air. "He's right here." They sat back around the table before Solomon clicked the send button yet again.

"I trust Mr. King is alive?" said the voice.

"What, a robot? I've stolen a lot of things for scavvys, butties, and spoiled tossers but never a robot. A sign of the times I s'pose."

"Good. I'll take that as a yes."

Solomon pressed the com button, interrupting. "What did you mean the other day when you said there was more than one reason to get off this island?"

Another static-bathed sigh came through the device. "I suppose it is only provident now to give you the relevant facts, and providence

51

bodes permanence. When Metzger and the Vorkämpfer fled Europe, they didn't leave their insatiable taste for science behind them. They built this place as a resort. That's true. On the outside it was a simple retreat for the last generation of the Reich to live and grow away from Jews, Slavs, or other 'undesirables.' But Metzger's true passion was the Kapitalzukunft, the fortress, and so much more. Here he and his colleagues engineered dozens of catastrophic marvels the likes of which our world, with our rules and laws, has never seen. Undaunted by fools impeding their work, they thrived here, until one day they started to die. They died quickly, but not all at once—the soldiers, the doctors, the wives and the children. You've seen some of them already. But that is not your concern, Mr. Solomon. Your concern is spending too many nights locked tightly in your basement, thinking you're safe. They are your prison, the safe-zones, and not meant for you to linger long. Dr. Metzger has seen to that."

The room fell silent. Then, "What in the ever-loving bloody fuckin' hell is he raving on about?"

Another sigh came over the hands-free. "One of the less tactful of the Vorkämpfer's innovations was a virus—airborne. It's rather thick in oxygen and fatal in concentrated doses. Fascinating, really. It's not actually a nerve agent, not like VX or Sarin gas. It's a microorganism of some kind, really impossible to know if Metzger came across it or if... he engineered it. If I had to classify the species, I'd say it's not far from the Filoviridae family, with cousins in Ebola and Marburg, for which there are no cures. However, it attacks you quite differently, it singles out only a single organ, the lungs, and it doesn't appear to be communicable in any way. Its more like an area of affect weapon than a plague as it won't spread through a civilian population person to person, but it will linger in a place for decades and lose little of its potency. A deadly little cloud. I call it The Haze, as you'll see, after the way it bends the air around itself. A sort of blood mirage. And you've been breathing it now for two days."

Solomon reached for his throat and looked to Liliana and Chuck.

"As far as can be told, it was released through the ventilation ducts of every house in every villa on the island decades ago. What little of it remains lingers there still and is killing each of you. Slowly but surely, in time the alveoli in your lungs will corrode and you will die, rather painfully I imagine, choking on the blood that overflows into your esophagus. It will leave you quite literally breathless."

Chuck kicked over a chair and stormed outside. Liliana grasped her mouth and chin and looked at Solomon emptily.

"It seems many of the inhabitants were killed that way, or at least those who didn't take their own lives...or weren't hunted down by the Volksklausur."

Solomon could see the horror on Liliana's face and the pure, unfiltered confusion on Cledwyn's.

"Those are the things in the streets at night?" he asked.

"Yes, the streets, the jungle, the coast... They're rather large beings and they require a lot of...sustenance. I doubt they're squeamish about cannibalism at this point."

"Cannibalism? So they're human?" asked Professor Ferreira.

"Genetically, yes, they're essentially identical to us. But far more dangerous. Volksklausur means 'isolated people.' They're another experiment of the Vorkämpfer. A glaring success, it would seem."

King turned to Solomon, mouthing the word in silence.

"Pioneers, Nazi scientists," he informed the thief.

The voice continued. "If you've seen them, chances are they've seen you and know you're here. They can smell you, hear you, see you in the darkest spaces. One of their many gifts, however, is their greatest curse. Their vision. Metzger managed to engineer the human eye to receive light at a ratio of ten times that of any bird of prey. You will not evade them. But because of this improvement, firelight, flashlight, and direct sunlight cause them severe pain, and I've yet to see one outdoors in the daytime. The only chance for your survival is to avoid them at all costs and never stray from my safe zones at night."

"Those same 'safe' zones filled with deadly gases? Fuck off."

"Yes. You see, you have a decision to make, Mr. King. All of you do. It's the same decision the last people to sit in those chairs you're sitting in now had to make. Do you stay in your houses, locked in and breathe till your last breath? Or do you take your night-lives outdoors

53

and risk the hunger of the Volksklausur?"

"I say we get into that fortress and break open that vault," barked Chuck from the doorway.

"A wise sentiment. Mr. King, there's an electric generator in the Villa Vienna to the south. I suggest you take Mr. Polanski and see about fixing it before another night is upon you. The light will be invaluable, and power is one of many keys into the fortress. Ms. Ferreira, Mr. Solomon, I have another task for you. Do these things, and soon I will be in the vault. And you will have your freedom."

Act II:

Join, Or Die

Chapter VI

Another sunny day in paradise, hey there, Solomon?

Chuck led the expedition southward to the Villa Vienna. On Solomon's map it looked nearly identical to the outlay of the Villa Roma, only a little larger and without the signature clock tower of the previous domain. He could see the boxy pattern of the roads stretch outward from Karl Braun street, that long, winding snake picking up from where Hermann Oberth left off running down from the North Docks, or what was left of them, and extending out through the Villa Roma to Vienna south and the Kapitalzukunft east. Among the streets in the latter resort he mouthed aloud were Von Zeppelin, Hertz, D.G Fahrenheit, and Konrad Zuse, whom Solomon recognized as the man whose blueprints for the first programmable computer had been destroyed by the Allies when they had bombed Berlin in the war eighty years before. *At least they didn't name the streets after themselves.*

Karl Braun brought them along a scenic path parallel to the beach. The wind-swept salt air grazing their faces struck the travelers with bitter sarcasm. There were no bodies along that stretch of road, no signs of a rampant plague or a horde of mutant monsters, just the stone walkway slowly being unearthed by the dirt, sand, and seashells of San Magnus island. Staring off into the sky, Solomon had to block out the sun's reflection with his hand lest it reflect against his glasses as he watched the seagulls duck and dive along the shimmering silver waves. Between the birds, the palm trees, and the bright white sand like clouds at their feet, Solomon couldn't help but feel a pull to stay on San Magnus island. "It's a damn shame."

"Yes, it is," said Liliana coming up beside him. She'd picked up a walking stick along the road, just short enough for the reach of her arms. Solomon frowned and looked her over. In the light of day, washed of the grime and disease of the butchery, Liliana Ferreira was an attractive woman in her own right. Her long, brown hair was a tangled mess for sure, no less in need of conditioning than Cledwyn's beard, but Solomon's frown dissipated with the chance to admire her form. She couldn't have been more than a size four, twisted locks falling halfway down between her waist and bosom. There was something there, however, maybe in her stare, which gave off the impression of power, of authority.

"So what did you do?" he asked, eyes meeting hers as they walked along. "To lose your tenure?"

"I haven't lost it yet," she replied.

"Is that right?"

"Yes, that's right. What did you do to go to prison?"

A few yards ahead, Chuck's neck turned around, evidently uninterested in Mr. King's half-comprehensible stories about "the knockers on this Venezuelan broad" so huge he "needed a blowtorch and a crowbar just to pry them from her brassiere."

"Me? Nothing. I did nothing," Solomon replied. Chuck shrugged and turned back around to Cledwyn, his hands out in front palming two massive, invisible breasts.

"Nothing? Is that right?"

"Yup, that's right."

Liliana smiled and turned her head to the jungle on the other side. Ten yards into the underbrush, her vision disappeared, kept from protrusion by dangling vines and crescent-curved trees. Compared to the collapsing of waves on the beach, the jungle felt quiet, undisturbed, isolated. She wondered if that was how the Volksklausur had gotten their name.

"Can you show me that map again?" she asked Solomon. He held it out as they walked, the Villa Vienna just beyond a clearing and a bend. "This island is still mostly forest, here between the ridge-line and the houses."

"And here, to the south along the shore."

She studied it closer, brushing against his arm.

"What's this?" she asked, pointing to a circle drawn over the jungle

58

a few clicks from their position.

"Huh, I didn't see that before. I don't know, a pool maybe?"

Liliana looked at him skeptically.

"No doubt there'll be some cockamamie reason to go out there and get ourselves killed soon enough. Have patience."

She smiled again. On their right they spotted a wide, light-colored board lying flat in the dirt. Walking over, Chuck flipped it upright.

"Die Villa Vienna."

"We're here."

From a glance, Vienna was identical to Roma, from the red ceramic rooftops down to its cracked and decaying foundations. The streets were covered in the same placid turquoise cobblestone, with the same rusted copper fountain, though the boy atop this one carried a double helix the size of a peach in his cupped hands rather than a torch. The implications were more or less the same. Solomon noted that in place of a clock tower on the far end of the square stood the power station, a fortified structure with similar roofing but with no windows and built of thick concrete. He was not surprised to find a red painted mark on its wrought iron door. As he approached the building, Chuck found it was not laden with a mat or a rug.

"What do we have here?" said King, facing a red arrow at the corner of the building, pointing toward the fountain.

Chuck walked passed Liliana, pardoning himself with an, "Excuse me, little lady," and jumped up on its rim to study the bronze boy over, looking for a crevice or a crease where the key might be hiding.

"Where is it, where is it…?"

Liliana held it out in her hand before him and pointed to a small hatch under his feet.

It took two of them to pry the door open after unlocking it, and even still, it shifted with a deafening screech. Solomon reached around and felt along the walls on both sides of the building, outside and in. It was indeed thick, maybe five or six inches thick. "Don't spend too much time in here during the day," he said.

"Or at all," Chuck mumbled.

Liliana took a washcloth from Solomon's sack and threw it to

King.

"This must be the presidential suite." The Welshman coughed, putting the towel over his mouth.

Solomon looked at Liliana slantwise.

"It won't do any good, but it'll make him feel safer," she shrugged. Solomon gazed into the dark of the building, fixed his glasses and, holding up the hands-free receiver, looked back at her.

"That's the kind of thing I expect from this," he muttered and walked into the narrow darkness.

Affronted, Liliana stayed back as Chuck went into the blackness of the structure after Seek and Cledwyn. While not a medical doctor, she had taken courses in the basic medical practices when pursuing her degree in genetics. While she loathed to think it, the creatures sounded—from what Solomon and the demented demigod on the line had told her—like forced evolution. There was no reason for such a drastic increase in the optical output of the human eye. Mankind, she thought, had survived just fine as diurnal beings and worshiped from its earliest days the sun and feared the night. Now there lived a contradiction on an isolated island off the coast of a first world nation, a human offshoot of unknown population who hunted and lived in the night and feared the sun. This unsettling thought kept her occupied as her eyes scanned the distant corners of the plaza.

It was silent. The villa, yes, but the generator too, and Liliana, panicking, ran to the doorway of the power station. Gasping for breath, she shouted in, "The virus!"

No reply.

She stood motionless, staring into the black, swirling Haze. Without warning, a face from the shadows collided into hers, knocking her down. Looking up she grasped for the pistol in her pocket.

"Do not pull that thing on me again," said Chuck, walking past, hauling the legs of a heavy body behind him. Liliana helped herself and stood as Solomon came out next, holding its head in a basket with his hands, pushing his mouth into his sleeve to avoid the stench.

"What is that?!" demanded Liliana.

"That," said King, strolling out last, "is our monkey wrench foulin' up the gears and all."

Liliana and Chuck studied the body as Solomon fled to the fountain to relieve yet another blood-soaked yack. The body wasn't like the others, decomposed and dressed in Third Reich regalia. This specimen was intact, its fingers and toes still wrapped in rubbery flesh, arms and legs still boasting the muscles which had failed to keep him alive. The face, however, was beyond recognition, coated in a dry bloodbath. Liliana bent down to examine the mouth, an empty hole still gaping wide. A gloss like a red runway ran down its jaw from the throat. She turned its neck, careful not to let the blood splinter in her palms. Aside from the sticky crimson discharge, its throat was bare and missed the signature azure mark of inmates to San Magnus Island.

Chuck paid closer attention to the rifle hanging by a strap across its chest, a piston-driven, gas-operated HK 550. He grabbed hold of it by the stock and scope and lifted it over the head of the corpse. "This doesn't belong here…" he whispered under his breath.

Liliana looked hesitantly over to Chuck, suddenly aware that his firepower now outmatched her own.

"It's German, all right," he explained, "but I doubt if he was. This rifle has only been on the market for three years." Liliana let the body go and sat back, watching Chuck as he expelled the breadbox-sized clip, a one-hundred-round circular beta-C magazine for the 5.56×45mm NATO cartridge. It was a godsend or a terror in a barren place like the one they had found themselves in, where a long, sharp stick might constitute high-grade weapons technology. Chuck poked his finger into the magazine, a tube spaced between the two drums of ammo. Carefully, he flicked out a spacer round, an empty cartridge signaling the drums had been run dry.

King stood over them, looking around the sky and then back into the dark of the generator room. "He fell over the turbine. It's clogged up with his blood and teeth. Just give me a few minutes and some ammonia and we'll have enough power for toast and a bubble bath." He nodded upward toward a mass of clouds off the sea. "Storm's comin'," he said, covering his mouth again and strutting into the generator room.

Solomon came back from the plaza, massaging his throat, and stopped cold when he saw Chuck rummaging through the dead man's pockets. "No dog tags, no wallet, no ID patch on his jacket, no nothing," Chuck said. "Not even any ammo." He tossed the magazine into a dirt patch behind them.

"Well, let's get to it." Solomon asked Chuck to stay behind and help Cledwyn with the generator, taking turns in the station so as not to let either of them take in the full force of The Haze. As thick as it was, the men could literally see it lingering, like a gas leak tinted with a dark violet floating in the air around them.

Liliana had to remind herself of what the malicious hands-free device had told them earlier that morning. The generator in the Villa Vienna provided power to both it and the Villa Roma but ran on a completely different circuit than the fortress. The former village, it had said, served as the center for San Magnus's civilian population, those refuges of political dignitary or intellectual importance. "In other words, the sick bastards who are still trying to kill us," Solomon had said. The latter had been the living quarters of escaped Schutzstaffel, elite Special Forces of Hitler's Nazi guard and their families. Only Vienna housed a bombardment shelter, which lay under the ruined mansion of biologist and dental practitioner Albert Vogel.

In the shelter under his house, the voice assured them, they would find his body along with that of his wife, children, and three others the sinister static had described as "irrelevant."

Liliana and Solomon made their way from the plaza toward the center of town. They walked and scanned silently, looking up and down the walls and windows for the Vogel practice. The Villa Vienna came fully stocked like its northerly neighbor, a separate and self-sufficient village so as not to combine the ranks of soldier and master. It possessed a series of shops, rows of residences, a garden, presumably of imported foliage, now overrun by the native species, a small church, and even a playground.

"And a dentist's office," Solomon smirked, pointing to a stained gray wooden tooth hanging from the entryway of the great big house at the end of Karl Benz. A fifty-year-old Jeep laid deflated and crippled just around the corner. He examined the truck carefully. It looked as if it had been left out on a day when rocks hailed instead of ice.

"That's a practice? Looks more like a castle," Liliana retorted, drawing his attention back to the matter at hand. The doorframe was marked with the signature crimson-colored spat, but they could not see why. Vogel's house was huge, but its windows were broken and unsupported, its front door falling off the hinges. Looking up at the sky to watch the storm clouds nearing, Solomon noticed the mansion's defenses: two large spotlights hanging from the balcony above, pointed not up but straight downward, staring at the street below their feet.

The mansion itself was a complete mess, its carpeting stained and ripped, littered over by torn pages from medical journals fallen off the high shelves of eight-foot-high hardwood bookcases propped against the sides of the interior structure. Two such shelves nearly covered the walkway from the foyer to the hall, and Liliana had to inch through and help Solomon push it aside from both sides. The corridor itself opened into many small rooms, each with a single beige dental chair, padding pushed out from the seams, tiny metallic probes and mirrors littering the floor around them. But no bodies could be found lying lifeless in any of these chairs, and indeed no one had died in one. The house was empty.

The second floor was more of the same, except stationed in every room along the walkway was a single bed. They were tucked in neatly as if they'd just been made and their owners were out at market, the children playing in the playground. At the end of the hall, by the balcony, sat the master bedroom, but the master was likewise absent, and his bed was likewise made. A tall glass sat on the nightstand by the far end, with a copy of Quick Magazine, its cover stories all written in capital German lettering. Solomon turned its cover and found the publication date, nineteen eighty-three. He ran his hand over the bedding. It was soft and inviting. He pushed down to test the springs, his hand falling straight through the mattress. *Figures.* From the hallway he heard Liliana's voice calling out.

"It's quite a view, no?" she said turning from the sky-rise railing toward him. From the second story they could scout the horizon in the distance, where the ocean rolled over and the clouds began. Solomon gripped the handle of one of the spotlights wrapped around the rail with electrical cords and heavy-duty black tape. He could shake it only a few inches from side to side, covering the left hand corner and the center to the entrance of the mansion.

"Hey!" shouted the Brit from way down the block, standing atop the fountain in the plaza. "I'm about to light this place like Christmas, so get the fuck back from those things!" he bellowed. Cledwyn walked back to the generator as Liliana and Solomon fled the dentist's house just in time to see the searchlights spark and light for a moment before exploding, sending glass and debris flying over and on top of their heads. Unconsciously, Solomon dropped into a cocoon and wrapped his arms around Liliana, pushing her to the ground.

Pinned against the cobblestone, Liliana whispered to him, "I'll stop pointing my gun at him if you stop jumping on me…"

The lights were completely blown out and had become two gravely out-of-place, twentieth-century gargoyles to watch over Albert Vogel's house. Solomon dusted off his jacket and let go of Liliana. Chuck and Cledwyn came running over but slowed when they saw their companions were unhurt. "This is the only safe house we could find," he informed them, "save for that damned plague-infested mole hole."

"Ay, that tells you something, don't it?" said the Welshman pointing up at the blown spotlights. "The last buggers to hold up here left those on when the power blew. They were safe in there while their buttie in the generator room was choking somethin' awful."

"He stayed in there and suffocated rather than risk coming outside?" Solomon asked.

"He was out of ammo," Chuck replied.

Solomon felt a vibration in his pocket and reached for the receiver. "I see you've got the generator working again. Good. Very good. Your next stop is indeed the basement of the house in front of you, not like the cellar of the butcher's, I assure you, and I tell you this now because you'll be alone when you go down there. No frequency can penetrate the bunker."

"Finally, some peace and quiet," said King.

"With the power back on, the key code to Vogel's outer shelter door will be online. It's a rather thin layer of steel compared to the one and a half meters of concrete behind it. The password for the outer hatch is an unimaginative *überlegen.*"

"Superior," said Liliana.

"Go down into that hole and set up shop. It has everything you need to begin your search. And don't worry. Its air is stale and foul but harmless. The Haze was pumped through the office and the bedrooms, but ventilation in the blast shelter seems untouched. It's the second safest place on the island."

"If you know so much about it, why don't you just come out here and do it all yourself?" asked Solomon.

"You tabloid slime! Did it not occur to you that I already had? You think you're the first team to come ashore in San Magnus in search of answers? I've done this before, again and again, but you people always manage to get yourselves killed. My own men even, loyal, obedient enough to follow me so far and so long only to fail me here. Casualties are always expected. You lose a few to the night, a couple here to the Haze, but eventually you make it into the fortress. And do you know what happens then? You turn on each other like the animals you flee, killing one another just as soon as you realize all the gold and riches can be yours and yours alone."

The group paused and looked at each other. No one's eyes proved a safe harbor for the intents of any other. King spoke first, but to the hands-free. "What gold and riches?"

Solomon's face sunk into his shirt. He dropped the device in the street closer to Cledwyn and walked back to sit on the stoop outside Vogel's practice.

"Oh? So Mr. Solomon didn't tell you?" asked the voice. "When the Nazis fled Europe, they didn't do it with pennies in their pockets, Mr. King. No, they took with them five point two billion—that's billion with a B—pounds sterling worth of stolen relics. It's the greatest treasure trove of the last four hundred years. That's roughly one billion per each of you, should you complete your work, or none and a gaping hole in your necks should you not. That's what they're for, of course.

Your little threats of death. Promise someone a billion dollars and they'll do as you say, but threaten them not to take six billion and you'd better be ready to blow their heads off."

January 2ⁿᵈ, 2021 2100 hours

Tomorrow I go to prison. The dog will stay with you at your mother's new place. My old place… Do you remember when Daddy used to live there with you? Is it too far now from your memories? I can't think of a better time to get divorced, really. There won't be any of that lingering "who gets what" or running into each other at the supermarket with some stranger. They'll just be notices every other week from the warden or guard captain or whatever saying, "I'm replacing the sofa," or "I've thrown out your Ween collection." I wish you could stay as children. I know I can't fathom it, but statistically speaking, one of you will have been divorced at least once by the time you read this. So you know.

As you're older now and no doubt know already, I think it's fair time to tell you about your mother. The woman stands for nothing. To her, convictions are creeds to live by for living's sake, not for truth or ethics but the next day. If our places had been reversed, do you think she would have stood her ground as I did? Do you think it was the right thing to do? Was I wrong? What I am sure of is that she'd never put herself on the line, let me raise you instead so *she* could face down a murderer, a psychopath like Salazar. She doesn't have the gumption to stand for the ideals she lacks in the first place. Maybe that's changed. Maybe I've changed.

I'm confident in my assumption; she would have turned in [our friend] and explained quaintly to you girls that some things are more important than principles or trust, that she had to provide for you first and foremost. Did she have that talk when you asked her? Did she say it just like that? I hope your opinions of me aren't shaped by the news headlines, the rumors at school, the hushed whispers of your teachers, or the ranting of your mother. And if they are, if I'm that man to you, I hope this log finds you in time before you no longer care at all.

As for Salazar, it looks like he'll be in prison himself soon enough, with a far longer sentence than mine. They've given me two years for obstruction, impeding, and wiretapping but they'll probably give him the chair or the needle or whatever it is the federal government deems "humane" these days. He doesn't qualify anyhow. That said, two years is a long time. Samantha, you will be thirteen and Rebecca eight. Seven hundred and thirty days of gruel and sleep and rise and gruel and sleep and rise. That's what Daddy's putting himself through to be right, to protect what's right, and so much more.

I'll have sweet dreams of the Lieutenant Colonel every night, trapped in a cramped iron box in a hole someplace under Guantanamo Bay. Or maybe in a shabby plywood casket marked by number rather than name. Feel free, as always, to make notes in the margins as to the outcomes of my speculations. What they should do is stamp a big red T for traitor on his chest and parade him through the cities and the countryside riding a mule. These types of men, these Nixons of the future, must be hunted, girls. I hope you realize that. Daddy didn't do it all for nothing.

That's what'll get me through. I love you very much and want to live long and grow old to see you become successful and happy, to see this entry and all the others irrelevant and unnecessary. I'm satisfied with my choices; I couldn't get by in this world where my children live if giving in to corruption and hypocrisy is norm. You'll be on my mind night and day, and I'll write as often as I can, two letters, one for you now and one for you then. But it'll be Salazar, disgraced, imprisoned, euthanized, and finally exposed, who'll be my ward. The righteous hunt drives me. I don't know what you do now, what you've grown up to learn, where you work and how or if you're married at home; that's all fine. But that drive—do you ever get that drive? Does your stomach turn when you hear a lie? When you watch the news, when a war report is stifled by a dog show or Superbowl ad? Do you have it in you?

All of the utilities here are turned off, so let this be the first official day of my sentencing. I'll store the Kindle with a few other things in my lock box and continue writing from my cell. Looking out the window now over the neighborhood, it's hard to think about the future and how different it's about to be. The snow is falling. It just missed the holidays, but it's coming down in force now. At your mother's you'll have already lit all the candles. You're now just putting away the menorah, and the rest of mankind is recovering from a rowdy worldwide New Year's party. It's been a really lovely winter. The other apartments all have wreaths on their doors. The houses on the other side of the boulevard are draped in red and green lights. The street curb is lined with piles of bushy white. The kids on my block are out there starting their snowmen and snow angels, and I am going to prison for making a mass murderer prime-time news to a nation who'd never even heard his name before.

I love you, girls. See you in two years. Happy Holidays, America.
Seek Solomon

June 27ᵗʰ, 2025 1330 hours

Where to start? Well, I'll start with this, since it fell and cracked on the beach three days ago, my Kindle seems to be malfunctioning. Not horribly—it's not making roaming calls to China, though I wish it would. Only every time I try to open a new file it opens two, an old one and then a new one. The good news is that with the power back on I can plug her in, though I had to test three outlets with an old vacuum and two analog clocks to find one that wouldn't spark. Whatever. So long as I can put down in words the insanity and absurdity that I'm about to.

Girls, Daddy's in trouble. In the three days I've been a "guest" on San Magnus, I've been implanted with explosives, chased by monsters, suffocated by poison gasses, and shot at by a ninety-pound anthropology professor. This place is a tropical resort for ghosts. They lie relaxing, letting the sun's rays tan their bones in the streets. Something terrible happened here to these people, not as long ago as it should have. Upstairs, in the live-in dental office of Nazi War Criminal Albert Vogel, I found a trashy gossip rag in German, with a date halfway between now and the Second World War. Many of the island's supplies, the expiration date on the milk in the iceboxes, publish dates in the medical journals, the old radio sets and cans of salted fish— they're all dated around the mid-nineteen-eighties. I was three or four when it seems most of these people were killed, either by choking to death from a super-strain of weaponized Ebola or these things, these nocturnal behemoths that roam the streets looking for me every night. They are the masters of San Magnus island now, save for one apparition: a digital god who orders us around under the promise of riches and threat of death.

There are four of us here including myself and Hiroto's contact, the man I met on the mainland, Chuck Polanski. Adding to our "team" as the voice refers to us over the blue-tooth I found in my hat, are Liliana Ferreira, the aforementioned professor, who I admit surprises me with her strength but must always be watched. A doctor on an island of horrors constructed by doctors is something to be fearful of indeed. The last of us is a colorful Welshman named Cledwyn King, a self-described larcenist with his eyes on a great big pot of gold. King seems decent enough, if not aggressively personable, and we would not be where we are now without his skill, but a man with a mind of money is always dangerous. I don't trust him either.

Why are they here? Why are any of us here? King claims he was coming to scout the resort and make off with a few sets of silver cutlery and old ladies' pearls. He doesn't seem as shocked by his predicament as the rest of us, but he does seem genuine in his aspirations. He was just tipped off forty years too late. Dr. Ferreira similarly claims she's here for research, and if true, that makes us colleagues. Or rivals. It seems she got herself in some trouble back on the mainland and is in the process of losing her job without the interference of a grand breakthrough, and in that I certainly sympathize. But there's something about her I can't quite grasp. She's more than she appears to be. I've never seen a bookworm take so quickly to firearms before.

My empathy, however, lies with Chuck, who is trapped here with the rest of us because of that damned Hiri. He's not after the casket of gold. He's not here for a study or a story. He's just a poor schmuck who got dragged along for the ride. Though I'm guilty in thinking it's our benefit that he was. In a place like this, we need as much muscle and armed know-how as we can get. So far we've found the bodies of soldiers from two different centuries. He may not be the brightest man on the island, but he hasn't spent a minute complaining, and we'd all be much worse off without him.

There's been no sign of Hiroto. It looks like he hacked into something he really shouldn't have. If he has been killed, then he's spared the torture of this vacation. If I ever get out of here, I'll do well to visit his mother and sister. I'd do better to bring them a billion dollars. That, the money, is sticking in my side. I don't understand it. Why both threaten to kill us *and* promise us fair shares of the plunder? Certainly the pain of death is enough motivation. And who is this invisible overseer? What do we know about him? He's cold. He looks out for us just as far as it keeps us alive and doing his work for him. He's smart; he has every step planned out ahead of time. He knows this island. I wonder how long he's been here, up in that tower looking over the villas like a ghoulish Rapunzel. And he said something—something I've heard before someplace. "Providence bodes permanence." Where do I know that from? I've control+F'd that phrase through my log and notes but came up with nothing.

In any case, he was right. In the bottom of Herr Vogel's house, we did find a trap door leading down to the blast shelter. The coded electric lock on the hatch itself was a great surprise as there's not an appliance bigger than a toaster around town that looks younger than sixty. But that lock, as Cledwyn, the expert on locks, said, "Would have taken a bloody long time to pop." It couldn't have been put in closer than forty years ago. The air-conditioned decomposing bodies of the Vogels speak for that. Did they invent it? And here is the most gruesome part of this trip to come. The voice laid out his plan for us in full. To get into the vault, he needs another password—three words. Apparently, it's something a lot harder to hack than "superior" in the father tongue. But before that we need access into the fortress itself, the Kapitalzukunft, this indestructible concrete stain in the jungle hills. With these Nazis, their obsession with racial supremacy dies hard; the biometric lock into the fortress requires the blood of its top scientists, or rather the DNA of its Vorkämpfer members. They had their genes tested, and no drop of blood but the four of theirs, Vogel, Jung,

Ebersbach, and Metzger, will open those massive iron doors. Vogel's diary confirms it. I found it under his empty mattress in the bunker's bedroom. Vogel was one of the worst, not a mad genius of genetics like Metzger, but a fanatic anti-Semite planning his retirement by plucking the teeth from his living victims and sipping mojitos. His body, with his wife's and his little girls', were huddled together in the corner. Chuck found another pistol, empty, beside their bodies. I quickly became sick again.

Vogel's diary is all in German of course, so I took a picture scan of the last few pages with the tablet and ran them through Adobe Translation. I've posted the most promising passages below:

Gerhadt is mad! He's killed us all. He's killed the future and all humanity! I was at Roma, pulling a molar from Captain Baer, the cripple from Buchenwald who never leaves his house. I expect now he will never leave it again. I was just finishing up when the ventilation duct started to pour Gerhadt's V12 toxin. He had displayed it with such pride last year, claiming that he could engineer it further to affect only peoples of lesser genetics. It devastated the test subjects in moments, and I expected I would last about as long when I saw the Captain spitting blood in the drain pan after his tooth. I tried to push him from his chair but he was too heavy, and I felt the blur, that nauseating death sensation seeping into my soul, so I left him there and ran back to my Jeep. Men and women, grasping their children, good Germans, soldiers and citizens, ran from their houses with that purple fog, that murdering cloud chasing them. One woman covered in blood tore out in front of me and tried throwing her baby into my backseat. I just kept driving.

When I got to Vienna the V12 was washing out into the streets. At the playground I found Teresa and the children coddled with the Kirchmann's and their son from next door. I shouted for them to jump into the Jeep and I drove to the house with our hands in a chain. The haze was so thick in my office I felt I was sleepwalking through a nightmare...

...In the shelter we have air running from a portal close to the beach. I'm assured that V12 is dependent on air flow, so it could not possibly blow toward the beach and then back down into the air ducts. But that is the good news. Surely the house is flooded with it and shall be for some time. We were running so fast to get down here that there was no chance of opening the windows, and even if we had it might still take years for the wind to blow out the last of the gas. And what if it

71

just keeps pumping into the house? Gerhadt. Why, Gerhadt? This was no accident. Senior Researcher Gerhardt Metzger 'does not make mistakes!' We are his test subjects now. We, his own people, his rats in the cage. Is this why he led us all here to begin with? Was this his plan since the war? If I ever get out of here, Gerhardt...

...Today is the twenty-second of October, meaning that Teresa, I, and the children have lived uncomfortably in the shelter for one whole year. The Kirchmanns did not make it. They were old and frail and could not survive, and they have left us their son, Klaus, with a large mouth to feed. He eyes my Trudi insistently, and I may have to kill him and dump him in the incinerator with his old crow of a mother and father...

...Teresa and I have decided that this is the end. Our supplies have run out faster than I'd hope they'd last what with the Kirchmanns and their filthy pervert of a son. The shelter was never meant to last more than two years, and it's now been two and a quarter. There is no food; what water we have will run dry by month's end, and the air ducts are too small even to fit Gerta, our smallest. I confronted Teresa about the possibility of opening the hatch, and she asked if there was a chance it might be safe. I could not lie to her. I had been monitoring the door outside for some time on the visual machine, and so I showed her. She told me it was like a moving painting of our house, smeared with a violet oil.

In the storehouse there is but one supply in ample stock, that of bullets. It is my greatest regret that I shall live, starving long enough, to eat the very last one. For the Fatherland, for her people, and for Hitler. May god forgive me.

Albert Hermenegild Vogel, D.D.S M.D.

Chapter VII

The first thing Solomon and his compatriots discovered in the blast shelter was the smell. Its previous tenants had lain together in a huddled mass locked off in a darkened bedroom someplace under Karl Benz Street for nearly half a century. The airtight locking systems of the rooms themselves, a testament to the advanced construction of the old subterranean retreat, had kept the odor of the Vogels from reaching the surface, but inside it could not be ignored.

Looking in through the door-frame at the huddled mass in the corner of the bedroom, Solomon could almost make out the expressions on the faces of Albert Vogel's three little girls. "That one there, the tallest one, that was Trudi. And the little one there, with the flowers on her dress, that was Gerta," he muttered.

"What of the other girl with the sandals? What was her name?" asked Chuck.

"I don't know," replied Solomon, taking off his glasses, wiping them over with his shirt and walking down the hall.

King spat something along the lines of, "Dentists and their suicide, aye?" and followed Solomon. Chuck crumpled his lips and closed the door after them.

The submerged safe house was now powered, drawing from the generator down the block. Cledwyn checked and found that it indeed had its own means of power generation, a geothermal system like the station above, but that its small alternator had blown out long ago. Though its supplies had been drained and required electricity from outside, it would be impossible to smell, hear, or for that matter know if anyone was hiding in the cellar from the street up above. The dentist's bunker was barren and rotten but indeed the safest place to sleep they had found yet on San Magnus Island.

"It's more than just a hole in the ground," Liliana said, walking down the hall leading toward the beach, closest to the air duct's exit point. She motioned for the others to come look, and there they found what the voice had sent them for. Along the white brick walls around the room lay great metal tables littered in varying shapes hiding under dusty white sheets. They walked into the room for a closer inspection. Above the tables hung framed photographs of teeth, thousands of teeth, sharp and dull, wide and small.

"Panthera leo nubica, Ursus arctos horribilis, Crocodylus nilo…ticus, Carcha…rodon carcha…rias," Cledwyn read, his thick accent treading heavily through his broken Latin.

"Those are Great White Shark teeth there, and those are bear's teeth," Liliana corrected.

"And these?" asked Solomon, pointing to a selection along the far wall above another table covered in a long white sheet. Liliana eyed the photographs as Solomon's attention turned tentatively toward the hidden, cloth-covered contents of the array before them.

"These…are all human teeth," she whispered. Liliana traced her finger along the edges of the prints, gathering a trail of dust from under her nails down to the inside of her second knuckle. "Nineteen-fifty, this one says. And this one, nineteen-sixty." Liliana brushed aside the lettering on all four the photographs, ending on nineteen-eighty, each displaying a progressively more menacing set of incisors than the last. Solomon whipped the white cloth from the table before them, revealing two sets of dark leather bracers chained tightly to the corners of the furniture. Liliana took a step back, but Solomon just stood and held out his hands as if to imitate the size of a gargantuan fish he'd just caught. He reached from one side of the table with each arm and stepped back, raising them but keeping them the same distance from each other. A distance of about four feet. Solomon dropped his hands.

"How do you grow fangs in forty years, Doctor?" Chuck asked, tilting his head up, nose level with the last of the photographs.

"I… I don't know. They could be *falso*, artificial, but then why have so many of them? Why not just implant the last ones?"

"This doesn't make any sense. Vogel was a Nazi purist like all the rest. They believed they were the superior beings. They believed they were perfect. Why were they trying to improve? What were they trying to build?"

"Soldiers," Chuck answered. "Numbers." He and King pulled the sheets off the remaining tables, spotting one with a sink on the far end. They stood gazing at it like fallen idol, a reminder of the last few drops of water they'd poured into dirty old bottles from melted iceboxes and storm drains. Liliana approached it, their representative scientist in the field. She tested the nozzle on the lab sink and, after a few hisses and moans found it leaking a weak but steady flow of clear, seemingly clean water. She dipped her head gently under to have a sip.

"Oh, God," she falsetto'd, slurping it down like a grazing water buffalo. King, Solomon, and Polanski quickly lined up behind her. When they and their bottles had been filled to the brink, they helped her to gather the newly found supplies. The room was fit enough for an amateur chemist, a veritable laboratory lair cliché to make any madman proud. Liliana collected all the instruments she would need onto the central table, the only one not decorated with a collection of black-and-white fangs.

There were some tiny polyethylene syringes, slides, clamps, swabs in plastic bags, beakers, a petri dish, a thermal cycler, a hybridization probe, a box of potentiometric dyes, and one massive electron microscope, nearly three feet high off the table. Liliana required a stool to reach the microscope while holding herself up by pressing her palms on the table.

And above that particular table Liliana stared at four printings of something she found very familiar: double helixes. The intent was not lost on her. They were framed like portraits of distinguished family members. On the bottom of each were the chartered lines of genetic code, the makings of each man in each picture on the wall. She could read them, sure, but the charts didn't distinguish any of them from Adam, though only one of them could have been. "What's the point?" she asked herself. "The only good these do is separate them from each other. And everyone else. But they're just men." She sighed and looked back to the team of men she had with her. *Four samples, three men.*

"Okay then, Doc." said Cledwyn. "Now it's your turn." Liliana smirked and turned to her equipment. Every frame and lens was decades older than she, but the age gap felt non-existent yet again. Somehow, before the rest of the world, the inhabitants of San Magnus were able to devise the tools and apparatuses of twenty-first century laboratory science. What could they have done, she wondered, if they'd continued to live and produce? Liliana felt a watchful gaze looming over her and was surprised to find it was Solomon's. She turned again to face the gentlemen all waiting for some semblance of an order, all well aware they were treading out of their elements and into hers.

Liliana smiled. "Would one of you fine gentlemen tear a fingernail off of Dr. Vogel and bring it to me?"

King chuckled, muttering "I'm on it," and left the room to fetch her the macabre item in question.

"Mr. Solomon?" she asked, sensing both his skepticism and his hesitance. "Could I ask you for a sample?"

"A sample?" he asked, his eyes skewing to the side. He looked over at Chuck who chortled softly and went after Cledwyn.

Liliana became stern, running the cool sink water over one the cleanest-looking syringes. "A blood sample. As a test. For your DNA." She started walking toward him, needle in hand.

"That doesn't look very hygienic. Don't you think I could catch something from that?"

"Oh, you're worried about your health now, Mr. Solomon? Please, there are many more dangerous things here than me with my little needle."

Solomon backed up against a corner table, where the great animal teeth prints scowled just above his head. Liliana took hold of his arm and held it out, looking straight into his eyes. He felt a chill shoot up and then slide slowly back down his spine like a frozen elevator as he watched her big green eyes drop to spy his elbow. He bobbed his head back so as not to look as she grabbed below his bicep and slipped the pointed tip through his light-toned skin, hairs standing on end, and into his median cubital vein just shy of his hinge joint. She extracted a tiny two milliliters of blood into the syringe and pulled out, walking back to lab table while he massaged his arm and ran his fingers over the

76

injection spot. Shooting the blood back into a petri dish, she turned around to look him in the eyes again.

"Big baby."

Chapter VIII

The men watched impatiently as Liliana tinkered over her microscope. The mix of smells—burning fingernail, sterilized enzymes, and what lingered on of the Vogels—warranted the men wait on the floor in the hall with their legs propped up against their chests, making light chit-chat.

"What'd you do after that?" Cledwyn asked Chuck.

"Well," replied the Texan, taking a swig from his jug of fresh distilled water, "I said, 'Thanks, boys, for all the laughs,' and I took my ass down to the private sector. There's a lot of work still to be found there, what with all the meddling NATO's been up to. A lot of legal work, I should add."

Solomon paused for a second when Chuck winked at him. Seek feigned a smile and, pointing to each of them in turn, gave his rebuttal.

"So you're a thief, you're a mercenary, she"—his arm stretched toward the laboratory—"is clearly a madwoman, and I'm the only one who's been to prison. That's just peachy."

"Oh, no worries, buddy. I've been arrested countless times. Just never convicted," Cledwyn added with a great big smack on Chuck's back. "Now, what's the great big secret with your little sentence, aye?" Solomon slipped his glasses up off his ears, poured a little water on his sleeve, and wiped them clear. He sighed and looked down at his frames, rubbing the joints where pressure had left them wide and susceptible to slippage.

"I... I stood up for a friend."

"What friend?" asked Chuck. "Hiroto?"

"Yeah." Seek sighed again.

"Much good it did you," Chuck replied. Solomon gave him a sharp glance but made no rebuke.

"Right, and who is this Hiroto fella I've been hearin' so much about?" posed the Welshman.

Chuck put up his hands as if to pass the question down the line.

"He was a friend of mine. Ours."

"Oh, he *was* a friend of yours then? Well. I guess that means you might meet him again after all. You know, if I die in this stupid place, at least I get to see me mum. Great jolly woman. Always smile at ya, laughin', could make you grin if a Nazi'd just run over your dog."

Chuck nudged him for his attention and held out his hands to imitate the cupping of two massive imperceptible knockers.

"Oh, you sick bastard," yelped King, pushing Chuck playfully into the doorway. "That's me mum, you bloody scrut!"

Solomon couldn't help but laugh.

"If you boys are done with your toys, I've got something for you to see," said Liliana, her back to the commotion. Solomon stood as Chuck and Cledwyn bullied about on the floor. She signaled him over to look into the microscope, hopping down from the stool in front of it. Solomon lifted his specs over his forehead and squinted as he bent forward over the lens.

"Even if I could see without my glasses, I'd still have no idea what I'm looking at."

Liliana scoffed and gently tilted his head back.

"That was your DNA. It looks sort of like a squiggly necklace."

"Ooh, how girly," he joked.

"Dr. Vogel's DNA looks to you or me just like it, but in the thermal cycler"—she waved Solomon over to the massive calculator-like machine—"they're amplified, and no two strands of code are the same. I've tested yours and the nail from the other room. One of you is Dr. Albert Vogel. You'll be happy to know it's not you." She smiled. She had a frightfully charming smile.

"But how do you know that?"

Liliana turned and took down a portrait from the wall behind him. It displayed a double helix, clear as day, and a multitude of fine print Solomon couldn't make out, much less understand.

"Mr. Solomon, meet Dr. Vogel."

Seek shook his head, baffled. "He had his DNA framed?"

"Someone did. The nail matches the code in the picture. And there are three other pictures. Three more men." Liliana propped the portrait back up on the wall and ran her hand along, pointing to each. "Vogel, Ebersbach, Jung and—"

"Metzger," Solomon finished. He couldn't help but stare at the last frame. It looked like nothing to him—two squiggly lines connected by a bunch of straight lines, like a spiral staircase that'd been hung out to dry. The significance, however, was not lost on him. This was the literal essence of evil.

"It's a manhunt. That's why we're here. That's why he brought us. To hunt these men."

Solomon felt a resoluteness fill him. "That's exactly why I came here in the first place."

"Maybe it was fate?" Liliana posed.

"Fate?" Solomon repeated. "That doesn't sound very scientific."

"No? Either you were coming to this island or not. You wanted to hunt for these men, yes? And it looks like someone knew you would. Someone who knows you well. So you came. You couldn't avoid it. You couldn't stop it from happening. It was always going to happen. Only one thing can ever happen; there's only ever one outcome. The experiment will succeed or fail but it is always science."

Solomon slunk back against the table. He just stood there for a while as Liliana watched his eyes flickering in internal discussion. Finally he replied in a tender voice, "Then what's the next thing that's going to happen?"

Liliana smirked and continued. "We'll have to test this machine lock thing that's waiting for us at the fortress. We need to see if it can truly tell if this is Vogel's DNA. I will be very surprised if it can."

"And why is that?" asked Solomon, shaking off the softness in his voice.

"Because that kind of electric identificação...er, profiling, has only been around for ten or twenty years. Alec Jeffreys was the first to profile DNA, and he did it by hand forty years ago."

"That's right. He used it to identify Joseph Mengele's body when they found it. In Brazil."

"Yes, and if we find your Dr. Metzger, we can use it on him too."

"All right," Solomon concluded. "I'll get the boys."

The team gathered in the common area of the bunker. Solomon checked the time. It was five p.m. "Okay," he started, spreading the map he'd found over a Swastika emblem on the coffee table, "there are about two hours of sunlight left. That should be more than enough to take the Jeep out. Cledwyn, you said you fixed it up, right?"

"Well, yes but—" King was cut off.

"And drive up Karl Braun through the Villa Roma," Seek continued, following the trail with his index finger. "To the gates of the Kapitalzukunft just over this ridge in the mountain crest, so we can test its lock mechanism," he concluded, pressing his eyeglasses back against his nose and locking them in place.

"Didn't the voice already say it works fine? Sounds like lot of extra risk we don't need," Chuck added.

Solomon paused. "Liliana has her doubts."

Cledwyn rolled his eyes.

"And frankly I'd rather not take at face value every little thing the man who's trying to kill us says."

"Friend, I think if he was trying to kill us—"

Solomon cut King short. "He is trying to kill us. He put bombs in our necks. Do you really think he's going to hand you a billion dollars and give you a pat on the back? We are not his friends. We're his tools, and you're not going to get any of that damn money listening to him!"

Cledwyn reached across the table and pushed Solomon down, pulling back a fist, but was tossed against a sofa by Chuck before making good on it.

"You, sit," said the big Texan, staring down at the tiny Welshman.

"Well, that was pleasant," said Liliana. "Do you think we could go now before it gets dark?"

"I think there's one other thing we need to discuss first," said Solomon, crawling off the floor. "I think we should vote a leader."

"A leader? What leader? You have the map. You have the wireless. You found us. You're the leader!" said Dr. Ferreira matter-of-factly.

"I agree," said Chuck, still staring down Cledwyn, "I'm only here because of you, anyway. I mean. You know what I mean."

"Was kind of hoping you wouldn't say that, but yeah," replied Solomon. "And you?" he asked the man who'd just tried to clock him in the face.

"Aye, well, I'm hardly in a position to disagree with you fine, very large fellas..." he mumbled, putting out his hands.

"I think that's all fine in here, when we're thinking ahead and we have air and our skin, but out there is a combat zone, especially at dusk when it starts crawling with hostiles. Is that an accurate depiction, Chuck?" asked Seek.

Chuck raised his eyebrows. "Well, yes, I suppose it is."

"Okay," continued Solomon, "I've been in a few combat zones in my life, and I know well enough that I shouldn't be in charge of our little troop when we get in one. I vote that when we're out there, in danger, Master Sergeant Polanski be in charge. I'd feel much safer with my life in his hands than he should with his life in mine."

Solomon looked around the room for confirmation. Liliana nodded and smiled lightly at Chuck. Cledwyn let out a great big sarcastic grin and stuck out his hand.

Chuck grabbed it and helped the man up to his feet. "Well then," he said. "Let's move out."

When they opened the hatch they heard a very familiar sound. Indeed, drips poured down the cracks in the ceiling and onto the carpet in the hall, the office, and the waiting room by the front door of the Vogel practice. Stepping out last, Solomon couldn't shake the shock and horror of his first night on the island, the streets drenched, torrential rain whipping his face like a towel, his glasses thick with fog and his clothes damp and heavy. He pulled his baseball cap down hard. Then the lightning struck. "Make that about an hour of daylight!" Chuck yelled back at him as they made out for the Jeep.

Their newly elected leader jumped into the driver's seat with Cledwyn passenger and revved the engine of the old war relic as it fought, coughing, against the rain. Solomon, a city-dweller all his life, had not spent much time behind the wheel, but he could appreciate the sound of a rotor turning over despite the odds stacked against it. He and Liliana climbed in back, using their free hands to point out the road signs leading back to Karl Braun and up to the Villa Roma. Cledwyn's jury-rigging held her together, but just barely, as she shot and sped, spitting fumes into the downpour and propelling them down the bumpy cobblestones. "There! Should be enough time to get there and back!" Solomon shouted, nearly tipping frontward and then back off the cart into the mud on the sides of the road.

"This thing had better work!" Chuck yelled back.

"Yes, it better," Liliana replied. They sped past the generator room, and Solomon spotted the still-open door.

"We have to lock up the generator!" he yelled.

"We'll get it on the way back," said Chuck as he turned the corner and flew out of the villa.

As they drove up the road, Seek took a look back at the beach they had passed on the serene walk into town earlier that day. It no longer tepidly beckoned him to a long-awaited retreat but screamed as the vanguard of hell, black waves crashing on the beach to the sounds of thunder soon after and streaks of lightning crashing down into the ocean from on high. He looked the opposite way toward the jungle crawling with a wall of rainfall, so dark not even the brief and sudden crashes of chained fire in the sky could illuminate it. Beside him in the Jeep, grasping hold of its rusted metal rails, sat the dark-skinned professor, water trickling down her face, hair thrashed from side to side by the wind. Seek found little difficulty in selecting comfort. He wrapped his arm around her as they turned the bend into the Villa Roma, and feeling this weight pull her down, she did the same. Their eyes may have met, but he couldn't be sure. It was only then that they noticed that the ringing sound on the wind was Cledwyn King in front of them, waving his hands about and chanting some Celtic ballad about the Bristol Channel.

As they flew into the Villa Roma, the Jeep began to pout, spurting a great black cloud from the muffler and stalling at the corner of Gottlieb Daimler.

"What the fuck?" Chuck muttered, slamming his foot on the gas and clutch, wiggling the starter and cursing in the downpour. She started up again but just barely, and Solomon and Liliana shot back in their seats, holding each other aboard. They skidded past the fountain with the boy holding his drenched copper torch and the clock tower whose rusted hands, though beaten down by the rain, refused to budge a single second. Though the fortress could be seen from miles away in any Westerly direction, and the tower from any direction at all, they held fast to caution in approaching it directly. To their relief, as Chuck drove up to the fortress's massive iron doors, they found no bodies, no signs of battle or struggle, just the wind and rain-battered entryway and a large standing terminal beside it.

Chuck pulled over at the curb and motioned the group to peel out and make for the stairs, lightning flashes lighting their way. Solomon and Cledwyn stopped and pressed their hands along the tiny gap between the colossal six-inch-thick wrought iron doors standing three times their height at the top of the steps. "A fortress indeed!" Solomon yelled to King, who shook his head in agreement. At the terminal Chuck struggled to figure out its controls.

"They're all in German!" he shouted into the wind, grabbing Solomon's attention.

"Let me take a look," said Seek. With a few taps the computer came to life, a small fifteen-by-fifteen-inch box that ejected a keyboard downward. With the flashing light from the display illuminating the keys, he instantly noticed the double *a* and *o* vowels with the accented diacritic marks above them. He looked up at the flashing red screen and read the words *Eintragen Probe*. "Eintragen Probe?" he repeated. "In probe?"

Liliana pointed out the receptacle on the side of the keyboard, a finger-shaped push print with a small hole in the center, ruling out the possibility of fingerprint analysis. Liliana nodded in its direction and put her hand over Solomon's. Her grip was tight, a match for his when they'd rolled around in the dankness of the butcher's basement. She held out his hand and pressed his index finger into the slot, triggering the small needle-point in the hole to stick out, puncture a fragment of skin in his finger, and retract. Solomon wiped the pin prick over his thumb and stuck it in his mouth to suck, feigning a scorned glance.

Then they watched the screen closely, edging for results. When a largely printed *Untergebene* flashed in red across the monitor, she knew her experiment was at least half successful.

Liliana reached into her pocket and pulled out a brown cloth bandage she had taken from the infirmary, holding it under the curvature of her body and then the terminal to protect it from the wind and rain. She pulled Dr. Albert Vogel's fingernail from within and pressed it into the center of the print slot. She and Solomon pressed their faces close together, just close enough to witness the small needle point extend from the hole and puncture the nail before retracting just as it had with Solomon's finger. Liliana took the nail back into the bandage and then her pocket as they stood huddled over the machine in the rain, waiting anxiously, tracing with their eyes every blip and imperfection on the screen.

"Does it work?" asked Chuck standing behind them with Cledwyn. Neither of them answered, just stood hunched, shaking as the gusts and the cold rocked them back and forth.

Solomon could hear himself saying aloud what he had been repeating in his head. "Come on, come on, come on…" A lightning bolt struck across the sky straight above, drawing their gaze for a second. When their focus returned, the display flashed again, this time slowly spelling out a stream of German in bright white lettering.

Willkommen bei Dr. Vogel. Wo sind die Ärzte Ebersbach, Jung und Metzger?

"What's it say?" petitioned King.

"It says it works!" concluded Solomon.

"It wants the samples from the other doctors," Liliana added.

"We already knew that!" shouted King. "Are you satisfied now?"

"Let's get back to the shelter," said Chuck. He checked the time on his digital watch. It was now a quarter to six. Sliding back into the soaked broken seating of the Jeep, Chuck flipped the starter and felt a kickback in his wrist. He tried it again and again, but the engine wouldn't turn. He got up to flip the hood, but Cledwyn ran around and grabbed him by the arm.

"No, if you open the hood you'll flood the whole bloody thing.

It'll never start!"

"It's not starting now!" Chuck shouted back.

Cledwyn motioned back to the cab and jumped in the driver's seat, shooing its passengers out and flailing his arms. "Fuck if I've got to do everything! Push, damn you, push!"

With the combined legwork of Ferriera, Solomon, and Polanski, but mostly the latter, they were able to twist the half-flat tires around in the rain and the sludge and point it down the hill back toward the Villa Roma. Slipping and falling as they did, they pushed it hard down the ramp with Cledwyn straining with the ignition until they fast ran into cobblestone, stopping the Jeep dead in its tracks.

"It's no good!" Liliana yelled.

Cledwyn cursed and pleaded and prayed and cursed again at the clutch and pedals, but he couldn't get the engine to turn.

"Fucking American piece of junk!" Cledwyn bailed and fell flat in the mud but was nabbed and pulled up by his shirt by Chuck.

"Come on. We're running."

"There's no way we're making it back to the shelter on foot," cried Solomon, breathing hard and hanging to the side of the beaten four-wheel.

"We're not going to the shelter. We aim for the townhouse."

"And breathe in all that poison again?!"

Chuck grabbed Seek by the collar and wrenched him away from the Jeep like a life-sized man-doll. "It beats waiting out here to get killed by God knows what. Now move!" Chuck threw Solomon onto the road in front of him and kicked him up onto his feet and into a washed-out jog. Lightning struck above them again and again as they raced along the cobblestones down the hillside, their boots screeching, chests pounding, the rain refusing to quell its fury. Solomon could hear however a sound like chanting. No. Counting. Chuck was counting. "Six...seven...eight...nine..."

"What are you doing?" he yelled, nearly giving out in the expenditure of breath. Then he heard another sound, a clash of thunder from behind the rocky cliffs they fled.

"The storm. It's almost twelve miles away. The lightning won't keep the road lit for long. Come on!" Chuck tried to whip them into a long-distance fervor but there was little to it. Solomon quickly lagged behind and was astonished at how well Liliana kept pace with Chuck, leaving Cledwyn's scrawny ass to keep his own eyes company. He had to continually wipe his glasses down just to make sure they hadn't slipped off his nose and lay crushed on the ground behind them. He tried to picture the map in his head. *How long is this road?*

Running along the cracks and bumps of Karl Braun, Solomon and the others could see the lightning flashes becoming less frequent and further from sight. The rain kept on after it, but slowly, it too began to lesson to a dull drizzle. The sun did not follow close behind. *The road to Roma. Yes, that's right. Two miles. No, three.* Solomon's heart pushed through his leaking lungs, forcing the blood within up to his esophagus. He had to stop and cough, spitting up red that the rain quickly washed into the brown dirt at his feet.

Chuck signaled for Liliana and Cledwyn to keep going before dropping back to Solomon.

"You gonna…kick me again?" Seek asked, smearing the blood off his lips.

Chuck flinched at first but then ducked his shoulder under Solomon's arm and wrapped his own around Solomon's waist, hoisting him up like a flag on a pole. "Come on, buddy," he said as the men jogged at a slowed pace together with Chuck in lead and Solomon in tow. His head throbbing and bobbing up and down in the run, Solomon gazed out into the pitch black of the jungle. They kept on the cobblestone, the only discernible marker of their path to safety, but Solomon could not help but feel his heart pound even faster at the sight of nothing on either side of them. In pairs they kept on, Liliana in front, followed by a winded Cledwyn and then Chuck and Solomon in the rear, pushing along in persisting solidarity. Darkness plagued them all along the path. Liliana stuck her hand in her jacket pocket and clutched her pistol. Solomon leaned over in case he had to quickly grab Chuck's Luger in a hurry.

As the rain cleared, they could hear only their own intense, winded coughing, the sounds of prey in the open, shouting their location to lazy hunters. *Where are they coming from? Where are they coming from?*

As her nerves and exhaustion got the better of her, Liliana slowed her steps, meeting Cledwyn behind her, whose steps slowed in turn. As they congealed together in a collected, sweaty mass, Chuck began to whisper.

"Synchronize your breaths. I'm taking the left. Liliana, look out to the right. Train your weapon; take it out and check it slowly and quietly."

Liliana did as she was told, extracting the clip from her Luger as Chuck instructed. "It's clear. No water, no jam," Liliana whispered, her pace slowing to a brisk walk.

Three quarters of the way to the Villa Roma the rain stopped completely. Chuck checked his watch again. It was ten after six. The sun was nowhere in sight. The group walked along, ever vigilant for the slightest sound, their guns hanging by their hips as they moved, scraping their blistered and bleeding feet along the cobblestones. Solomon found himself missing the anonymity of the storm, the rain, the flashing violent lights like fireworks. Now they were uncovered in the night. Naked. Solomon whispered into the center of the slowly treading mass, "I hear movement."

They froze, looking frantically about. "It's just...a little while...further..." Slowly, Chuck got them to move again in a slow stride toward the villa. A twig behind them broke. A branch to their right creaked. A clap pressed on the stone road in front of them. They stopped again. Solomon handed Chuck's pistol to him. Liliana raised her weapon toward the stepping sound on the road in front growing closer. Blackness. Nothingness. The void. Then, at the cusp of dusk under the shade of the fleeing storm clouds, eyes, eyes from the darkness.

Solomon reached into his breast pocket and ducked down flat in the road as Chuck and Liliana opened fire at the wide pupils staring them down from the night. The flashes of muzzle fire lit up his face, and more importantly, the small box of matches Solomon pulled from his inner jacket pocket. In seconds Chuck and Liliana's pistols ran dry and the eyes reemerged, squinting unharmed from the void. Solomon, fumbling with his fingers, struck a handful of matches along the box and stood, raising them above his head. Thinking quickly, he ripped Cledwyn's coat off his back and undid his own belt, tying it around a sleeve, throwing the jacket to the ground and tossing the matches on it. The hungering figures emerged from the darkness, mammoth men with dark gray skin, fangs, and eyes that wrapped along the sides of their heads. Liliana threw her gun at them and collapsed in the road.

Solomon pushed past her, swinging the flaming vest through the air as a wraith ablaze. He shouted and yelped at the Volksklausur screaming "flüchten! Schnell! Flüchten!" Chuck lowered his gun and watched as this crazed little man with glasses swung this flaming shirt at their foes, and was amazed to see them back away, covering their eyes in pain or fear. Solomon kept yelling, focusing on the creature in the road in front of them. He could see it in the firelight, with its arms over its face and a long scar running down its torso like a shoulder bag across its chest.

"Ya!" he continued. "Run! Flüchten! Schnell!" Unable to spot their attacker through the circling tormenting fire, the Volksklausur slipped back into the darkness, one by one. As their claws trod out down the road and into silence, Solomon yelled his last bit of German after them. He caught his breath and turned slowly, droplets of sweat as big as Reichmarks falling down his face, his hand still grasping his belt hard and the flame burning the jacket to ash on the cobblestone. Solomon stood, exhaling heavily. The others stared at him. He slowly raised his other hand and straightened his glasses. The night was silent yet again, not a stirring in the woodland or clawing at the road ahead. Solomon leaked out a smirk.

"Jesus, gent," said the Welsman. "That was me fuckin' favorite coat!"

Chapter IX

From the street, the Villa Roma safehouse stood just as decrepit as it had almost two days before. Careful not to return the attention of the Volksklausur, Solomon had dragged King's burning coat the whole way until the last of its embers burned out on the far side of the bronze boy fountain. His legs and lungs had been run half to death, but Solomon was triumphant in retreat. His heart still racing, he pushed his way inside, stumbling down the rickety wooden stairs and into the newly furnished basement. He pulled the cord on the swinging overhead light bulb, and with a click, his eyes widened. Across the room, lying on the old sofa, he made out the body of a man—a short, thin man grasping his chest in pain.

Solomon paced forward and dropped to his knees before the figure, a middle-aged familiar, blood creeping down his lips and across his neck, staining his lapel.

"Hiri!" Solomon exclaimed. Hiroto reached out and grabbed hold of Solomon's shoulder, tossing his head back in pain as a large glob of crimson was expelled from his mouth. Solomon took his friend's hands in his own and pushed the wounded man up the couch to prop his head up over its arm. Hiroto let drool another ounce of blood from behind his molars.

"Stephen... Stephen..."

Solomon slid his hands under Hiroto and tried to lift him, but he was exhausted from the run. His friend fell down on top of him, pinning him to the cold cellar floor. Hiroto spit his blood in little pellets all over Solomon's face, his fluids seeping into Solomon's eyes. "Find me! Find me!" Hiroto yelled, his lethal breath coughing ruddy paste into Solomon's mouth. Seek rolled, pushing Hiroto's body over and onto the floor beside him. Struggling to his knees, Solomon put his hands

91

over his friend's chest, but Hiroto convulsed horribly, shoulders twisting and shaking.

Solomon couldn't think fast enough to put his feelings to words and proved unable to stop Hiroto from spitting blood by the quart like a geyser from his mouth. Then, suddenly, he stopped. His life-juice spilled all over the ground at Solomon's feet, on his pants, his shirt, riddled all over his hands and face. Solomon inched forward, putting his ear to Hiroto's chest, but the beating of his heart lay silent. Slamming his fists down on the dead man's ribs, he bawled out an anguished cry, a soulful moan that echoed along the walls of the basement. Defeated, Seek collapsed over the body of his friend with only his own breaths for company.

"Seek..." He heard a voice like a gurgled whisper behind him. Solomon fell back on his heels and turned. Before him lay three more bodies, convulsing and spitting blood from their faces. Chuck, Cledwyn, and Liliana stretched outward on their arms and legs like animals, plasma flowing from their mouths and hanging from their nostrils like twisted flypaper. "Seek..." they burbled. Solomon reached back in himself for the strength to press forward, unsure of whom to approach first. Going with his gut, Solomon reached out his hands and held up Liliana's face, a long red drool dripping down between them. He screamed out as she suffocated before his eyes. Then he blinked. Liliana's face vanished, but her bloodied, broken body remained. Solomon squinted hard, wiping Hiroto's fluids from his eyes. His little girl, Rebecca, lay before him, frail and trembling, blood trickling down her like a red snake slithering along front of her yellow sundress. He panicked, thrashing his arms and legs backward as if to claw a hole in the sofa and crawl through to the Earth's core just to escape San Magnus Island.

"Nooo!" He looked back as Samantha cried out, her long brown hair drenched in sticky carmine. Solomon fell flat as his ears popped under the sound wave of a small detonation in her throat, sending pints of her blood washing over him, a waterfall of his daughter's gore flooding the villa cellar. Solomon felt himself drowning in it and grasped his neck in terror, feeling the lump throbbing bigger and

92

bigger. His ears popped again.

Solomon felt a pair of hands cupping his cheeks. Opening his eyes, he saw that it was Liliana.

"Hey, hey, hey," she repeated, running her hands behind his ears and over his forehead to check for fever. "You're awake. You're awake now." As his vision cleared, Seek looked around and found himself lying in a chair in that very basement. It was surprisingly clean and free of the river of blood he had felt topple him over during the night. He did, however, spot Chuck in the chair opposite him waking up, coughing and spitting red over his left armrest. Cledwyn stood over him on the left, eyeing him with contempt.

"Good morning, King," Seek said, checking his mouth and face for blood. Cledwyn huffed and walked up the stairs. "I really hate this island," whispered Solomon.

"You haven't heard the bad news yet," Liliana replied. She walked over to a small nightstand where they had set up an old glass lamp plugged into a utility outlet by the defunct industrial sink. She pulled the string hooked to its bulb. Nothing happened. She pulled it a couple more times just for emphasis.

"I thought we fixed that problem," Solomon groaned, dropping his head backward behind the chair.

Chuck stretched and wiggled out of his chair, his expression a combination of withheld rage and steady determination. He stretched his legs, wrapped his arms behind his head and cracked his knuckles. "Come on. Let's not spend any more time down here."

With the storm and night dissipated, San Magnus Island once again resumed its perfect, relaxing weather with cool salt breezes coming in from the sea and sunny skies dotted with swooping gulls. They left the townhouse on foot, walking back down Karl Braun Street. Chuck decided, under suggestion from Cledwyn, that they make the hike back to the Villa Vienna and forget about the Jeep or risk a walk twice as long. When Chuck pressed him on the issue, hopeful of the convenience an automobile would bring in such an isolated place, Cledwyn just shook his head and glared back at Liliana, who walked with Solomon behind them.

"Chuck!" Solomon shouted up ahead. He ran up to stride beside his colleague. Cledwyn dropped back, walking side by side with Liliana. Then he dropped back some more.

"Chuck, I saw Hiroto last night."

"You were dreaming, Seek."

"I know, but it made me think about something. He kept screaming 'find me.'"

"Find him? That was it?"

"Yeah, that was it. He was lying on that couch. I had him right there, and he asked me to find him."

"You think he's on the island somewhere?"

"Well, yeah, it could mean that."

"It was a dream, Solomon, a dream. Hiroto didn't speak to you."

"Well, isn't there a chance he could be alive here somewhere?"

Chuck stopped in the middle of the road and stared point blank into his companion's eyes. As Cledwyn and Liliana walked past, he waved them forward. Liliana looked back as she trailed down Karl Braun but left earshot. Chuck turned back sharply to Solomon as if disciplining a man of inferior rank on the march.

"You're a journalist. Think like a journalist. Your source is a dream. It doesn't mean anything. Hell, Hiroto is probably sitting at his desk in D.C., completely oblivious to all of this."

Seek jerked his neck back. "How do you mean?"

"Did you call him before you came down here? Actually speak with him?"

"I can't. Our phones are probably tapped."

"Paranoid as always. You didn't talk to him. He's probably never even heard of San Magnus Island."

"You're saying he was hacked? That someone else sent that email?" Solomon posed.

"He was a hacker. What are the odds he got into something over his head and someone hacked him back for it?"

"No, Hiri was crazy into encryptions, there's no way—"

"No way what? That he didn't dig into something he shouldn't have? Right, he never had a history of that. Jesus, Solomon, Hiroto was as much my friend as he was yours, but open your eyes, dammit. He wasn't God's gift to journalists."

Solomon paused and took in a deep breath. He turned his head to face down the road and spotted the silhouettes of Liliana and Cledwyn disappearing over a ridge into the sun. He thought he could see them yelling too.

"You were taken in, Seek, just like I was," Chuck continued. He barreled up fluid from his throat and spat into the dirt, his rosy saliva sinking into the soil.

"How did you hear about it, Chuck?" Solomon asked.

"What, the island?"

"Yeah, the island. If Hiroto wasn't Hiroto, how did you hear about this place?"

Chuck sighed but stared unflinchingly at Solomon.

"Hiroto, or rather Hiroto's email address, sent me a message. It sounded like him. He asked how I'd been and how Chile was treating me. Then he asked if I wouldn't follow a lead for him. He offered to pay me for it. I agreed. I crossed the border to talk to that man I introduced you to and a few others. He didn't answer when I sent him a reply back saying he was right. Instead he sent me *you*." Chuck made sure to emphasize the last word.

Cledwyn started running when he came to the welcome sign of the villa. He raced up through the plaza and to the generator room. Its door still hung wide, and a small stream of blurry gas-like air flowed out from the archway and up to be taken by the wind. He took a deep breath, spotting Liliana jogging up into the plaza behind him and turned, putting his mouth in his elbow, into the bunker. He hollered first before trudging back into the plaza, his finger posed as a weapon with which to aim at the professor.

"You've ruined everything!" he shouted across the square. Liliana stopped in her tracks, bewildered. King raced forward until he planted himself just inches from her face. "It's gone, destroyed, fffffucked, you tart. We're fucked now because of you and your incessant questioning bullshit!"

Overhearing the commotion, Solomon and Polanski came running.

Calm in the face of fire, Liliana responded. "We had to make sure. If we didn't know—"

"We knew! He told us. We knew the whole time. Why would he lie? He wants us to succeed!"

"You shouldn't be so trusting Cle—"

"Oh, that's right, I shan't be. I shan't be too trusting of you," he yelled sardonically. Cledwyn spotted Chuck and Solomon running towards him. "Or any of you!"

Chuck ran up between them, pushing Liliana back toward Solomon.

"It was the right call," Chuck interluded.

"Your call, you stupid fucking brainless Darren," Cledwyn continued. "You could have stopped. You could have let me out to lock up before going on to your merry stupid escapades!"

Listening intently, Solomon raced past them to the generator room.

"Oh, that's right, touchscreen man. You go and fix the machine what's older than you are."

Solomon didn't stop to face him; he simply tucked his mouth into his collar and squinted into The Haze. There, in the middle of the room, lay the dilapidated, mutilated body of the generator, spitting sparks and steam, nearly wrenched from the floor. Solomon had no idea what he was looking at, but the impact of the destruction was not lost on him. He inched closer, still hearing Cledwyn yelling from the plaza, and spotted something out of place—not metal. It looked like ivory. Not ivory. Nail. A massive human nail, like a claw stabbing into a spiral wheel. Solomon tried to yank it out with his open hand and nearly cut himself.

"No, I can't fix it, not with my hands and not with a bloody mountain of duct tape, which we don't have. The converter is mashed potatoes and it needs replacement conductors which we also don't have," Cledwyn explained, spotting Solomon walking from the generator room. "Would you agree, Mr. Solomon? Or have you just fixed it already?"

Seek shook his low-hanging head in defeat. He inhaled deeply, as he'd been holding his breath, and said, "How will you ever get your money now, King?"

Cledwyn dropped his fists and charged at Solomon, slipping Chuck's grasp.

"Why don't you stop your bitching and go house-to-house, stealing earrings of the bodies of little girls?" As he retreated backward, Seek lost control and his glasses slipped off his ears. King reached out to him, grabbed Solomon's white collar and snapped his fist dead flat into Solomon's nose. Seek fell on his back, blood trickling from his nostrils, and stuck up his hands to deflect the blows of the Welshman, who shouted as he swung his fists in rage..

"Your gold is just as gone as mine parasite!" he yelled, hooking Seek in his ribs, drawing up a coughing squall from the journalist. Chuck reached over and grabbed Cledwyn by the shoulders, pulling him back off Solomon and dropping him on the cobblestone. Liliana stood watching but didn't say a word. Cledwyn kicked back at Chuck, nailing him in the genitals, causing him to fall over the thief into a chaotic brawl on the ground. Cledwyn screamed and bit Chuck on the wrist as the Texan tried to hold him down in an armlock. The fighting went on, scaring off the birds sitting in the trees nearby. Their yells were caught by the wind and carried to the beach.

Then they heard a beeping. It was a steady beep, low in volume but high in pitch, like a sharp screech muffled by a rug or a towel. Chuck and Cledwyn's standoff slowed as they looked up in the direction of the sound, steady, beating like a heart, an electric pulse. Solomon froze, lying on the ground, his hand over his bleeding nose, split to the right side of his face. He stopped breathing. The beeping was coming from him. He lowered his hand and traced along his neck to the lump in his throat. He could feel it for the first time, vibrating ever so slightly against his skin.

Liliana walked over, passed the boys on the ground, and approached Solomon, holding out her hands to his neck. "It's glowing," she said.

"Are you done now?" asked an equally high-pitched voice from Solomon's pocket. The beeping man slowly pulled the hands-free from his hip and held it between himself and Dr. Ferreira. The voice continued. "Mr. Polanski, I did not invite you here to throw punches with the other guests. And Mr. King, you will get nowhere rolling around in the shadow of that fountain. Get up. Now."

The voice echoed around the plaza as Chuck and Cledwyn did as they were told, separated, and walked over to the device. Cledwyn saw the blood trickling from the blow he had laid on Solomon.

"Good. Good doggies. Despite what you may think, I do not revel in your displays of animalism. Nor did I enjoy the show you put on last night. Ms. Ferreira, when I tell you something is so, that something is so. And I'm telling you now, I'm tempted to blow your fuses and start all over again with a new team who'll do what I say and when! You've attained one of the four DNA keys, yes?"

Solomon arched his head forward and leaned over to pick up his glasses, his neck still vibrating. "Yes."

"Good." Solomon's neck ceased beeping, and his skin settled. He dropped his head back down against the cobblestone. "That makes three more," the voice continued.

Cledwyn interrupted. "E'scuse me sir, but we've got ourselves a bigger problem."

"The Volksklausur had their way with your generator last night. Always keep the safe zones locked. Always. Especially that one. They're not animals, not children. They're as smart as you or I. The former at least."

"So what's our next move?" Cledwyn asked.

"So impatient to succeed. That's good. You need to get that generator back online. More important than just a safehouse, it has the lab Ms. Ferreira will need to test the Vorkämpfers' DNA. Now, it just so happens that you're in luck. To the east, in the jungle, there is a camp. There you will find both the body of Dr. Jung and a second generator. I suggest you take what you need from both and rebuild what you've lost. A few more nights in the dank San Magnus air and you won't be good to me any longer."

The hands-free clicked off once again.

Chapter X

"Stand still!" **Liliana** demanded, her hands on either side of Solomon's nose, trying desperately to slide the cartilage back onto the bone as red, runny puss excreted from his nostrils. Solomon shrieked in pain, grabbing handfuls of bloodied khakis, wiggling on the ground like a worm in the sun.

Cledwyn looked down on him and scoffed. "This is no good. Come on. There's clamps and morphine in the bunker."

"Good luck getting down there, princess," Cledwyn snorted. Liliana looked back at him with fire in her eyes.

Solomon managed to wave her off his face long enough to squeak. "He's right. The power's out."

"Then we need to get moving toward that camp," said Chuck.

Solomon tried to stand but didn't get far. He'd been hit over the head, sprained his ankle in a darkened fit, coughed up almost a cup of blood over the course of four days, and his face was now indistinguishable from mashed grapefruit. Desperate to get any and all thought and attention away from the bleeding, he slid his medical backpack off his shoulder and started to rifle through it for the map.

Liliana put her hands back over his face. "Just hold on," she said, pushing the crest of his beak. Solomon shouted again.

Chuck sighed and pushed the doctor aside, positioning himself face-to-face with Solomon. He stuck his index finger in Solomon's face, moving it side to side. The wounded man's eyes followed. "Good," Chuck said, dropping his finger toward his legs. When Solomon's eyes gave chase, the big Texan stomped hard on his bad foot. Solomon cringed and bent forward to grab his toes but was blocked by the sergeant's wide, outstretched hand that grabbed him by the hair and held him still. Chuck pinched the septum and pushed his hands together, snapping the bone upright. "There. Better," he said, holding the journalist's face up toward him as he smiled and picked up the man's pack.

Chuck rolled the map out over the fountain in the plaza. "It's not far," he said, running his fingers between the square of the Villa Vienna and the little circle mark in the jungle to the east. Liliana helped Solomon over to where Cledwyn and Chuck were going over the upcoming trek.

"What did I say about that circle thing, huh?" said Seek, trying desperately to rub or itch his nose but being batted away by Liliana in every attempt.

"It'll take maybe an hour to get there on foot in the jungle." Chuck looked up at the sun and saw not a cloud in sky.

Solomon checked his watch. "It's oh-nine-hundred. Sarge," he squeaked through a nasal drip.

"From here to the other safehouse is about half an hour, so make that about an hour and a half to get back there from this...circle thing," Chuck continued.

"I don't want to stay the night there again," Solomon muttered.

"Neither do I," Liliana seconded.

"King, how long do you think it would take to repair the generator?"

"Ha. If I had all the parts and they worked, an hour. I'd say two, for shite happens."

"That's cutting it close," Chuck said, looking into the eyes of his three companions. "Real close if you can't get the thing back online." Cledwyn tilted his head in agreement.

"Not a hell of a lot of choice in the matter." King rubbed the lump in this throat.

The four stood lined up along Karl Braun, parallel to a tiny hole in the jungle before them, stretching into the dirt and sand only a few yards out from the cobblestones.

They were armed and prepared, if only physically. Despite the injuries they had come out from their hovel well equipped. From the butcher's in the Villa Roma and a disheveled general store just outside the plaza in Vienna, Solomon had accumulated a supply of lighter fluid and matches, several towels, and a long-desired single bulb flashlight. He also carried the hands-free receiver and his old model Kindle. Liliana likewise pilfered the infirmary and the house of Albert Vogel and carried with her bandages, tweezers, scissors, a small scalpel, and an assortment of ointments and purifying agents in addition to her Luger. Chuck carried the other pistol in his belt, followed by a long-rusted chopping blade from a counter in the butcher's and a pair of binoculars he'd found hanging in a novelty shop in the Villa Roma. Lastly, and possibly most importantly, Cledwyn had armed himself with a complete tool belt that had been wrapped around the waist of a body he'd found hiding in the closet of the generator room. They all had bottles or makeshift canteens of Albert Vogel's distilled lab water.

And so they stood against the backdrop of the unknown, hearing the chirping and creaking sounds of wildlife from the depths of the wood, farther in than their eyes could spot the beasts who made them. Solomon and his group had seen the best of San Magnus, its resorts, its pleasant skies and cool weather, the serene slopes of her cliffs, and the calm, crashing waves of her beaches. All those things were discerning enough, riddled in bodies and decay, filled with toxic fumes and trampled over foot by a legion of nighttime killers. Now they faced the strange of the jungle.

Cledwyn exhaled. "Do you think they're in there?"

"They could be anywhere," Solomon answered, looking over at the Welshman and scratching his nose.

"They're hiding someplace during the day. Maybe it's in there?" said Liliana.

"No, they wouldn't be. The voice said, 'Go into the jungle'. He wants us to succeed. He wouldn't send us to our deaths," Chuck chimed in.

Solomon scoffed, standing next to him. "You sound like him," he said, indicating Cledwyn.

Liliana squinted and moved first, walking over the road toward the small opening in the woodland. Solomon watched her form as she strode over the dirt and laid her hands on the nearest branch. *In her element.* He followed suit, followed by Chuck and then Cledwyn.

After a few hundred meters along their grossly overrun dirt path, Liliana had a revelation. She slowed up to walk just ahead of Solomon. He wasn't wearing the strain in his foot well, so she turned around and looked along the sides of the path. Twenty feet in, the vines and tree brush obscured any view. Small, green plants opened like pods from the dark beneath their feet, crawled over by little red and blue beetles. Ants traced down the sides of the spiny, thick Pindo Palm and lengthy evergreen trees. Liliana stepped over the thin skin of a deceased spotted snake, no longer than her arm, as she bent down to split a curved branch off a Chilean Myrtle trunk that lay slantwise across their path.

"Here, use this," she said, handing him the stick. He nodded and took it under his right arm, leaning against it to test its strength. Solomon found he could put his whole body weight on the limb with only a slight bend. He reminded himself that he'd been eating one meal of canned sardines a day for the past half-week. His stomach ached.

"It's funny," Liliana continued. Solomon turned his attention back to her quizzically. "People came here. They cut down the forest, built houses and shops and a great big *mausoléu* in the mountain. They had electricity and medicine and guns. They had children. And now there is more life in the jungle than the rest of the island."

Solomon smirked. His foot dug in to a stretch of vines. Way out in front of them a macaw cried. "You've been to the villas. They *are* the jungle."

"And the air," Liliana said, ignoring Seek. "All the oxygen we need is here, coming from these plants." She rubbed a big, hanging leaf in her hand.

In the rear of their column, Cledwyn tripped over the fallen myrtle trunk. The sound of his fall shook the local birds from their nests and into the skies above the jungle canopy. The Texan looked back and chuckled. The farther they trod through the jungle, the closer the walls of shrubs and vines came around them. King felt claustrophobic and Solomon swore he saw the man feign to push a low-hanging limb or protruding leaf from his way so as not to get nature on his fingers. Chuck's time estimate was not inaccurate. Seek wiped down his sweaty forehead with another dishtowel he kept in his pack. The end of the winding snake trail from the Villa Vienna opened, just as it had started, into a clearing of dirt and sand. Liliana stood in the gap before him with her hands on her hips. She didn't say a word. Solomon couldn't spot what she was staring at through her figure, which he found himself repeatedly ogling. As he neared, he ran his gaze up from her legs, her ankles and calves covered in a green-stained pitch. He couldn't help but wonder whether it was just the similarity between the island and prison or whether she truly was as attractive as he found her.

As he neared, he raised his eyes from Dr. Ferreira's hips over her back and beyond her greasy brown hair. "Jesus," he whispered, close enough behind her to share the sentiment. They stared at the spiral spindle towers rising from the shrubs like conquering metal warriors with their feet over the necks of the defeated vegetation. Along the towers Solomon immediately spotted a familiar sight: great big glass searchlights pointing in his direction. He swallowed and pointed them out to Liliana in front of him. Chuck lined up behind them, peering over Solomon, who peered over Liliana. His first impression was not the towers, but the fifteen-foot wall of double chain-link that stretched between them, dug in at the base and reinforced with concrete. Rows of barbed wire covered the tops, flowing over the sides like a waterfall of iron spikes. Dr. Ferreira spotted the remains of a body on the inside of the fence, a blackened skeleton with its hand outstretched through the links of the chain.

Cledwyn bumped into Chuck, pushing them all forward. He said nothing as he stretched through the opening by them. Liliana followed him as he traced along the sides of the camp. "Some circle," he muttered. The camp was indeed circular. They walked around its perimeter to the front and only gate. Four guard towers, tall steel based with concrete footing, about thirty feet high stood tall at equal lengths, making a smaller square inside the robust gates of the iron-gated ellipse. Solomon ran his fingers along the rusted metal and peered upward. At the top of every barbed wire barrier slunk a walkway, a wood-plated suspended bridge to link each tower. It wasn't until they reached the gate, torn from its hinges and flayed open, that they bothered to look inside.

Although the gatehouses and the wooden longhouses stood intact, the jungle had struck back in force over the course of decades. Tall grasses rose from the compound along every lane and gap. Shrubs grew along the wood panels of the rows of enclosed huts in the center and up along the legs and stairs of the towers themselves. The chain-link had been mingled with vines from the jungle, a casual mix of flaky brown rust and bright forest green. Along the back, on the opposite side of the clearing they'd come from, was a bunker not unlike the power generator room in the Villa Vienna. Solomon picked up half of a massive iron lock from the dirt in front of the gate. Worms and tiny beetles squirmed around in the soil underneath. It was the bottom half of the lock, a simple construction unlike the electric barriers they had been confronted with so far. He looked around but didn't spot the arm clamp that should have run over the top, wrapping around the thick iron chain he'd found in pieces by the side of the fence.

Cledwyn held his arm up and pointed to the concrete bunker in the distance. "That's what we're lookin' for," he yelled, skipping toward it. Liliana turned her attention to another bony figure in the dirt, its tibia and fibula bones dismantled and flung about. She couldn't find the toes. As he followed Cledwyn to the bunker, Chuck picked another antiquated weapon from the dirt. He expelled its clip. Empty.

As they regathered at the cement structure, Cledwyn smiled. He pointed out a chalk-marked arrow on the side of the building, pointing upward into the hut of the tower.

And a red blotch above the tall iron door.

Chapter XI

Solomon looked all over but couldn't find so much as a sign with a name for the camp. Likewise, the pilfered map that had led them to the site was bare of even its basic description, just a small, light gray circle surrounded on all sides by little trees marked in the key. There wasn't so much as a spot for hanging a display over the gate. The cement structure to the rear of the camp was blank of any signifying markers. He couldn't even make out the numbering on the wooden huts that populated the center compound. Near the northwest portion, opposite the concrete structure, he found a large sandpit cornered off by wooden planks in the shape of a hexagon. Where he expected to see a mound of dead bodies spread along a firing wall, he instead came across a row of tall wooden dummies of varying degrees of battle fatigue. There were no bullet holes, just chunks of the figures missing or pierced and slashed into shards and splinters.

Then Seek focused his attention on the huts. He counted six in all, though one was little more than a smoldered mound of ash and charred metal. They aligned in a row three by three.. When the party split up in their designated searches, Solomon felt obligated to be the first to scout those buildings, great, tall longhouses with curved archways, not built to withstand the blast that never came, the blast San Magnus expected to outlast in its concrete bunkers. Solomon found that not one of the structures in the center of the camp hosted a painted red blotch.

"It's just like Dachau," he said to himself. "Or Belzic. There's just one thing out of place…"

Liliana came up behind him. "And what's that?"

"All the bodies are the guards, not the prisoners."

"Then they got what they deserved," she concluded. Solomon was surprised to hear such a cold-blooded tone in her voice. He surprised himself with his response.

"You know, the more I see of this place the harder it gets to think like that. A lot of these people were monsters—you won't hear an argument from me—and it looks like they didn't change any when they got here. But after what we've been through I'm starting to feel myself—"

Liliana cut in. "And you said your family was locked in a camp like this? And you feel sorry for these murderers?"

Solomon pounded the underside of his fist on the side paneling of the northeast longhouse. "And you don't? You've been hunted by these creatures, you've breathed in the poison air, and you can't sympathize for what these people went through?"

She scoffed. "These people made those creatures. They made that poison. They wanted to release it on the rest of the world! They all deserved to die."

"Did their children deserve to die? The infants, those too young to know how to hate?"

Liliana paused and walked closer to Solomon, resting her back up against the longhouse.

"They would have grown up just like their parents. You do not think so?"

"I'm having a hard time figuring out what I think. First I thought you were a scientist like them. I saw the way you eyed their instruments and results."

"That was shock, not admiration," she snapped.

"Uh-huh. And then I thought, 'She doesn't have any stake in this. Why wouldn't she be impressed'?

"I am a doctor, Mr. Solomon."

"Yeah, exactly, so how can you think that way? How can you think it's better for the children to be dead? I thought you would come out on the side of nature, not nurture. How can you think that their minds were doomed from the start?"

"It is because I am a doctor that I think that," she replied, taking a deep, calm breath.

Solomon took a different approach.

"What would you do with their findings?"

Liliana sighed and turned away.

"If we walk out of here and you have all their secrets in your hand, all their advancement, what would you do with it?" he asked, walking around her back to confront her. She looked up tiredly.

"It would not be proper science."

"What would you do with it, Doctor?"

"Their results are not founded within the parameters of sound research."

"What would you do with it, Doctor?!"

"I don't know!" she shouted in his face. "I don't know."

"Would you hesitate to destroy it?"

"Probably."

"Would you hesitate to use it?"

Another pause. "Probably."

Solomon sighed and glared at the door. "Come on," he said, taking her by the arm and dragging her to the entrance of the rotting, mildew-covered shack they'd been resting against.

"Let go of my arm!" she yelled. At the doorway he let go and looked deep in her jade eyes. He moved to jiggle the door handle, but she reached out and grabbed his wrist, shaking her head as she returned the glance. His expression was stern and solemn. Then he opened the door and walked into the darkness.

Liliana stared blankly inside as Solomon's figure was covered in shadow. There was silence. She dared not whisper for fear of waking what might be sleeping within. Solomon reached ever so gently into the pack hanging from his shoulder and pulled from it his withered antique flashlight. He looked back at Liliana and held it out in front of him. His thumb pressed into its rubber button, and the hut was lit. And empty. He looked around. Bunks, dilapidated wooden bunks only five or so feet long each, were stacked in rows along the sides of the structure. There were no scraps, no clothes, no bodies, no other furniture, no signs of cognitive life. Just the tall island grass creeping through the dank, rotting floorboards and round brown mushrooms gathered in clumps at the corners. He turned around to face her, holding the handheld torch up to his face.

"They would not have come back here."

He moved to walked out and stopped just shy of her and the entryway.

"How did you know?" she asked in a soft, nonthreatening tone.

He was just inches from her now, and her arms grazed his chest.

"Because *I* wouldn't have come back here," he said and continued on.

Neither Chuck nor Cledwyn heard a single word of this from the soundproof confines of the concrete structure at the far end of the compound. Both were pleasantly surprised to find that the air was clean, if not stale and smelling of mold, for the Haze had not been pumped into its facilities. The latter of the men stood over the geothermal generator on the ground floor of the structure. He made a clicking sound with his tongue against his cheek and folding his arms against his torso.

"What's the matter?" said the sergeant coming up behind him.

Cledwyn turned around and grinned a sour grin, then walked to a switch on the wall and flicked it on. Nothing.

"I'm getting really sick of that," Chuck replied.

"That makes two of us, mate. However, this here generator hasn't been torn to bits like the other one. Looks like the great gorillas never got to it. That said, she's in bad need of a repair, say, fifty years ago, and it'll take me some time to see if I can even get the parts we need for the other one to work on this one. Luckily for you gents, I have some experience workin' in the dark."

Chuck sighed. "Well," he said, "take your time, we've got breathable air in this one. Just not too much time."

Cledwyn nodded and turned his attention back to the machine. He took out his pilfered spanner and his thick gray work gloves and wondered what he should approach first. He had not expected to come all the way to Argentina just to renovate a few electrical generators. But he worked diligently and hummed a tune in G major that Chuck couldn't recognize.

"More Celtic folk songs?" he asked.

"Mate," Cledwyn replied, a shocked expression on his face. "That's the Beatles." Cledwyn shook his head and went back to applying pressure on the partly detached ventilator. Chuck, oblivious to his offense, passed into the next room to scout the rest of the structure. He quickly found it not unlike the blast shelter under the Vogel residence, a small, livable domicile, though three stories high rather than entirely subterranean, complete with its own independent ventilation system. He found the thick metal hatch leading to the basement already ajar but dared not venture into its halls alone and poorly armed. He was far more interested in the upper levels, stocked with eight-foot-long beds lined with proper blankets and a small kitchenette and pantry still stocked with more of the delightful canned rations they'd taken advantage of. Clothes, unworn or stained by the coughed-up blood of their former owners, hung neatly in the small, cramped closet space, and a metal locker stood tall with a tiny keyhole on the latch.

He rifled through the clothes, mostly uniforms too small for his stature and of a nation he'd rather have forgotten, but he took the opportunity to change his undershirt and his fatigues into something far older but less foul-smelling. He didn't bother to test the bedding or search through the icebox. Instead he took a swig of water from his pouch and slammed his foot into the lock on the tin storage cabinet, breaking it into pieces down to the tiniest spring. The door to the locker swung open and revealed to him a sight more beautiful than any he had yet seen on the island. Stacked up in rows before him stood an array of Old World weaponry, polished and untouched for generations. One scoped rifle caught his eye, and Chuck lifted his binoculars off from his neck, threw them on a bed, and slung the rifle down from its holding spot on the right wall of the cabinet. Its leather strap was faded but fit tightly around his shoulder.

He peered over its sights, aiming at a tattered propaganda poster of Adolf Hitler hanging beside a bunk bed near the far wall. On the smooth, laminated stock he felt an engraving and saw that it had been printed in gold lettering. "Karabiner 98, Württemberg Waffenarsenal, 1940," he read aloud. He ran his index and middle fingers over the print which began peeling in flakes as they passed over it. Chuck slid the bolt handle out and checked the breach. It was clear, almost pristine, as if it had never been fired before. He walked over to the closet and held out the sleeve of a hanging uniform, spitting over it and wiping down the scope's receptor lens. With the exception of a massive amount of dust, its sights were likewise brand new and lined up nicely with the misprinted speck above Hitler's left eyebrow. Chuck held it down around his waist and smiled, then went to the locker to grab a box of 8mm Mauser stripper clips and walked back down the stairs.

He passed Cledwyn at the generator. The man wore a blast helmet over his face, and a blowtorch burned away in his hands.

Solomon spotted Chuck coming out of the administration center with the long rifle slung over his shoulder and sporting a fresh pair of dark brown fatigues. Seek's heart skipped a beat. As he marched nearer, Chuck waved his hand up for Solomon to join him. "Nice gun you've got there, Chuck," Solomon said nervously, limp-skipping over. "Where are you going with it?"

"There's a hutch full of that tin-canned fish up in the tower there. I say we go out and catch us something fresher."

Solomon and Polanski left the camp without a word to Liliana, who they passed by the gate. Solomon checked his watch and stretched his arm around so Chuck could read it. It was just after noon. Several yards down the trail they differed from the path, the hunter in lead, the journalist in tow, pushing aside vines and tree limbs, stepping over brush and fungus. Solomon whispered ahead of him, "What is it we're hunting for?"

"Boar. Great big, fat, delicious bacon-y boar," Chuck whispered back, licking his lips. They moved quietly through the trees for a while before coming to a spot where the rifleman told Solomon to lie down flat in a small clearing in the brush. Chuck took his pistol from his belt and handed it to Solomon, then double backed around to collect some of the wide, frilly green leaves that fell to the floor from up in the canopy. Solomon lay silently in the grass with his legs stretched out and looked the Luger over. He'd never had a gun before, never fired one either, so he was cautious to point the barrel end outward into the wilderness and away from himself. He kept his finger off the trigger, even away from the trigger guard, and inspected. It had a little gray Iron Cross icon on the butt and two twin brass swastikas along the handle. Solomon felt dirty holding it. He dropped it in a patch of soil beside him and waited patiently for his companion to return. He half-expected a snake to slither along and devour his foot, but the chirping and cawing of exotic birds above again reminded him that he was indeed on vacation.

With a rustling Chuck plopped down beside him, tossed the rifle down, and laid the great leaves over Solomon's legs and body and then his own. Solomon chuckled when he saw his friend had drawn mud across his face and around his eyes. "Shut up," Chuck whispered as he drew the rifle back under his arm, grappling the stock and scope with his hands.

"Will they hear us from here?"

"No, I just don't like backtalk," Polanski joked. He peered down the microscopic sights to another small clearing about four hundred feet out in front of them, where the grass was beaten down. "This is not my first pig hunt," he continued, rotating the aperture on the top of the scope. "In Peru, pig hunting is like NASCAR and just about anyone who knows how to hold a gun has gone on a pig hunt at one time or another."

Solomon shrugged with feigned interest.

"Not so bad for an uncultured good ol' boy?" Chuck laughed.

"Ha, do you think I think that?"

"Well," said Chuck, "maybe not you. But the good doctor?"

"I don't know how good a doctor she is," replied Solomon. "Then again, I've been finding a whole lot worse doctors as of late."

"I think I know what you mean. First that Salazar business and now this whole…"

Solomon put his arm out and grasped Chuck's hand still adjusting the sights.

"You know about that?"

"Of course I know. I may not have been back there in a while, but I'm an American and I get imported television. You're the most famous man on San Magnus Island."

"It's a real honor. Why didn't you say anything? When she was asking me about my sentence and all?"

Chuck raised his hand in protest. "That was none of my business to be interfering in. What you want to tell those other two is your prerogative. I already knew you were harmless." Their eyes met. Chuck looked down in the dirt beside Solomon at the Luger he'd thrown aside. "See?"

Solomon squirmed his lips in false protest and kept quiet, watching his comrade take a five-round-long clip from his pocket and slide it snap shut into the top breach of the Mauser. He slowly and quietly drew the bolt handle forward and back and rested his head on the butt of the gun.

"You know, that gun probably killed a lot of Poles," said Solomon. "Possibly even a few Americans."

"No sir," Chuck replied. "This gun hasn't killed a soul yet."

They sat quietly in the brush for some time, the sun drifting by over the trees and running a shadow trail across the jungle. They continued to whisper about this and that, the last Super Bowl, the last election, but most importantly the value of clean water and their extreme longing for toilet paper. Solomon found that they were much alike. Neither had any love of any particular person in higher office, nor any political party, American or otherwise. Chuck had not voted in any Chilean election during the seven years he'd lived there, not even the last two for which he was eligible. Solomon understood well enough when he said his time in Bolivia had both disillusioned him to the idea of free elections and gave him a deep-seated feeling of guilt for thinking of participating in one.

"I don't see myself having any right in telling them how to run their country. Did enough of that already with one of these," he concluded, patting the Mauser on the stock. Solomon managed to drag out of Chuck his loathing for football, or soccer, as he refused to call it anything but. He was a Longhorn. "Spent two years at the Uni of Texas. Class of 2010, majored in Criminology. Dropped out 2008. I was gonna be a cop like my old man. He was killed on the job while I was in

Afghanistan. Didn't leave the military after that."

The more they talked, the more Solomon found Chuck agreeable, just as he had on the mainland. It was as if they were indeed on a long-awaited holiday, hunting in the woods, just a couple of men on a tropical paradise with hot, roasted red meat on their minds. In reality, what they desired most was Charmin two-ply, though Chuck admitted he'd grown used to the thick brown sheets of knock-off brand found in most small town cantinas below the equator.

"So," said Polanski, changing the subject. "If she's no good, what about her has your attention?"

"Liliana?"

"It's not that she's the only woman on the island, is it?"

"I've been wondering that myself. What gave me away?"

"I'm a marine. We pay attention."

Solomon sighed. "I don't know. She's smart. I think she knows more than she lets on."

"That's why I don't trust her," Chuck muttered.

"And you trust King?"

"No, I don't trust him either."

"Oh," said Solomon, "and what about me?"

Chuck didn't lift his gaze from the sights, just continued speaking into the stock of the rifle with his attention trained forward. "Well. I trusted Hiroto, and here I am."

Solomon snorted. "Yeah, me too."

"But," Polanski continued, "I've taken you out into the jungle, I put a gun in your hand, and I turned my back. And here we are and you didn't so much as put a print on the finger guard. I'm not worried about you."

Solomon shrugged. "I guess that's good news. I'm not sure why, but I can't help feeling she's not a threat. She's hiding something, but I don't think it's dangerous. And King, he's clearly not hiding anything. He gloats over being an international criminal and doesn't even bat an eye. So I'll keep mine on him."

"You want my advice?" Chuck said.

He heard a rustling in the woods ahead of them.

"Of course," replied Solomon.

"You're a journalist." Chuck inched forward and pulled on his trigger. The shot rang out through the woods, silencing the birds taking flight above the canopy. He waited for the echo of the round to disappear behind the hills and looked up at his companion. "Don't trust your instinct," he continued, standing up slowly. He lifted the rifle between them as if to put it on display. "Trust your training. Come on. Let's eat."

Chapter XII

It was a quarter to three when Seek and Chuck finally dragged the razorback, its limbs tied with vines, through the gates of the camp. A little bloody trail marked their path through the jungle from between the great big leaves they had wrapped the boar in. Proving his vaunted marksmanship, Chuck had caught the animal right below its ears. The eighty-five-year-old bullet had expelled down the barrel of his rifle, exceeding the speed of soundto meet with the skull of the cute and fuzzy Sus Scrofa Scrofa, otherwise known as the common wild boar. The round, meant for the battle-stricken grounds of Eastern Europe, had passed through the pig as if it were the stick of butter Solomon imagined it'd taste like. Liliana was much appreciative when she looked down from the concrete tower and saw them lugging the beast toward her.

"Now that is a meal," she called out, running her fingers along her lips. Chuck and Solomon carried two sets of long sticks tied to their chests with more vines. They plopped the animal down when they'd reached the center compound, and Liliana climbed down from the tower to aid them. Chuck motioned for Solomon's branches, which he unwrapped and handed over. Sitting down in the dirt, Chuck took out the knife he'd found in the butcher's shop.

When Liliana was close enough, she saw him carving the ends of one of the long sticks into a spike. She smiled. "You look uncomfortable. I'll get chairs."

Solomon looked at Chuck in surprise before he lifted the leaves off the boar and gathered the other pieces of wood they'd hauled from the wild. "Right here good?"

Chuck nodded.

"I've never even been camping before," Seek continued, laying down the sticks like an X beside him.

"Hmm," Chuck replied, a piece of vine in his mouth, holding the sharpening spear straight with his feet. "Ges sum gas."

Solomon walked over to the side of one of the wooden longhouses and ripped some of the long roots out from where they grew along its sides. With Chuck's woodwork and shooting and Solomon's matches and gathering, they put together a quaint cookout in the middle of the slave pen. Liliana came out dragging two old oak rocking chairs under her arms.

"How's King coming with the generator?" Polanski asked.

"Power's still out. I told him we were having pork loins. He went to wash his screwdriver."

"What time did you say it was, Solomon?"

"It's three forty-five, *grand rôtisseur* Polanski."

"We've got less than four hours to get that thing working and take it back in pieces to the shelter," he said, sticking the finished pike in the dirt and starting on the second. "If he doesn't have it online in two, I say we head back to the Villa Roma safe house. Agreed?"

Liliana nodded. Solomon was less agreeable but retorted with, "We voted you leader. I'm not going to second guess you now, especially after this."

"Okay. Let's string her up."

As the sun began to creep away from them, the four sat in complete comfort around the fire. Not bitten by a single mosquito or fought over by a single ant, they lounged in their chairs and dug into the big half-burned slabs of boar meat Chuck had sliced from their makeshift rotisserie. They'd pilfered some plates, a couple knives, and sheets to use as napkins from the nearby shelter. Solomon had found a bottle of hundred-year-old Argentinian wine still corked in the cabinet on the second floor. It had settled poorly in storage, however, facing the heat strokes of a concrete structure without air conditioning in eighty tropical summers since nineteen forty-five, and it tasted more like spiked raisin stew than Chakana Malbec.

Still, they had water to wash it down with and had gotten a little drunk, all except for Cledwyn who explained politely that his liver had been replaced with a hydroelectric conductor years earlier. He nonetheless tried acting drunk, and it was impossible for the other three to notice a difference. Solomon rocked back and forth in the rickety rocking chair, chewing on the end of a rib. He watched Liliana across the crackling fire as she licked the ends of her fingers. So did Chuck and Solomon. She caught them all staring when she looked up.

"What?" she exclaimed.

Chuck muttered something to himself and looked down at his feet. Solomon gazed up at the sky. Cledwyn just smiled and kept staring. She gave him a soured glance.

"You know," she said to no one in particular, "this pig isn't a native either."

Chuck sighed. "No pigs are native to South America."

"Yes, Mr. Polanski," she continued, "but this island wouldn't have any pigs on it at all."

"Is that right?" Cledwyn asked sarcastically, waiting for her to lick her fingers again.

"The Spanish brought their pigs to the mainland. Did this one just swim across from there?" she posed instead.

"So they imported wild pigs and let them roam around in the jungle?" Chuck asked.

"Just like the wine," Solomon countered, "and the supplies and the appliances."

"And the slave labor," finished Liliana.

"Yeah, you know, that makes sense," said Solomon. He prepared himself for a speech. "Okay, this is relevant. It's a Hermann Goering story."

"Who?"

"Hermann Goering. He was head of the German Air Force during the war."

Liliana shrugged.

"He was one of Metzger's bosses. He'd been stripped of all his titles and ran to surrender to the Americans but killed himself rather than be hanged when they found him guilty of war crimes. Anyway, Herr Goering, not unlike Herr Metzger it seems, was big into wild imports. What he really liked was fashion, and he had his eyes on the wily old American raccoon."

Chuck chortled a little behind his pork slab.

"Apparently their pelts make for great coats, so he had a bunch of them sent over from the states and put into little breeding farms for their skins."

"Huh, like this one," Liliana muttered.

"Exactly. This is all before the war you see, but eventually they got loose and now, eighty years later, there are huge populations of American raccoons all over Europe. They gave us the tasty pig and we gave them the pesky, meat-eating, nocturnal raccoon."

Liliana put down her plate and looked over at the longhouses, then back across the fire to Solomon.

"You know, if these things ever get off this island, that's exactly what will happen." She stood. "Come, I have something to show you."

She motioned for him to follow her, grabbed his flashlight, and sped toward the concrete offices. Chuck and Cledwyn returned to their meals.

"First a meal and then a show, aye?" Cledwyn said as Seek passed just beyond earshot.

The bulkhead door to the structure's basement was open, just as Chuck had found it. Down below, Seek found a construction not unlike that under Albert Vogel's dental practice, a massive concrete reinforced bunker built to withstand a bombardment…or the wrath of the camp inmates up above. As they entered the common room, he turned to face the hallway leading toward what he knew would be the sleeping quarters. Liliana turned back around and grabbed him by the arm, shaking her head and walking him in the opposite direction to the laboratory.

The glass door to the lab opened with a hiss, releasing a gray, stale mist across their faces. Solomon held his breath. When the air subsided he scanned the room. This was a very different lab from the malicious orthodontia in the previous shelter. For one, it was littered in broken borosilicate glass and discarded, strange-looking medical apparatuses. A handful of syringes stuck into the wall where the four tall double-helix strands had hung in the sister blast shelter. Cupboards lining the floor lay open and barren, their contents strewn about the floor. The stands along the walls held bits of shattered beakers and flasks, their dried contents drawing long stains down the wall under them. To his right on the counter there looked to be a fire pit made in the industrial sink, ashes and charred bits of paper stuck to the lining of the enamel around the drain.

In the corner to his left, splayed out like an animal skin rug against the huge metal frame of a forty-year-old operant conditioning chamber, lay the well-preserved and still discernible body of Martin Jung. Solomon stepped very carefully over the carpeting of splintered shards, holding Liliana and tilting her equally gently to the side as he passed. He looked to make sure her already deeply worn loafers found safe spots on the floor before approaching the body. Dr. Jung was clutching a single reagent bottle of thick, dusty glass. Whatever liquid it held had long since evaporated and dried someplace off into the ventilation ducts above their heads. Seek covered his face with a cloth from his pack as he neared but was surprised to find that the decomposition of the former doctor had hardly begun. His stench barely mirrored that which could be found in countless other places—closets, bathrooms, basements and sidewalks all over San Magnus island.

Solomon felt tempted to touch him, as if he were uncertain if the man was dead at all or possibly made of wax. His skin was glossy enough and his eyes, while absent-looking, remained nearly undisturbed by time. Dr. Jung sported a straight, lengthened goatee, the hairs from his lip propelling almost as far toward his chest as those protruding from his chin. A hint of gray remained in his facial hair though he was completely bald atop his head.

Solomon turned to Liliana. "He looks like he died just yesterday."

"Look at his hands," she replied.

They were red, stark red, unlike the pale whiteness in his face. Solomon looked closer, careful not to touch his arms which were riddled with fragments of glass still sticking into the lining of his blood-stained lab coat, trapped as if embalmed in his skin. They stuck in his hands and arms, the tips of his fingers, and into the corners of his knuckles.

121

"He did all this," Solomon muttered, turning back around to Liliana.

July 1st, 2020 2100 hours

How fitting: the trial is scheduled to start on the forth. I had a moment to glance at the news between lawyers and got a hearty laugh at the field day they've been having. At least now they've put away the *Which talentless millionaire heiress isn't wearing underwear?* segments for a rainier day. CNN has released a 3-D graphics campaign (what else is new?) depicting me under such headlines as "Crossroads: Seeking the Truth" and "Truth Time: Crossing the Line." A wonderfully creative staff they have over there at CNN. Could be worse though. There was an editorial on the New York Post's Facebook wall the other week that read "Solomon: Not So Wise." As if I didn't get picked on enough in Hebrew school, now every tabloid in the Western Hemisphere is taking shots at me.

Then there's Fox News. Oh, how I love my dear old friend Fox News. I spent almost an entire day watching Fox News, except for quick breaks to piss and vomit, often in the same place and once at the same time. Nearly every segment on that feed is bemoaning the violation of one man's rights with one outstretched twisted little hand and beating my career into an early grave with the other. "Stephen Solomon is a violator of the Constitution of the United States and a traitor to the great nation for which it stands!" preached one indiscernible big-boobed, blonde talking head. "Colonel Salazar is the finest of American patriots and he has been thoroughly wronged in all this," continued an actual talking boob. I swear, maybe it's me, but the hair gets blonder and the boobs bigger as the day goes on. It's like at noon they get bleached and by 4 pm the producers stuff their bras with cabbages. And all that Aryan-izing makes them all the more maddening. By six their heavy hitters came on, men with bigger breasts than the women, and they hurled a red, white, and blue flag graphic barrage salvo that would sink the Statue of Liberty in New York Harbor.

"Stephen 'Seeeeeek' Solomon has desecrated not only the

founding principles of objective journalism, but also those of this, the greatest nation on Earth." I didn't even make it to the bathroom on time with that one. "For God's sake, the man's name he's harassing is 'America!' He's a national hero." It's a good thing my laptop is reinforced. There was one glimmering light at the other end of my streaming live news feed, fifteen minutes of fame. ABC Nightly reported that the military tribunal is now investigating Salazar on suspicion of war crimes. You'd think that would be the headline all across the internet and broadcast waves. "Suspicion of war crimes." Instead they've centered the chopping block on one lowly journalist whose article brought that man to their attention in the first place.

The irony of course, which seems lost on the good folks at Fox, along with ideas like decency and "less is more," is that when the government invades your privacy, taps and traps your phone, monitors your bank accounts, hacks your email and Facebook page, it's all in the interest of National Security and violates not a word of the founding fathers' document of righteousness. But when a citizen does it to bring a corrupt government bureaucrat to justice, that's not National Security. That's unlawful. That's treason. And when he refuses to name his "accomplice," that man is a traitor.

Living in the now seems impossible. The last time I felt brave enough to leave the apartment, I ran into my neighbor Rick who said he hoped they'd give me the death penalty, because that's "what we used to do with traitors." I used to doggie sit for that bastard. It's amazing how powerful the wrong words can be and how easy it is to hide away the right ones. I won't deny breaking the law, and I'll plead guilty in court if the charges read likewise. But I won't submit my source and I won't admit to wrong-doing. That son of a bitch would still be operating if it weren't for our story, and no one seems to care that he's been stopped.

I'm sorry, girls. I can't help but be coarse. My biggest worry in all this is what you're seeing and hearing at home. I hope this hasn't defined me; it was not my intention. You know by now from reading that all these things, all my searches and stories, are for you and in your names. That's more than just an excuse for my actions. It's the purpose for them and everything else for which I'm bound to come under national scrutiny for in the coming weeks. Do you remember this? I wish you could tell me; tell me you didn't hate me. I suppose all parents embarrass their children, hell, grandpa grew out a Jew-fro, and when he picked me up from school my friends called him Disco Dad. And this was in '94. It must be another thing altogether for Dad to be plastered on the morning news minutes before Sesame Street.

I moved out of the house last month so the press wouldn't ambush you girls playing on the swings in the front yard. It didn't seem to help at first, but there's only so much time a managing editor will let their agents sit out in front of the wrong house without getting anything juicy. And for that I am grateful to your mother. She gave them nothing of me, for the sake of you girls, and I could expect nothing less. That said, I'm getting the not-so-subtle suspicion that she's using this all to split you away from me. Fox News would love that, no? "Disgraced malefactor left by own wife." Not that they could spell malefactor. But what she doesn't understand is that all of this is for you. This country will never be safe for our children, all of them, with men like Salazar in positions of power, behind blacked memos and invisible, limitless investments. For Christ's sake, most of his work was based on children no older than you are now as I write this!

I'm confident his days are numbered, though maybe not as few in number as mine. The Post's lawyers have been working non-stop trying to put out fires, and for that, too, I am thankful. I think Paula sent them as reinforcement *because* I didn't name names, not that her name was particularly indictable. But because of this, the lawyers say I can expect added charges of impeding a federal investigation, interference of justice, and withholding evidence. It's not as if I can plead the fifth. I'm not even the one who broke the law! I mean, I know. I know that if they investigate him as I investigated him, they'll find what I found. They'll cut through the red tape it took me years to wrangle out of in just days, and they won't need any of my sources. It's too late for that, though; this is a media frenzy now, and the nation wants blood it didn't even know could be spilled. This poor, deluded, mistaken nation is simmering with vengeance like the crowds at the Colosseum. Caesar's pilfering their pockets for his war coffer, but they couldn't care less. Well then, come Independence Day, I say feed me to the lions and let history sort itself out.

June 28th, 2025 1750 hours

It's amazing how much can happen in a day. Since finding Vogel's underground tomb we have finally come to the heart of the matter, that age-old question: why are we here? We're here to hunt down the remains of four men, the Vorkämpfer, fugitive Nazi warmongers, and use their blood or body parts to open a grizzly lock and break into the Kapitalzukunft, the last remaining fortress of the deported Third Reich. It's a massive structure whose front doors look completely impenetrable, even to a nuclear blast, and I suppose that was the point. We invent the A-bomb; they invent the A-bomb-proof vest.

So far, we've extracted and successfully tested the DNA of Albert Vogel, chief of dentistry and murderer of his own children. On the floor in the other room, here in a similar concrete bunker buried under a New World concentration camp hidden deep in the jungle, is the second of the four, Martin Jung, psychologist and pediatrician. His lab and remains are of an even more gruesome nature.

Lily, that is Dr. Ferreira, confirmed his cause of death, an overly obvious self-inflicted set of wounds he sustained from destroying his lab with his own bare hands. We know this for sure because the lab's overhead camera caught it all before the power went out. And more. The time and date stamp from the last recording (They're in analog, ugh.) read *8:00 Uhr; Zwanzig zweite, Oktober: 1984.* That's eight PM on the twenty-second, the same date The Haze was released in the ventilation systems in the Villa Roma and Villa Vienna.

The outdoor footage is grainy but discernible, displayed in a green hue. It looks like some of what remains were taken from a position on this very structure, maybe hanging from the guard tower it stands perpendicular against. There is no camera there anymore. The feed shows a mob of men and women, some dressed in uniform, others not, some with pistols and rifles, others with lanterns and flashlights, hammers and knives, storming the gate to the camp. One of them carries a tall pair of wire cutters. This part gets easier to see when the guard tower searchlights find the commotion. When the mob breaks into the camp, some of the guards come out from the building over to them. I think I can see the bald dome and white lab coat of Dr. Jung following behind them. The tape is muted, the cameras had no audio pickup, and they'd be speaking German anyway, but it looks like they talk with the guards for just under a minute before the mob starts the shooting.

Dr. Jung was not shot. He sort of just stands there stiffly. He watches the mob overrun the guards in the camp, and one of them tosses a flaming lamp on the inmate hut closest to the gate. We've seen what became of that hut. It's completely burned to the ground. After I'd seen the video I ran out to look it over again. I could only make out two things. Child-sized bed frames and scattered rows of razor-sharp little teeth. For a while the mob watches the hut burn, half-expecting someone or something to come running out. But nothing ever does. The roof collapses and the mob jumps back, raising their weapons and hands in celebration. When we watched it Liliana put her hands over her eyes and said, "Thank God there are no microphones."

Then a couple of those with rifles walk to the next house, carrying burning planks from the wreckage. They move and are about to throw their torches on the second building when Dr. Jung snaps out of his daze and runs up, throwing himself on them. One of them tosses him to the ground where he lies begging. The men don't burn the second hut. Instead they beat and kick Dr. Jung on the ground until he stops wiggling, and then they open the longhouse door. Dr. Jung looks like he takes something out from the inside of his lab coat and kisses it, maybe a cross hanging on his necklace? One of the gunmen holds up his machine gun, and we're still in debate over whether or not he fires it into the longhouse. I'm pretty certain he does. His body shakes as if reacting to the gun's recoil. I don't know how, but through the fuzzy video Lily says she can see his hands drop away from the gun and the shaking is simply an adrenaline shock.

Whether flight or fight, the man stands there for a moment and then—whoosh. Just like that, he's gone. His buddies run in after him, but they don't come out. Dr. Jung scrambles to his feet and runs back toward this structure. That's the last we see of him outdoors. On the interior camera he comes barreling into the lab, flailing his arms and legs. I've never seen an old man so animate. He tears the place to pieces, chucking bottles and needles, thrashing about in a berserk rage, and then collapses in a heap on the floor where we found him.

By then we can see them pouring out of the cabin and blocked from the camp gates by the mob. A few of them back up and run to the other huts. Soon all the longhouses are spilling out these little gray children with these huge black eyes that span around the sides of their sharp, pointy heads. They look like birds, their faces pressed back as if hit by the wind, but they don't have any wings. And they're all naked, not a single scrap of clothing on any single one of them. They gather in the center of the camp and the mob starts to flee back toward the gate. The one with the wire cutters tries to make a new hole in the west side, but he's electrocuted by the fence. It looks like a couple of the armed invaders stand their ground and shoot at the children, the creatures. That's when it happens. They zig-zag, sort of like crossing in and out between each other and jumping side to side like monkeys. They charge the mob. That's at 8:24:05. It's all over by 8:24:30.

Afterward, it sort of looks like they try putting out the fire on the burning hut, but none of them really get close enough to it. They hold back their heads and try to walk forward. It's the light from the blaze. They can't look at it. Eventually they give up and scatter, some leaving through the gate. The others look like they're running toward the structure under the camera. That's when the power goes out and the feed ends.

By then Jung is already dead. He's bled out in the corner where he remains still, mostly intact. With the generator knocked out, probably the same way it was to happen later in the Villa Vienna, this place fell into dark obscurity with the rest of the island, and no one has come to disturb the doctor's remains in all this time. Except for the man we know as the voice. He must have come through here, maybe taking a sample from Dr. Jung. And he might have found what the doctor forgot to toss in the bonfire he made in the laboratory sink halfway through cutting himself to death. The room next to this one is a server room, possibly one of the first ever built. Its towers are old and corroded and probably hold as much memory as your little pink iPod shuffles, but they still work. With the power back on, Cledwyn managed to extract a few hundred megabytes of information from them. They're all in German, of course, but this old Kindle can translate any written text. If you speak slowly enough, it can even translate spoken speech. I'm sure you're not impressed.

Of the uncorrupted material the following will be featured highly in the book I'm going to write if I ever get off this island alive. If I ever get to see you again.

Logdate: April 20th, 1974, Experiment Codename Volksklausur; Day 13.

Today, on the 85th birthday of the Führer, we begin construction of Camp Menschheit, the future site of the birth of a new peoples, a new frontier in human evolution. The site is as remote as one can find on this already most remote island colony, and will serve perfectly as our base for the social engineering phase of the experiment. My phase. We will employ only those most trusted officers who fled Poland with Herr Metzger, proper SS men loyal to the cause and with no families, to oversee the camp. But they will shan't be needed for long. None of them will be.

Logdate: February 4th, 1980, Experiment Codename Volksklausur; Day 2,128.

Initial behavioral modification for Generation A is enormously successful. Herr Metzger's first crop of forty-eight healthy males tests positively across the board, though I am disappointed in being unable to run tests on the one female whom he has requested at his labs in the Kapitalzukunft. A marvel that he was able to control the sex of the children, doubtless he is working on a simpler, more productive method for producing them with Hera than reverting to mass stock, which will soon be impossible. Additionally, they have adapted well to life inside the camp, a token to the good doctor's skill with the syringe.

I have begun schooling them in proper German, and they pick up our tongue very quickly. We have skipped written language completely for obvious reasons and have sped straight through intermediate vocabulary, cognates, and pronunciation. It is difficult to relay to them mannerisms, terms of speech, sarcasm, and humor, and I have had no success in getting them to laugh. Nevertheless, they are born for combat, not comedy. Their education has been molded for this purpose, and so we will not be approaching the finer points of Hegel and Kant but gearing straight for the fundamentals of the Fatherland's superior militaria, von Clausewitz, von Moltke, etc. etc. We have had only one setback during this phase of the experiment, though I feign to dub it such. I have discussed this with Dr. Vogel, and he assures me there is no way around their speech impediment, that the modifications made to their teeth, jaws, and tongues make it impossible for them to speak like proper Germans but instead with a great raspy lisp, an effeminate snakelike sound which grows more noticeable at every lesson.

Security is tight, as briefed. The camp is outfitted in case of an outbreak, but its defenses are just as much to keep in Generation A as it is to keep out any invaders to our progress. The fences are unclimbable, electrified, but more importantly, the subjects will be protected from premature attack by Captain Holtzmann and his troops, some of the best soldiers to come out of the Reich. For now, secrecy will be our greatest defense, just as it is with the rest of the island. In addition to myself, Dr. Ebersbach, Dr. Vogel, and of course Dr. Metzger, Captain Holtzmann and his men are the only other peoples who know of the camp's existence. Like this we will keep it until the time is right.

The issue with the light is not as detrimental as I had assumed. Training and reinforcement begins at eleven o'clock sharp and continues until dawn. Those ingenious engineering boys devised these spectacular goggles with a green glowing light with which to see during the night, making our operations here nearly invisible to the citizens of the Reich, tucked gently away, asleep just a mile off in the Villa Vienna. I had previously requested that the subjects be outfitted with light-dampening receptacles, but Gerhart dismissed this idea with impunity. "I shall fix this mistake in a more permanent fashion," he said before pointing out the value of covert nighttime operations. He seems to have a solution to every problem, for when I questioned him on the propriety of working nearly eighteen hours a day, he sent me a package of adrenal supplements he and Dr. Ebersbach had cooked up, and now I feel like I sleep ten hours a day when in fact I sleep for three. It's truly incredible what those two are capable of. They've managed to turn a seventy-seven-year-old man back into a restless medical student!

Logdate: October 28th, 1982, Experiment Codename Volksklausur; Day 3,125.

Behavior modification continues to surpass my expectations. We've started them on reinforcement, using whistle tones of varying pitches to signify orders, and to great success. I've conditioned their minds to switch over to new ways of thinking, new neural pathways, the instant they receive the auditory signals. We plan on removing this line of conditioning and phasing it into another once their orders are memorized, a proper form of handling to follow military rank, so as they follow my directions first and the captain's second.

In keeping with this, the children have also begun combat training, and within a week we've requested new practice targets. Deferring to the expert opinion of Captain Holtzmann, they have been drilled in and mastered the techniques of light infantry tactics and hand-to-hand combat. In a year's time he will begin to instruct them on firearms and explosives, but for now their tiny razor hands will suffice. Last night's hunt went superbly, though I must confess I found myself quite shaken by the jungle after dark. The captain led them on their first of soon-to-be many assassination protocols. In the brush I blew the whistle to begin the protocol, and when they had returned with the bodies, I blew it again to end protocol. Results can be found in the official report, but what is not in the report was the deliciousness of Ebersbach's prized boar and the petrified expression it held while we roasted it.

I remember when he first saw the children, the captain himself nearly screamed, and I relieved him, sympathizing that I too was taken aback by their form and the solemn blackness of their eyes. But in truth, after these few years, I have come to admire the children as my own family of negroes, and I find their features adoring rather than frightful. Yesterday I rested my hand on the chin of 32 and he smiled at me. Or perhaps it was 33. It makes me think of my own wife sitting alone by the fire, sleeping every night while I toil in the field with the children, and of my boys, lost someplace on the soiled battleground of bloodthirsty Stalin's Communist Europe. With this we could take back the human race. If every good German family of five has as its fourth child one of the Volksklausur, they would never need worry about intruders or the keeping of firearms or the worry of conscription. Their intelligence is constantly impressing, each as bright as the next and were their role not a militaristic one, I dare to say they could replace us old men in setting the stage for the science of the future.

Next week the hunt will resume, but we will switch our form of prey and finally do away with the last of the locals.

Logdate: October 22nd, 1984, Experiment Codename Volksklausur; Day 3,850.

Heinrich just messaged. Metzger's poison gas released in the houses and streets. Everyone not dead has fled to the beach. Says Talia is not among them. Says he has told them everything. They are coming here now for the children. We must not let them have the children. It is not yet time. They are not ready for the world. It will be dark soon. I fear the light is all in vain.

Chapter XIII

Chuck flipped on the laboratory light, took out the knife he'd used to cut his boar meat, and sliced off the end of Martin Jung's right-hand pinky finger. He stopped for a moment before passing the appendage to Liliana and looked down on Jung's left-handed pinky finger that had already received the same treatment, lying bare past the second knuckle. "It's almost six," he said, looking back at the gang in the doorway. "There's beds upstairs."

Solomon nodded. No one said a word. They retreated one by one, Chuck lastly making sure to lock the generator and shelter doors before trotting back up the stairs to the vacant guard quarters.

Solomon picked a bunk next to a thick double-paned glass window facing the camp interior. He tapped it with his finger and felt reassured in the strength of its reinforced metal bars split down the middle of the glass. Looking out at the compound, his eyes drifted and Liliana, sitting on the flattened mattress beside him, could tell he was replaying the security footage in his head and through his eyes on the camp floor below. He blinked and turned away to see her staring at him.

Cledwyn's jump and collapse on the bunk above broke the silence. He released a deep sigh of comfort, arching his head back and talked up at the ceiling. "This is truly a grotty-like shandy van, ain't it, Solomon?"

Seek lay on his pillow, staring up at the frame supporting the Welshman. "A what, King?"

"A place fucked in the head."

"Oh. Yes, yes it is, King."

"You know, I've been thinkin'," he continued from the top bunk. "Those generators are lush, the same make and model. The Germans didn't bring them over. Hell, most of the stuff 'round here is bought

American or Chinese or a cheap knock-off of one or the other."

"Yeah? And?"

"That means they was getting help from people. A lot of people. We've not seen any quarries. Someone must have built their houses. We've not seen any farms. Someone must have brought them food."

"We met one of those people on the way over here, isn't that right, Chuck?" Solomon asked the Texan as he walked into the room, taking a look at the remaining bed space. He didn't respond, just looked at Liliana on the bottom bunk, the wooden frame holding up the top bunk, and sat himself down in a chair beside the metal gun locker.

"You met one of them?" Cledwyn asked.

"That's right," retorted the bottom bunk.

"Well, then you already know."

"Know what, King?"

"Money. Money's not bad. Greed's not evil. All that work, all those toys, these assholes bought them all right, but from who? Poor brown fellas living in shacks on the docks or in the shanty part of some dump town along the coast."

"You're saying money's not evil; it just pays for evil things?"

"It paid for those people to feed their families. This place is all fucked and dirty as the road, but it wasn't made by dirty people. Those are all the science types and the soldier types. No offense to my esteemed colleagues."

"No offense taken," mumbled Liliana.

Chuck started to doze off.

"But they didn't have any Nazi carpenters or Nazi masons on the island."

"They had engineers," replied Solomon.

"Yeah, and what happened to their engineers?"

"Haven't found them yet."

"Not bloody likely to," finished King.

Solomon stared up at the top bunk. His fingers whittled on a thick splinter hanging vertically from the bedpost on his right side. He tried jimmying it from its slot, first with one nail, then with two, and found he couldn't break it off without first getting out of bed. Finally, he flicked it with the tip of his middle finger and pulled his hands back under the pillow.

"And what is your billion dollars going to pay for, Cledwyn?" asked the journalist.

"Huh? Well, I don't know. I won't be buying no Nazi concentration camps."

"Yeah, well, I'd hold off on your shopping list until after we find the next two bodies."

"Jeez man," spoke the top bunk. "You sure know how to take the piss out of everything. Hey, miss, er, Miss Ferreira, what'll you spend your billion on?"

Liliana turned over to face the direction of the question. Her answer surprised Solomon.

"It's not my billion to spend. Or yours. It belongs to people I've never heard of in a place I've never been."

"Rubbish," Cledwyn retorted. "All those people are dead and gone. It's ours for the takin' now. What about you, big man?"

Chuck, sitting back with his feet up on a faded blue cushion, slowly opened his eyes.

"It doesn't matter, King. It doesn't matter at all."

"What do you mean, you brute? A billion dollars! How can't that matter?"

"A billion, a trillion, a hundred trillion. It doesn't matter. Those numbers are too big to make any damned difference to just one person. They've no meaning."

"No context," Solomon added, as surprised with the sergeant's answer as he was with the doctor's. "Nothing matters without context. It's the most powerful force there is."

"Spoken like a true linguist," said Liliana. "Are you forgetting genetics so soon?"

"What good is evolution without life?"

Cledwyn shook his head and pushed a pillow over his face.

"Without context, genes, DNA, it doesn't mean a thing."

"Tell that to the last person who slept in that bed," concluded Liliana.

Solomon suddenly felt very uneasy. He slipped out of bed and leaned over to the window. The sun was closing to its lowest spot on the horizon, half submerged behind the towering canopy of the jungle. He stared down the walkway from the tower above them to the farther one to the south. There was no wind, no movement at all on the chain or in the high grass fading into the darkness below. Solomon turned back and gazed down the hall to a small metal ladder leading up to the guard tower, just a few meters from their beds.

"It's locked," mumbled Chuck, one eye open, watching Solomon's worrisome expression.

"What about the spotlights? Should we put them on?"

The Texan sighed. "And announce that we're here?"

Chuck turned over, putting his back to the room. Within moments he was asleep. Solomon counted himself reassured. He looked down at Liliana facing away from him, lying on her side in the bed beside his own. He watched her breathing, the sloping line of her waist sinking and rising into the mattress, and wondered if she could feel his eyes watching her. Then he turned back to the splinter in the bedpost.

Several hours later he awoke, sitting up against the concrete wall, his butt slipping off the nightstand, head pointed out the window. A thin line of drool ran down his shirt. He shook off his exhaustion and wiped his lip, squinting in the night. With the darkness in and outside, only a sliver of the moon to keep watch, he struggled, searching for the signs of movement he'd expected would follow them back to the camp. But he saw nothing, only black, the silver shimmer of moonlight across the jungle canopy where the sun had rested. He inched off the nightstand and climbed back into bed quietly. Turning over, he stuck his second pillow beneath his legs.

Liliana, her eyes open just a bit, thought she could hear him whisper to himself, "They're just children," before falling back to sleep.

In the morning they locked up the structure and made back for the Villa Vienna with the camp's most valuable contents in tow. The other three helped Cledwyn push a dirty, rusted wheelbarrow he'd found in a ditch behind the camp through the small gap-like trail in the trees back to Albert Vogel's house. With the bits and pieces of the camp's generator filling it, the tin cart weighed more than he did, and though he acted as a captain at the helm of his vessel, Cledwyn did little in the way of actual pushing. Chuck, the brawn behind the chariot, took with him the Mauser rifle he'd used to kill their mid-afternoon meal the day before, along with a second pouch of ammunition and a pair of Martin Jung's precious night-vision goggles, twice as worn as the scope mounted on his bolt-action. Guiding the tipsy caravan was Solomon, trying desperately not to get his foot stuck in a hole or vine patch, having logged in another entry to his tablet. Leading the expedition and feigning sympathy when they reached the sprawled tree across the path halfway through the jungle was Liliana, who came away with the most prized possession of all, the distal phelange of Martin Jung's remaining pinky finger.

Each carried a heavy ration of thick, poorly dried strips of boar meat and had made a point to swap out into what of the guard tower's closet they could stomach to wear. Solomon had refused to change except to finally take off his tie and to switch his heavily worn loafers for a size nine leather-strapped boot. Liliana had done the same and found little of the masculine attire to her liking but nevertheless made do with a white undershirt in place of her torn and sweat-stained blouse. They both wore white. Cledwyn, having lost his overcoat in a flailing torch-fire, felt strangely comfortable in a khaki cotton field blouse with a double-lined downward triangle on the sleeve and a double lightning bolt *S* mark on the collar. Chuck maintained his green with brown-green fatigues and sleeveless button-down regalia.

Their relief came in the form of collapse upon reaching the plaza after crawling and pushing their way through the jungle. Chuck slung his rifle around the tall brass boy and hunkered in the dry, rusted fountain with Liliana beside him. Solomon signaled that he'd be right back and went to relieve himself in the grass behind a townhouse on Konrad Zuse street.

Lying atop his replacement parts in the wheelbarrow, Cledwyn spoke up at the clouds. "Well, at least with that door open a while the air should be better." By the time Solomon had zipped up and returned, the Welshman had already wrapped a ripped sheet around his mouth and gotten to work, echoing clanking and cursing sounds from the generator room.

Solomon crashed beside his companions at the fountain and found his eyes could rest nowhere else in the sky but the tower of the Kapitalzukunft behind the jungle from which they'd just emerged. He stared at it, pushing back on his glasses, and felt as if his gaze could pierce the structure, destroy it. He fantasized about watching it tip and fall, with great explosion, on top of the rest of the fortress. He pictured the struts failing at first, a few shingles falling from the roof as a gull took flight from its perch, sensing the collapse. A cloud of dust would build at the base and a strong wind would give the last push, as if nature herself had had enough of *the damnable Nazis*. In his mind he could see a single body, some crippled specter falling from the dome at the top, having climbed and jumped from the window just at the point of tipping over. He tried to imagine its face, its gender, the sound on the air as it screamed, falling story by story, followed closely by the concrete structure like the slab of a tomb.

He didn't notice the mumbling coming from his pocket until Liliana had laid her hand on his shoulder.

"Mr. Solomon? Mr. Solomon!" demanded the voice. "You can stop staring now."

Seek shook off his daydream and pulled the hands-free from his pocket. "So you are in that tower?"

"No, Mr. Solomon, I'm in that little capsule in your neck. I'm in that pocket of blood building in your lungs. I'm in the fear that bottles up in your gut every night."

Solomon stood and stared harder up at the top of the tower.

"So you're Metzger?"

Chuck and Liliana looked at each other and rose to attention. There was no answer. Thirty seconds of silence moved like molasses in their veins. Then a sound came through the receiver, like static drum rattling, a repetitious, low, grinding roar like an engine in slow motion. Laughter. The voice was laughing.

"I would be well over one hundred and twenty years old!" it said through the bouts of robotic hysteria.

"Then who are you? How did you find out about this place? How do you know us?"

Slowly, the laughter subsided. "You really are an annoyingly persistent rodent, Mr. Solomon. Why would I answer any of those questions?"

Liliana stepped forward and seized the device. "Then never mind those questions," she intruded, signaling for Solomon to back down. "Would you answer questions about the island instead?"

A pause.

"Have you a sample of Dr. Jung?"

"He was the old man who went mad in the laboratório?" asked Liliana. "Yes, we have his sample."

"Good. Then you should waste no more time today. The third sample is Dr. Ebersbach. His coordinates are in a small file located on Mr. Solomon's tablet computer entitled: "And You Shall Receive"."

Solomon rolled his eyes and searched his files with Liliana watching from over his shoulder. There it was, at the top of the search, capital A. "How can he be playing us so hard?" he muttered.

Liliana turned back to the tower. "How is it the island doesn't appear on any satellite maps?"

"I don't know."

"What happened to all the people they kidnapped here?"

"I don't know."

"Why did Metzger turn the gas on his own people?"

"I. Don't. Know. Ms. Ferreira, you're starting to sound like your pencil-pushing colleague Mr. Solomon. You're not here for any of those things. You're here for the samples."

She sighed. Solomon reached out his hands for the device, but she stuck up her index finger. *Wait.*

"If we have Jung's sample, why do we need the lab open to test it?"

"You don't. You need the lab open to test Dr. Ebersbach's. It will take you all day to find him, and there's no cozy bed to sleep in once you get there."

Click.

139

Chapter XIV

Solomon ran his fingers back along the faded map he now wished he'd never found. Liliana held onto his Kindle and read him the coordinates. He traced his hands along the corners of the paper, making a bony compass with his index finger and thumb. Liliana kept her amusement under wraps as he deduced the location of Dr. Ebersbach. "It's nothing. Just a blank space near these docks," Solomon concluded, pointing out the southerly location to Chuck and Liliana. The former shouted out for Cledwyn and strutted over to swap the news.

"Why is he out there?" Solomon asked.

"Maybe he was chased? Heading for a boat?" replied Dr. Ferreira.

Solomon shrugged and shrunk his head between his shoulder blades. He was exhausted, worn, chased, and asthmatic. With the sun on his back he watched his shadow cast down on the map, like a huge darkness blanketing San Magnus island. Then he noticed it, handwritten on the corner of the page. Seek leaned back and held up the paper to let the sunlight shine through it.

"What is it, Stephen?"

"Here. This is his map. H.E. Heinrich Ebersbach. He was in the village with Vogel when it happened. Vogel might have even driven right by him on the street without even noticing."

Solomon passed Liliana the map. She took quick notice of the initials, folded it up, and slipped it back in his shoulder pack.

"Vogel, Jung, Ebersbach. Metzger. Where's Metzger? If he really released the gas, where did he do it from? Did it kill him too?"

Solomon took one last glance up at the tower of the Kapitalzukunft. Chuck marched over.

"We're moving out. It's almost ten. King says it'll take longer to get the generator fixed than it did to take the other one apart. He's going to stay and work. I've left him my pistol. We are going to track down the next sample."

"Heinrich Ebersbach," replied Solomon to his orders.

"Yeah, whatever," said Chuck as he reached up and grabbed the rifle, slinging it over his back. "Let's move".

Without so much as a wave, the party of three took off down the south side of the plaza on Karl Braun's cobblestones.

"You know, I'm really starting to hate this road," Solomon murmured. "Hard to believe it's been less than a week." He sighed. Chuck walked beside him on the left, staring ahead, Liliana to his right with her eyes to the western shore. "Eight days ago I was in my apartment. There's a pizza place two blocks the street, clean clothes, a running tap." He drew Chuck's attention.

"Weren't you in Afghanistan?" came the soft voice to his right.

"For two years," answered Solomon. "This seems like three."

"How much combat did you see?" asked the sergeant.

Solomon shrugged. "The closest I came to combat was a ricochet off the Humvee. It was almost ten years ago."

"What happened?" Liliana continued.

"You don't really want to hear this. It's nothing important."

"Please tell it," Chuck pleaded. "Anything but another damned Mateses story."

"Matsés!" Liliana snapped.

Solomon smiled. He looked at his companions and saw that they were smiling too. *What a strange sight to see in a place like this.*

"Well. We were a little ways out from Qalat. There was an airstrip there in the militarized zone about a hundred miles from the Pakistani boarder. It was a month after the Dean David Jensen massacre; do you remember that? He was the private who chucked a grenade into a schoolhouse. After they released his name and put him on trial, I secured an interview with him. It was my first big report, my breakout story. They stationed a few men outside the room, but it was just him and me in there, this tiny concrete box in the sand."

"What was he like?"

"Stoic," Solomon shot back as if rehearsed. "No emotion. He

142

looked like shit. I asked him what had happened that day, and he told me about the week before it. His platoon had been ambushed while on urban patrol. They were all killed or wounded. Dean came away with some shrapnel in his back. I remember he said, 'They just kept shooting,' even after all his friends were all down, and, 'The more of us were hit, the more they fired.' So one day the next week he left the med station, put on his bandolier, and walked up the hill to the school. Those walls are like hard clay, and the fragments just bounced from one side of the room to the next. He killed thirteen kids someplace between seven and ten years old, their teacher, plus another five wounded. My wife was six months pregnant with my second daughter. I just remember looking at him the way the rest of the country was looking at him."

"Why did he do it?" asked Liliana, kicking over a rock into the dirt.

"He said he had to 'thin them out'. Kill as many as he could. Didn't want them to grow up and 'ambush any more of us'. It wasn't until after his sentencing that I read the dispatch about his kid. He had a little boy, probably just out of high school now, ready for enlistment. A month later the Post still had me in Afghanistan. The coverage of Jensen had been huge. People were paying attention to the war again, whether for the right reasons or not. When we got hit on the Kandahar Ghazini highway, I just froze and thought about what he'd said. They just kept shooting. It shouldn't have phased me. Big fuckin' surprise, people shooting at other people in a war, right? I didn't go back after that. Rebecca was born twenty days early, but I made it back stateside in time. Named her after her mother's mother. I remember thinking that I needed to do everything in my power to make sure my children had a safe world to live in."

He looked over at Liliana. There was that smile again.

"Do either of you have kids?"

"No," came the response, almost in unison.

Solomon shrugged, and there was silence for a while. On the far southern side of Karl Braun, the shoreline was only partially visible, blocked by a small bluff that came up from the dirt and then dropped steeply under the waves. Liliana struggled to see and hear the water, being just beyond reach.

"Do you remember when you said I had no stake in the war?" she asked casually of Solomon.

"Yes."

"You were wrong. My grandfather was killed in it."

Seek looked at her slantwise. "How?"

Liliana scoffed. "You Americans always seem to forget. It was called a World War for a reason. He was a...how do you say, a mercantil...fuzileiro? Boat soldier?"

"Merchant Marine," Chuck interceded.

"Yes, that is it. In nineteen forty-two he was killed by the Germans in those torpedo submarinos, along with just about everyone else on the ship."

"I... I, ah...don't know what to say. I'm sorry. Did you know him well?"

"Stephen, how old do you think I am? He was twenty years old when he died."

Solomon blushed. "I...wasn't thinking. I'm sorry."

"Seek's great with women," Chuck murmured.

"My nana would talk about him often, though. She was seventeen, raising my mother and uncles by herself. Even when I was growing up I remember her saying, 'What a brave avô you girls have. You come from the stock of saints.'"

"Your grandmother raised your mother and her brothers all by herself?"

"Yes. She was a housekeeper."

"Wow. And here you are, a doctor, in genetics no less. Ha, that's the American dream."

"The what?"

"Oh, it's just this stupid thing we have in America. This grandiose ideal. People get there and they think as long as they work hard, they can raise their kids to do better than they did. The American dream."

"I am not an American, Mr. Solomon."

The walk to the South Docks took longer than their trek through

144

the jungle, though it felt considerably more like a stroll and less like a death march. In place of the cumbersome foliage and occasional slither from the underbrush, they had, to contend with, the chirping of seagulls and bright, clear skies. Karl Braun seemed to break down the closer they came to the beachhead, opening into a cracked cement road that withered and vanished under the sand. The docks themselves were barren, sticking out like twigs in the Atlantic, a single-man rowboat sunk to the bottom between the dilapidated, rusted struts crawling with coral. But that was all. Solomon half-suspected to see a squadron of powerboats or maybe an old U-boat like the one that had sunk the *Araraquara* on her way to São Luís from Salvador more than eighty years before. He turned to Chuck, who stared, calculatingly, at the map.

"Maybe some of them escaped?"

Chuck lowered the map and looked over it at Solomon.

"Then why haven't we heard of this sooner? Come on. We're less than half a click from the coordinates."

They turned from the docks and walked east along the shoreline. The southern shore of the island was not the picturesque vacation postcard that could be found running along its western side, but a series of brief openings of shell-drenched beach between rocky crevasses. All the same, it didn't stop Liliana from taking off her boots and walking out ahead of them in the sand, feeling the chill winter water grace her footsteps.

"It's got to be fifty-something degrees. She must be freezing!" Solomon said to his companion.

"She's a big girl, Seek. She can take care of herself."

Solomon silently conceded and tried to turn the conversation around.

"Speaking of, how good an idea was it to leave King with your gun?"

Chuck pulled his rifle strap over his shoulder. "Pretty good, I'd say. It wasn't smart leaving him to begin with, but we need all the time we can get. I'm more worried the dumb bastard will fall asleep in the room and suffocate than I am him having to shoot anything."

"What if he shoots us?"

"Now why, oh why, would he do that? For a journalist you're really bad at making out people's character, you know that? Once he gets that generator on, his part is finished. He's done his job. He needs us to break into that vault. And he needs that pill in his neck not to go boom. Trust is about motive, Seek. What do you trust other people to do? For example, what do you trust me to do?"

"You, Chuck?"

"Yeah, me. What do you expect of me? How do you trust me?"

"Well..." Solomon thought it over. "I trust you to keep us alive. I trust you to get us around the island."

"And what do you trust her to do?" Chuck asked, nudging in the direction of Liliana, kicking up a large, pure white seashell pushed gently up the beach as if discarded by the sea.

"Well, I guess I expe—trust her—to get us in the fortress, get us to the vault."

"And I trust you to open the vault," concluded Chuck. "Just like I trust Cledwyn to turn the power back on and follow us all the way to the money he's looking for."

"Did you mean what you said last night? About the money?" Solomon asked nervously, setting the pace for a follow-up question.

"I already have all the money I need to keep me in liquor. I wouldn't know what to do with much more than that."

"Then why are you here?"

"What? What do you mean?"

"I mean, King and Lily and I were all lured here with something. I came for a story. You got suckered in just like the rest of us. How did they do it?"

"I wasn't suckered," responded Chuck. "I was doing a favor for a friend."

"Oh, well then," concluded Solomon. "You were suckered the worst."

Chuck mushed his lips together into a crooked smile and folded away the map.

After a few more meters Seek noticed Liliana had stopped dead ahead with her feet sinking into the sand. He reached out to Chuck and

146

pointed as she raised her hand to cover her mouth. Without thinking, Seek bolted toward her, nearly tripping on a shrub in the dirt. Liliana heard his steps racing closer and turned around with a quizzical look on her face. When he saw her expression he slowed. There was no emergency or fear in her eyes. She wasn't covering her mouth, but her nose. Then the smell hit him. A strong methane stench carried by a gust from the east. Solomon pulled his head back and put his hand over his nose, drawing pain from the break.

"We're close," Chuck said walking up between them. When he saw they weren't following him, he turned. "This is nothing. It's the fresh ones that really reek."

As they neared, the odor intensified. The coastline rose into a steep incline away from the beach and then dropped suddenly before them into a crescent-shaped gorge, its jaws facing out to the Atlantic. Away from the depression, many more smaller drops, like punches in the sand along the coast, dotted in a line to the East. Sinkholes were common in places thick with sandstone and water where chemicals in the bedrock dissolved in layers, suddenly or gradually, leaving large, gaping holes in the earth. They formed even faster when introduced to an abundance of acidic components, such as the calcium and phosphorous acid Solomon pressed hard to keep from his nostrils. He looked down and immediately spewed vomit into the gorge before turning and stumbling back down the incline.

"It's like a dig site," whispered Liliana.

Bones, skulls, cartilage, torn shreds and dried skin stuck to the walls of the pit like floral paper. They mingled indiscriminately with guns, blankets tusks, claws, and feathers floating in circles around the murky water basin. Chuck and Liliana walked around the crater to the next small one, and the next smaller still, each littered with a mass grave of its own, a compost of rotting things. In one of the holes Chuck spotted a familiar sight, a black Kevlar vest bobbing in shallow water. Covering his face with his elbow, he carefully climbed his way down. Holding to a root sticking out from the wall face, he dragged his foot across the body, hooking his heel in its side and pulled it toward him. When he had it stuck against the sides of the basin, he crouched down and lifted it out. It was damp but light as the vest wrapped only around a bloated torso absent of limbs or a head. Chuck dropped it with a splash.

Chapter XV

Liliana sat on a rock on the shore within eye-shot of the gorge pits, washed her feet in the salt water, and slipped her boots back on. She watched Solomon farther down the beach, his hands over his knees, spitting up in the Atlantic. Chuck walked up behind her and washed his hands where she had cleaned her feet. He glanced over at Solomon, still arched forward in the shallow ocean water.

"He does that a lot," said Chuck.

Liliana sighed. "One of those bodies is Ebersbach's. We're looking for a bone in a bone-yard."

"Son of a bitch. No wonder he said it would take all day."

"And all night," retorted the doctor. "I need to test every cadaver."

"Every one?" shouted Chuck. "Can't we just look for the one with the lab coat?"

Liliana stood, rifled through her pack, and pulled out an old pair of latex gloves from a box labeled *Wegwerfbar.*

"Did you see a lab coat?" she asked.

Solomon trudged through the sand toward her as Liliana made back up the bluff.

"You're not going to go through all of that, are you?" he exclaimed.

Without turning, she replied, "We need that sample, Solomon."

"Wait, wait, wait." Solomon gasped as he tried to catch her on the hill, his arm over his face, running straight into the down-rush, stench-filled wind stream.

"You're never going to find him in all that. You're going to have to take them all."

"Yes. That's right," she continued, climbing the top of the bluff. "You should go back to the town. We'll need the wheelbarrow."

Liliana disappeared into the sinkhole. Solomon walked backward from the hole where she had descended and turned to Chuck, scraping his hands together in the shallow waves.

"Chuck. Chuck, come on. This is crazy. She's insane."

The sergeant dried his hands on his fatigues and brought them up to his neck, highlighting the blue-veined pill stuck in the side of his throat. "And this isn't? She's right. You should head back and fetch the cart. Bring some towels or something while you're at it. I can't have you vomiting all over while we're trying to collect the bodies. Besides, I just cooked you that boar and now the ocean has it. Get with the times man. There's lots of dead people, get used to it." Reluctantly, Solomon complied and walked back toward the docks, kicking up water from the beach with his good leg as he strode.

To her discouragement, Liliana quickly found it impossible to prick a finger from every corpse in the San Magnus sinkholes, firstly because not every corpse had its fingers, and secondly because not every set of fingers had a corpse. Nor was she equipped with hygienically sealed packaging to store each sample or chiseling tools to root out every bone. *This is not like a dig site.* She sunk her feet into the mud of one of the lesser deposits and scoured around with her hands, pulling up a humerus, a whole bicep, an ankle bracelet still wrapped around its femur bone. With her hands wrist deep in sludge, she pulled out a set of tiny bones no longer than her ring finger—a mouse, maybe a bird, kept together in a sort of sticky clay. "Fala sério..." she muttered, dropping the clump at her feet and shuddering. "Chuck! Chuck!"

The Texan climbed up from where he was crouching in the dirt and raced along the edges of the gorges, looking in each one until finally he came to Liliana.

"This is not a grave!" she yelled from the bottom of the pit. "É esgoto!"

Chuck squinted down at her, confused, and then walked around the sides to step carefully over to where she hunched in the sludge. She pushed her finger around a spot on the ground, a mush of little red seeds and tiny fish scales. Chuck looked away. "I should have gone to get the wheelbarrow."

"Do you know what this means?" she asked, a mild excitement in her voice.

"It means we're wading in their shit?"

"It means they're omnivorous, just as we are."

"But there are human bones too. They eat people, Doctor."

"And wouldn't you if you had no other choice?"

"I don't understand," Chuck said, hitting his palm on the side of his head. "They had a choice. Look, they eat berries! Birds, rodents, the imported pigs... They don't need human meat."

"Vengeance maybe?"

"There are decades between some of the bodies here."

"Men with guns are always men with guns. That never changes."

Chuck scoffed and climbed back out of the sinkhole, muttering something under his breath. Liliana turned over another body, this one with legs.

"Mr. Polanski!" Liliana shouted up after him.

"What is it, Doctor?"

She tried holding up the midsection of the skeleton, pointing to the gap where its lungs once lay.

"Take the ribs. Of the bodies. If you find a ribcage, take a rib and toss it aside. It's better than rifling around for fingers."

"Ha," Chuck replied, a smirk coming across his face. "You feelin' biblical now?"

Liliana didn't respond. She just trudged through the pit and pushed aside another torso. From sinkhole to sinkhole they scoured, breaking marrow, collecting an excess of human vertebrae and piling them in a ditch over the bluff like a stack of railroad spikes. Although she tried, Liliana couldn't make out with certainty what was human refuse and what was deposited ocean chemicals. With the gorges open to the sky and the elements, the Volksklausur deposits had not petrified as she'd hoped. Even after poking around and studying their droppings long into the afternoon, she could not conclude that what the voice had told them was true, that they were in fact cannibals. *They certainly have the teeth for it.*

Solomon finally stopped talking aloud to himself upon arriving back in the Villa Vienna. He trod lightly so as not to draw the attention and distraction of King. Sneaking into a side-street house, he covered his mouth from the Haze and tore some sheets from the upstairs bedding. When he approached the generator room from the enclosed side and circled around to where they had parked the wheelbarrow, he saw that there were no more spare parts inside, so Seek tilted it off its back struts and started to quietly push it back to the south. As he passed, Seek gazed into the slightly hazy generator room. It was empty. He could make out some of the parts on the floor, others resting in the generator, a wrench and a drill sitting beside them, but Cledwyn was gone. Solomon put down the cart and covered his mouth again as he walked into the room. He checked behind the generator and in the closet where the skeletal mechanic had hidden, but there was no Cledwyn.

Running out of the building, Solomon looked around the plaza. He hesitated to yell after the man but was desperate to find him. *What if he's lying in ambush?* Seek remembered what Chuck had told him about trust but couldn't reason his suspicions from his mind. *He's a thief. Maybe he figures he can crack the vault by himself. He doesn't need me. I'm dead.* Solomon ran back to the wheelbarrow and rolled out fast toward the docks, ready to dive into the cart at the sound of a shot ringing out from behind him. But there was no shot. After a few hundred meters his feet tired and he slowed down, mumbling more to himself on the way back than he had on the way there.

The sun was halfway through its descent by the time he returned with the wheelbarrow and sheets. "King is gone!" he shouted, pushing the cart up the bottom of the bluff. "You'd better not be too!"

Solomon dodged a rib cage that came flying out of the gorge and rolled down the hill. A head popped up from the pit. "What do you mean King is gone?" asked Chuck.

Solomon parked the cart at the end of the largest sinkhole and looked within. He could already see the row of ribs they'd accumulated and stacked against the corner. He felt another urge pushing up from his gut but looked away and committed to swallowing hard. Holding out his hand and grasping the handle of the wheelbarrow, he struggled

152

to respond. "He's not in the generator room. His tools are just lying there. I didn't see him anywhere."

Chuck sighed, tore another rib from its cage and kicked it aside. "Is the generator fixed?"

"Doesn't look like it. Looks like he just picked up and left."

"And the gun?"

"Like I said…" A strong breeze nearly wiped him out. Solomon had to hold onto the dirt to keep from falling over. "Just picked up and left. I thought you said…we could trust him?"

"We can. That doesn't make any sense." Chuck tossed a rib up and into the wheelbarrow. "He can't leave. He'd be killed. You didn't see any sign of his body?"

"I've seen more than my share of bodies this week. I didn't see his."

Liliana walked up the other end of the bluff. "Did I hear you say King is gone?"

Solomon sunk his head. Chuck looked up.

"Let's just finish what we've done here. He'd better not be dead," said Liliana.

Solomon helped haul their collection of bones onto the unfolded sheet he'd laid out in the cart. He only vomited one more time and considered it a triumph. "How many is that?"

"Seventy-three," answered Liliana, tying off the ends of the sheet into a makeshift bag and leading the bone-filled wagon down the hill.

"So that's the rest of them? All the other Nazis who weren't killed by the Haze?"

"No. Those are just the adults."

On the road back to the Villa, Solomon took out his tablet. He had the inkling to write but realized he had no new information to add to the investigation. The German inhabitants were still dead. The Volksklausur were still loose. Metzger was still to blame. They were still prisoners.

Chapter XVI

When they rolled back into town, Chuck dropped the wheelbarrow in front of Solomon and ran up ahead to check the generator room. He could hear a rustling, clanking sound echoing out into the plaza. Solomon saw him run off behind the cement shack, and as he started to lift the cart, Chuck reemerged, a skeptical look on his face. He stared at Solomon for a moment as Cledwyn walked out from behind him.

"What do you mean I ran off? Chuck, I went off to have a shit, mate."

"Seek said he came back and couldn't find you."

"Well he wasn't lookin' very hard, was he?"

"I looked around the plaza and the backstreets," Seek interceded.

"Yeah, well, I wasn't in the backstreets. I wanted a proper shit on a proper toilet, so I used the porcelain in the house 'cross from the dentist's."

"You left your tools."

"I wasn't going to bloody need them in the john, now was I? What is your problem?"

"You're a schemer," replied Solomon. "I don't trust you."

"We've been over this, Seek," interrupted Chuck. "He needs us. And we need him."

"What does he need us for? He's a safe-cracker, a hacker. He said so himself. He could be biding his time, waiting to be alone so he can run off to hack that terminal and break into the vault all by himself."

"You've seen that lock, haven't ya? It's got no wiring, built into the wall, so there's no getting around it. It's not like I can fake someone's DNA."

"Solomon, if he was going to break in without us, why would he come back?" Chuck posed, putting himself like a barricade between the two men. Liliana pushed the cart around the generator room and

155

plopped it down next to the commotion.

"What the hell is that?" asked King.

"That," Liliana responded, wiping sweat from her forehead with a ripped piece of sheet, "is the haystack."

"You're going to test every one of those?"

"That's right."

"Then I suppose you'll need the power back on." Cledwyn strolled into the room. Within moments they heard a roar, and a popping sound went off in their ears.

"You fixed it?" Solomon asked.

"That's right. Spent every last second workin' on it. I work extra fast when I'm plottin' to kill some people and steal their money." King smirked at Solomon and gave him a quick wink in passing before hauling the wheelbarrow himself down the street toward the shelter.

"This isn't exactly the pile of bones I was hoping for." He laughed joyfully.

When he and Liliana had left earshot, Chuck turned to face Solomon.

"You have to stop doing this. I know it's what you do, accusing people of things—" Solomon tried to cut in but Chuck continued. "—but you need to stop. This is a team, a group effort."

"So you're taking his side this time?"

"He doesn't have a side, Solomon. He's with us. And you don't have one either. You're just paranoid. Look. The power is back. He did his job. Why can't you get past this?"

Cledwyn wheeled the macabre collection up to Albert Vogel's house, waited impatiently for Liliana to spell the password correctly, and then promptly disappeared inside. Out in the street, Solomon grabbed hold of Chuck's elbow to keep him from following.

"I've thought about it for a while. The voice is up in that tower. Why doesn't he just open the fortress gate from the inside? It would be a lot faster and safer than all this running around bullshit. It's not as if we could ambush him. He has the detonator, so what's he afraid of?"

"I don't know. Maybe he thinks this is fun or something. But what's it matter? We do what he says or..." Chuck made a bursting

156

gesture over his face with his hands.

"What if he can't come out? What if he's stuck in there?"

Chuck paused. His eyebrow flickered. "You mean…what if he didn't knock us out? What if he didn't lead us here?"

"Hypothetically," Solomon replied, "what if he's not alone? If he's trapped, and I'd say his behavior is good evidence of that, then someone else has to be working for him."

"Someone on the island?"

"Someone like King. He's been doing all the work. He knows all about the generators like he's seen them before. He's way too forward, too frank. I think he's hiding, hiding in plain sight, you know?"

"He was dying of dehydration in that tin water-house when we found him."

"Got better fast, didn't he? Didn't waste any time getting us to work."

Chuck sighed, looking over at the dentist's practice and then back to Solomon, who stood eager to be recognized. Instead, the big Texan undid the buttons at the top of his over-shirt. Solomon tilted his head back and eyed the man with grave suspicion as he peeled back the shirt to reveal a thin black jacket with torn threads and red stains around the collar and waist. "It's Kevlar," Chuck answered to the confused look on Solomon's face.

"I know what Kevlar is," Seek responded. "Why are you wearing it?"

"I took it off a body near the docks," said Chuck, pulling it over his head.

"So this whole time you were thinking the same thing?"

"Always err on the side of caution."

"I'd agree, but I don't think it helped the guy you pulled it off much."

"That's because—" Chuck tossed Solomon the vest. "—he wasn't shot."

"Wow, it's light."

"That's right. It's to…lighten the weight on your mind. Should you be right about King."

157

"So you do think he's against us."

"I think you think he's against us, and I need you focused. Put it on under your shirt. He'll only notice if he stares long and hard at your wimpy chest muscles."

"I think he spends a lot more time watching Lily's ass," Seek replied, pulling his shirt over his head.

"Yeah, well, that makes two of you."

With his shirt off, Chuck could make out the chromatic varicose veins stretching down Solomon's neck from the pill in his throat. More noticeable were the rosy red bruises over his upper ribcage.

Solomon looked down and rubbed the blotches, breathing heavily. "Who knows how many years this place has taken from us..."

Chuck itched his own throat and nodded silently.

Solomon changed the subject as he slipped the uncomfortable garment over his head. "This vest is like that other one in the generator room. The American."

"Yeah, I think he was. There were a few NATO shell casings scattered in one of the little sinkholes. Found a plastic stock sticking up out of another one."

"How are we supposed to survive if those guys got killed?"

Chuck raised his pointer finger to his head and tapped on the space above his ear.

"By being smarter."

"Good to be home," Chuck whispered as he collapsed on the sofa in the blast shelter common area. Liliana had wasted no time in bundling the ribs and distributing them into the laboratory sink. When all the candidates were accounted for, she addressed the men as they sat idly across from King.

"This is going to take a while," she said. "Feel free to go and make yourselves useful."

By eleven o'clock that night Liliana had gone through only one third of the potential Ebersbach candidates. Cledwyn lay still, asleep in a chair in the common area. After deciding against a late-night hunt, Chuck and Solomon had scoured the town and returned with three tins of canned beans and a quarter crate of Frankfurter Würstel. They sat across from one another on the floor in the hall, eating them cold with the old metal cutlery they'd taken from the camp mess, swapping war stories and waiting for the verdict to arrive.

"There's always a lot of waiting in covert operations," said Chuck.

"Is that what this is? Covert ops?"

"No one on the planet knows we're here. So as much as I hate to say it, yeah, this is covert."

"How do you think they'll react when they find out about this place?" asked Seek.

"Who, the planet? Hell. I think humanity stopped caring about people a long time ago. Nazis, war criminals, they've heard it all a million times. Now they just don't care. Here, take you for example. You've already brought a war criminal to justice."

Solomon looked down the hall to see Cledwyn still asleep, then to the lab to check if Liliana had turned to listen in. Chuck shrugged as if to say, *who cares?* "You brought him to trial. It's because of you that we knew what he and the rest of them were up to in the first place."

"Well, no, that was the attorney general and the justice department, but I get your point."

"You get out of here and write your article, and it'll probably make the tiny print on the Yahoo News page right next to the stupid pet trick videos."

"You're trying to get an argument from me?"

"No, just a reason. Why do you bother? Why expose what no one cares about?"

"Hmph," Solomon snorted, rolling his eyes. "Why breathe?" He plopped his fork in the tin can and put it on the floor beside him. "Why eat? Why care? Why love? Why make love? Why should we let murderers get away with murder? I believe in something more than that, and it's all that I can do but serve it. It's not a flag; it's not a god; it's not even me. It's knowledge. It's people. Yeah, they suck. A lot of us are assholes. Most of us live by house, block, and city and never think about that old fishmonger in Mar Del Sur or the dead school teacher in Qalat. It's *me-me-me* out there, and no one knows what it's like for anyone else to live, so no one sympathizes, no one cares, but most important, no one sees the big picture. I'm not about charity, giving money to strangers to make yourself feel better. I'm about information. We feel bad for ourselves and our forty-grand-a-year jobs. We get through every day just to come home to the microwave and the late-night programming.

"Now, what if we interrupt that programming, just once let's say, and tell them something true, something incredible or terrible that's happening someplace to people just as apathetic as them. And we do it everywhere. There's a whole planet of potential here, wasted, still squabbling amongst itself, thinking about nothing else but the next paycheck and the next tank of gas. Expose what no one cares about? We could have been colonizing other planets by now if people cared. We could have stopped all the wars and all the famines by now if people cared. We sent men to the moon. That was over fifty years ago. We defeated the Nazis; that was eighty years ago. Imagine what we could accomplish if people had continued to care, if they didn't go back home and leave the next fascist for the next person to deal with. Imagine what we could have done if people gave two fucking shits about the species and not just their life insurance policies."

Solomon exhaled deeply and felt the cough bellowing inside him. It rushed up his throat and he spat out a pinch of blood with disdain, staining the rug beside him.

"All that said, whether or not they do care, whether we go anywhere at all, won't stop me from doing what's right."

Chuck steadied his back against the wall. "And how do you know what's right?"

"That's the easiest thing in the world to know. You just look around to see what's wrong and you do the opposite."

Liliana stood at the laboratory doorway, listening intently. "Dr. Ebersbach cared. So did the others," she interceded, drawing their attention. "They were onto things the rest of us still haven't dreamed of. They were fugitives, hated, excomungado when the men landed on the moon. But they were united. United for revenge and destruction. I think they succeeded."

160

Solomon paused. "Have you found Dr. Ebersbach?"

"Yes," she replied. "And his family too."

Liliana showcased the rib sample of the doctor's DNA, matching the coded strand on the framed tapestry marked with his name on the wall. Neither Chuck nor Solomon had any idea how to read them, so her assurances had to do.

"All right, let's get this over with. I'll wake the bastard," said Solomon, pulling the receiver from his pocket, and walking to the common room with Chuck and Liliana in tow. "Providence bodes permanence," he whispered and pressed the speaker button.

It was silent for a few seconds before a rustling came through the static, and then the familiar voice. "What?"

"We've found the third sample," Liliana chimed in.

The voice's audio went in and out. Then a discernible yawn. "That was very quick, Dr. Ferreria. I can't imagine why your colleagues in São Paulo want to get rid of you so badly."

"That means there's one sample left," she continued.

"Metzger's," said Solomon.

Again the reception flickered. "Yes, that's right. A rather difficult strand to track down, although in great abundance."

"What do you mean? What are you saying? His body is scattered around the place?" asked Liliana.

"Oh, no, quite the opposite," answered the voice. "In fact, his body isn't on the island. It seems he's either escaped or has been buried under it. In the vault."

"The vault?" exclaimed Solomon. How do you know he's in there?"

"Eliminate all the variables, Mr. Solomon. I've been to every nook and cranny of this island, and I've yet to find him. The only place I have not been is the vault, which is why I've brought you."

"Wait," interrupted Liliana. "If his body is where we can't get to without his body, how do we get his DNA? You said it's all around. Are we supposed to scrub every comb and glass in the Villa?"

"No, I'm afraid it'll be much more difficult than that. I can tell you exactly where his DNA can be found. It's walking around the streets right now looking for you."

Solomon's pulse dropped. His eyes crawled over the wall, across Liliana's tanned face, her frozen green eyes, a pellet of sweat seeping from her forehead and slithering down the arch of her nose, dive bombing with her heart rate down to the floor.

"If those things..." She pushed herself to finish her statement. "...are his children, they won't have the s—"

"They're not his children," the voice interrupted. "They're the last variable. The independent variable."

"But still they'll be different. They'll have different genome sequences, varying repetitions."

"You're right. But the machine won't see those. The machine only reads twenty-three pairs of chromosomes, those we find in human DNA. It does not scan for the twenty-fourth and twenty-fifth chromosome pairs imbedded in the Volksklausur. You see, for all intents and purposes, those creatures, those monsters, they are Metzger."

Chuck rolled his head around his neck and went to sit down in the common room. Solomon scratched his chin, perplexed. "That doesn't make any sense."

"You're quite sure of your genetics education, Mr. Solomon?" The voice asked with a laugh.

"No, I don't know anything about DNA or their number of chromosomes, but I don't see how you could either. We've been to where you've been. I've seen and read all the things you have. How could you think, know, to try their DNA?"

A chuckle. "Do you think Dr. Jung destroyed *all* of the evidence in his lab? *I* burned the last of it. I left unscathed what I wanted unscathed. So now, when I wanted you to know, you know."

"They're children," Solomon replied.

"The children of our future," concluded the voice.

"What are we supposed to do, grab one of them and stick it with a needle?" demanded Liliana.

Solomon looked around for Chuck, expecting that kind of logistical question to come from the military man whom he found had silently left the room.

"There are two ways," continued the voice. "You can go to them in the daylight, to where they sleep, and outfox the foxes. Or you can wait for another night and get them to come to you. I have tried it both ways. If I had to suggest one or the other, I'd suggest letting them come to you. My men installed searchlights on the balcony of the dentist's house for just that purpose. In the morning we found blood, but not a body. Not one of theirs anyhow."

The voice dictated the coordinates of the Volksklausur's domain to Solomon, a spot in the ridge-line on the east shore, and signed off with, "Do this, and you will be rewarded not as kings or queens, but as gods."

Solomon collapsed with Liliana on the floor of the common room, not bothering to stuff the hands-free back into his pocket. They sat there silently staring at one another. He dropped his head in his hands and wiped his face down with his palms. She arched hers back and searched her consciousness for answers. They sat there for some time, their eyes slowly closing and flashing open to feign fighting the sleep they almost expected to end the week-long nightmare.

Static from the coffee table shook them in a hypnic jerk, pulling them back to San Magnus. It was just static at first, and Solomon felt himself drifting back to sleep despite it. He couldn't help, however, waking up over the speech that came through next.

"That is not the voice," whispered Liliana.

Its pitch was low, not robotic high, with a rumbling hiss, like a tenor's lisp. Solomon thought he was listening to an old horror show broadcast. Then he realized the sounds weren't effects or babble but German, squeezing through a valley of teeth.

"Jagen... Jagen... Wir sind die jäger. Jagen... Jagen..."

163

Chapter XVII

"That's not the smart play," Chuck advised. "You don't know what's waiting for you there. You could walk straight into an ambush."

"We've already walked into an ambush, but not by them. I think we might be able to reason with them," replied Solomon.

It was five in the morning, and they'd gathered in the common room, tapping their feet and rattling their fingers along the coffee table and ratty old sofa cushions, ready to make out at first light. Solomon had not slept a single minute that night, only closing his eyes in intervals of five minutes, fifteen minutes, thirty minutes, where he could only see the scarred torso of a boy, a mutant child, whispering those words in his ears. Liliana had watched and shared in his nightmare.

"They're still just children," he continued, "afraid, killing on instinct. It's like *Lord of the Flies* out there! They're people, Chuck. We can talk to them."

"How? How're you gonna talk to them?" interceded King.

"The tablet." Solomon took it out of his pocket. "It charged all last night. Listen."

Solomon rifled his finger over the display until he came across the program he was after. He tapped the glass and said aloud, "Jagen... Wir sind die jäger." Solomon waited.

The tablet responded in a synthetic monotone, "Hunt. We are the hunters."

"So you're going to have a conversation with them? 'You're the hunters. You want to kill us. That's lovely. Oh, and by the way, might I stick this needle in your arm?'"

"We don't need their blood," Liliana calmly interrupted. "Just something of size. A finger nail, an uncontaminated stool sample, a swab with enough saliva would do."

"You'll be sure to get plenty of their saliva when they're eating away at your bloody legs," said King.

Chuck took Solomon by the arm. "Why do you really want to do this? Why should I risk *my* life to bring you out there?"

Solomon sighed as if repeating himself and leaned over the back of his chair. "Because it's the right thing to do. They're prisoners here too. They're just like us."

Chuck spun around and walked to the hallway, planting his hand hard on the wall. Solomon turned to Liliana, who nodded and then glared back at the big Texan as he came barreling back into the room.

"They're not Jews, Solomon! That's why you want to go out there, isn't it? You think they're you, your people, your children. You think they're victims, is that it? They're murderers! Can't you see that?"

"They murdered Nazis, Chuck. Nazis." Solomon slammed his hands on the back of the chair. "Nazis who were bent on ending them, wiping them all out. I don't know who they are. Jews or not, it doesn't matter. This isn't about race. It's about people, and I won't have these people hunt me down too. I am not a Nazi."

Chuck retreated back to his corner. "That's not fair," he muttered.

"No, you're right. It's not. Neither is killing them."

Chuck wiped his hand down the wall and turned. "Killing them? I just want to survive them."

"I say let them go," replied King.

"What?" Chuck replied.

"And go with them, of course. I'll need time to re-reinstall the parts for the generator. I should have it done, just in case Plan A doesn't work, by the time you all come whimpering back."

"Are you sure?" Chuck asked.

"Shit I'm sure, man. I could build that thing with my eyes closed at this point. Just tell me it's the last time."

"Actually…" Liliana cut in. "I would really like to see the sample in the lab. Just…for…"

Cledwyn stared her dead in the eyes.

"All right, last time," she agreed.

"You're going to be at the camp all by yourself?" Solomon asked.

"Jesus, Seek, we're past this. You can trust him."

"I'll make sure to take my next dump out in the open this time if that'll suit you."

"That's fine," Solomon conceded. "That's just fine".

With the cool light of dawn rising over the island, the four collected themselves and marched out. Chuck issued orders to search the villa again for supplies but not for canned rations of which they were fully stocked. "When diplomacy fails," he explained, staring at Solomon, "and it will, we will be prepared to defend ourselves."

Chuck borrowed some of Cledwyn's tools and took Liliana and Solomon from house to house, wrenching up hardwood floorboards from the townhouses and ransacking the general store for nails and screws. Near the outskirts of the Villa, on Von Zeppelin Avenue, they came across a bicycle shop. Prewar bikes hung along the walls with bent, broken postwar bikes on the floor beneath them. Chuck dragged a couple of them into the street and dislodged their steel alloy chains, tossing them into the wheelbarrow with a quart of butane lighter fluid. After Cledwyn had pried out the replacement parts he'd installed the previous afternoon, they piled them all in the overflowing cart covered with oak boards and pushed it out once again for the long trek through the jungle. This time they did not talk. They did not relish recourse from the jungle or its wild dwellers. No one complained when they reached the fallen trunk. They pushed their joints together, heaved the rusted mass over the obstacle, and continued.

At the gate of the camp, Chuck pointed over the tree line to the east toward the rising sun. "There, Cled. We're going there. The coordinates are nearly on the coast around that ridge-line." He sighed. "If we're not back at fourteen hundred hours…"

"I know, I know," Cledwyn said, putting his hand over the big man's shoulder. "Go break into the vault myself and steal all the treasure." He winked at Solomon.

Cledwyn struggled to push the cart through the camp as Polanski, Ferreira, and Solomon walked around and watched him from the other side of the gate before passing beyond sight behind a pair of Chilean Myrtles. Chuck flung his rifle around his back to his shoulder and took the stock in his armpit. They used their hands, elbows, and the barrel of his rifle to push aside the vines to make a path much thinner, much weaker than that they'd followed from the Villa Vienna. This was uncharted territory, pure jungle, pure unknown, where the encroachment of concrete and the saw had not dared. Chuck kept his eyes peeled for predators, bipedal or otherwise. Solomon began to speak and was quickly shushed from their sergeant leading the way up ahead.

"Lily, Lily," he whispered back. "Looks like you'll be the first one to get what you came for."

Through the foliage and the bobbing of their heads as they trod forward, Solomon caught a smirk run across her face and suddenly drop into melancholy.

"It feels wrong, doesn't it?" Solomon whispered.

"No," he heard back in an almost broken tone. "You called me Lily."

"Oh." Solomon said, holding a branch in her path to the side. "Does someone else call you that?"

"Yes," she replied. "They did."

As they neared the coastline under the shadow of the rocky embankment and the fortress tower above, the three came across a clearing. Solomon immediately stepped into it, despite Chuck's warning.

"Swamp."

"Igapó," Liliana replied.

Solomon grabbed his leg below the knee and struggled to pull himself from the muck. His boot twisted and shot from the soil, spilling brown on his face and shirt as he fell back into Liliana's arms.

"Thanks, Doc," he said, retaining his balance. Liliana freed her hands of him to point at an imprint in the mud ahead. It was a footprint only a few meters from where Solomon had planted his own, but bare with the markings of toes stretched out like triangles.

"That thing is huge," Solomon said, careful not to fall in next to it.

"This is a freshwater swamp. That means the water here is from the rain coming off the mountain, not the ocean."

"So?" asked Chuck.

168

"It also means the soil is often displaced. These tracks are very new."

"Then we've found ourselves a path."

Chuck led them on, following the winding path of muck and swirling waters of the black-water forest until they rose to a small earthen spout sticking out from the steep, rocky incline. Liliana continued to explain the topography of the island while Chuck marshaled them forward around the base of the cliff, but Solomon thought only of what he might say to the Volksklausur once they'd arrived. *We come in peace* crossed his mind more than once. As they neared the horizon he could hear that familiar sound—waves on the beaches. Not the serene, gentle slips of water up the golden shores by the villas, but short, sharp crashes on hard rock face, one followed quickly by another. From the breach of the jungle, they emerged over the inlet, a curved semicircle pointing inward to the center of San Magnus. The waters of the Atlantic found safe harbor under its overhanging cliffs.

"Well, there goes all the mystery." Solomon's voice echoed out into the bay. "They're cave dwellers."

"They're nocturnal," said Liliana. "Where did you think they'd hide?"

They walked around a flat path from the jungle under the bluff. Salt water trickled down from the walls and pushed up the eroding submerged granite on which they stepped. Solomon let Liliana pass him and observed the way she walked, gliding on the end of her boot heels across the stone. He did his best to imitate. As they pushed farther in, hands running down the crackling wall space for balance, Solomon took out his archaic flashlight. With the sun blocked by the sedimentary enclosure of the sea cave, he pushed ahead of Chuck and pointed the light at the floor and along the walls as they shuffled, careful not to slip into the splashing water below.

They neared the mouth of the cave itself, and Liliana pointed out the perfection of their location.

"The water is dark but not too dark for them. This is probably where most of their diet is supplemented. They eat fish, seaweed, anything that washes ashore. The marsh behind us is freshwater. They've adapted to their environment."

"I'd rather eat that canned garbage," muttered Chuck. "No wonder they eat people."

"We still don't know that," Liliana shot back.

"Shh," Solomon hissed. "This is it." He pushed forward, his solitary yellow bulb light leading the way between a pair of glossy, jagged rocks. He grasped at the tablet in his pack between steps and reaching out to grasp the wall between slips. When he looked back he saw Chuck and Liliana trailing far behind, but rather than wait he shuffled faster into the dankness in front of him. By the time he had reached a small opening, like a naturally made door to the ancient grotto, he could no longer read the hands on his watch. He was entering pure darkness.

Without waiting for his companions, Solomon slipped through the gap and stared within. The dull light of his incandescent torch was consumed by the black only a dozen meters in. As he shifted forward for a closer look, Solomon dropped for what seemed like an eternity and crashed feet first onto the steely granite floor. The clangor echoed out in front of him, waking a battalion of bats from the heights, which circled around the wide dome above his head, their flapping covering the sounds of his panicked scrambling. On his hands and knees, he found the flashlight and sprayed its light around and above, scaring off the bats flying back to their perches beyond the unperceived veil of the cave. Then he pointed it behind him and saw that he'd taken a dive of about one foot.

Relieved, he raised the light and bathed the cave walls in its tungsten brilliance. The water running down its innards shimmered across the limestone. Small puddles in the distance mirrored the reflection of the bats hanging atop, and at this disturbance the Volksklausur, sitting cross-legged, their heads bowed across their chests, slowly rose like an army of solemn golems. Seek's flashlight flickered as if it were unable to absorb or understand the sight emerging before it. He crawled backward on his knees and smacked the torch back to life, drawing the Volksklausur's attention. In the light he could see their limbs, their bodies, bare, naked, gray and cold like anthropomorphic beings, gargoyles with their noses perched high in the air to catch his craven stench. They lined along the cave floor in rows like perfect soldiers, guarding the entrenchments of their lair from inquisitive intruders. His only relief was that he saw they'd covered their eyes with their bear-paw-sized hands and moved no closer to him. He sat up and slipped the Kindle from his bag, its light drawing a painful squint through his glasses. The Volksklausur said not a word, made not a sound, moved not an inch towards the light, all waiting for it to slowly die.

Solomon whispered into the device and read aloud, as best he could, the prompt it displayed in German. "Sie sind die Jäger. Ich bin die gejagt werden. Warum jagst du mich?" *You are the hunters. I am the hunted. Why do you hunt me?*

With the flashlight trembling in his hand, Solomon could make out the figure of a lone Volksklausur stepping softly toward him, its hands over its face, wrenched backward in anguish and disgust. It walked to the border where the rays from his bulb penetrated the tiny spaces between its fingers, and stopped, standing not ten meters from him. With the thick snake-like lisp Seek had heard the night before, it replied.

"Wir jagen weil wir sind die Jäger. Warum willst du laufen?"

Solomon could feel the quizzical nature of its response, the confusion in its tone, the change in pitch and what he thought he could make out as a tilt in its neck. He quickly ran the translation software.

We hunt because we are the hunters. Why do you run?

Solomon heard steps coming up from behind him, and he scrambled to his feet and backward to the slip in the cracks. "No!" he yelled. "Don't come any closer. I'm okay. Stay where you are." There was no reply. When he was confident in the backward-shuffling sounds coming from the outer cove, he turned back to his tablet.

"Ich habe ausgeführt, da ich habe keinen Wunsch zu sterben," he replied. *I run because I have no wish to die.*

The bulb in his torch began to flicker again. With every shake to keep it alive, he swore he could see the Volksklausur clearer and closer

171

than before. He backed up against the one-foot drop and waited for his reply.

"Und wir haben keine lust dich zu töten." *And we have no wish to kill you.*

Solomon wrestled with the torch again, smacking it upside his boot and slapping it side to side as the Volksklausur neared, like a cloud of concrete bodies rising over him. When the light flashed again he typed quickly for a response, sweat pouring down from his forehead and dripping like stalactite water on the tablet monitor.

"Warum wird sie dann?" *Then why will you?*

The flashlight flickered again and died.

"Denn wir sind die Jäger ist." The answer came through jagged rows of fangs slipping into the darkness. Panicking, he threw the torch on the floor, crashing glass at the feet of the creature before him and flashed it in the face with the dim light of his Kindle. He ran his finger up its side, and the light grew intensely, pushing the Volksklausur back over the broken shards. In that last moment Solomon could see the scar running down its chest before he was yanked from behind over the hump and through the gap of the cave. He desperately held on to the device, its illumination covering his retreat.

"Okay, time to go," said Chuck, dragging the journalist on his ass down the path toward the cove where they'd entered. The hissing chased Chuck, Lily, and Seek from the cave, emerging from the inner gap to slash blindly at Solomon's feet as he was pulled toward the light. They pulled themselves along by the cave wall with just his smell and panicked breaths to guide them. Halfway down the path, with the sun creeping in through a small hole in the cove ceiling, the gray men stopped and covered their eyes. Before he was lifted to his feet, Solomon could see the last of the Volksklausur turn around and slip back on all fours between the sides of the gap into the cave.

"Are you done now?" Chuck demanded, grabbing hold of Solomon's collar and screaming in his face. "Did you learn anything with this stupid fuckin' expedition? Get a swab of their DNA or anything? Huh?"

No," Solomon replied, cut off again by Chuck.

"Then we're doing it my way, the right way, God dammit. Come on." The Texan dropped Solomon on the saltwater-drenched walkway and shuffled out to the jungle.

Liliana looked down at Solomon and offered him her hand. "*Did you learn anything?*" she asked.

He reached out and grabbed her hand, letting her help to pull him to his feet. "I did," he replied, brushing off the crack in his tablet of cave dust and ocean spray. "I learned why they're hunting us."

He held out the device, lowering the light settings to make the font readable again. Liliana traced her squinting eyes along its broken screen.

Because we are the hunters.

Chapter XVIII

Liliana helped Solomon limp back to camp, his sprained ankle restating its dominance over him from a nick he'd received in the hasty escape.

"Go on ahead," Chuck said, pushing them toward the sickly path they'd carved in the jungle. Solomon saw the man emptying his canteen on the bank of the swamp they'd crossed before being tugged and shuffled across the jungle floor from view.

"You actually talked to them?" Liliana asked, huffing through the trees, Solomon's arm around her shoulder.

"It was more like a tennis match than a conversation. They're just as intelligent as Jung said. Maybe more. They're inquisitive. One of them asked me a question."

"One of them?"

"The leader, maybe: has a great big scar like a strap across his chest. Wanted to know why we were running."

"And that sounded intelligent to you?" Liliana scoffed.

"I couldn't tell if it was sincere or whether it was telling me that there's no point in running."

"What did you say?"

"I told it I didn't want to die. It said it didn't want to kill me."

"But they're going to anyway?"

"Yeah. I think so. I think they have to."

Solomon pushed a vine from Liliana's shoulder.

"They have minds but not free will?" she posed. "They're perfect soldiers."

"And they got my flashlight."

Cledwyn ran out from the camp and over to Solomon as they emerged from the jungle. Seek shuffled down his human crutch in anticipation of King's assistance. Instead, King rifled around through

175

Solomon's pack, took out the box of matches, and patted him on the back. "Thanks," he shouted and ran back through the gate. By the time Liliana had hauled Solomon to the wheelbarrow outside the generator for balance, they could feel the sweet sound of electric pop in their eardrums. Cledwyn threw Solomon back his matches.

"Sorry. Dark in there. Where's the big man?"

Chuck came marching up from the wilderness behind them, his face, arms, and neck covered in mud. He held out his finger and silenced Cledwyn, throwing the Welshman his canteen.

"They see in infrared. Before nightfall, cover your bodies in this."

Solomon's eyebrows raised as the Texan threw him a second brown bottle.

"And how do you know that?"

"If I was building a Marine and he could see in the dark, he'd see in infrared."

Cledwyn shrugged and put the canteen aside. "Generator's online. I take it things didn't go as planned?"

Again, Chuck spoke first. "We're making our stand here. King, test the system for power surges. We need the fences and the searchlights back up. They're the bait and our first line of defense. Doctor, we need all the supplies you have. Set up a med station in the barracks on the third floor. That's our fallback position."

"Fallback position from where?" she asked.

Chuck pointed up to the metal guard tower high above them, stuck in the earth with concrete struts.

"The hatch leading up from the barracks we slept in two nights ago leads up there. If we're overrun, we displace there and hope to hell they can't break the seal on that hatch."

"Solomon can barely walk," said Liliana.

Chuck looked down at his companion's leg. "He doesn't need to walk. Not yet. He's with me. We need to lock down that gate, my friend. Okay. Everyone understand their duties?"

The party nodded but stayed silent. Solomon grasped the handles on the wheelbarrow hard.

"Good. It's just past noon now. Everyone meet back in the center of camp in one hour."

They split up, Liliana and Cledwyn to the bunker, Solomon with Chuck and the cart as levy support for the gate. "Feels like the first time we got here, huh?" asked the sergeant jovially, shoving the wheelbarrow filled with boards foot by foot toward the entrance.

"It's gonna feel like the last if this doesn't work," Solomon answered. Chuck gave him a stern glance. "Sir."

"We'll do fine. We have everything we need to repel them."

"Like what, an army? Guns? Tanks?"

"We have something...better than that," Chuck continued, straining to drop both Solomon and the cart off by the interior side of the gate. "We've got information."

He pulled a hammer and a bucket of old, blackened nails from the cart and motioned for his compatriot to help prop up the long wooden pieces against the fence. "We know that this gate isn't electrified at the bottom, right?"

"Yeah, that's right. The Germans just chopped the lock and came right in."

"Exactly. So...they didn't expect those monsters to try opening it. They knew they'd try to climb it first."

"Unless it was already open," Solomon concluded.

"Right. So all we have to do—" Chuck closed the gate and latched it tightly shut, tying two sets of bicycle chain through the metal links and slipping them into an overhand stopper knot. "—is lock up this gate. Either they break it down or they climb and get shocked trying to go over it."

"And if they break through your chain and your boards?"

"Our chain, Seek, our boards. Don't worry about that. We move one step at a time."

With the gate locked they began to pile the floorboards vertically against it, forming a small concave opening between the chain link and the wooden wall. They built it on another set of boards, running horizontally against the earth, and Chuck ordered Solomon to nail that plank into the ground. The Texan took out the last bit of Old World salvage from the cart, Cledwyn's pilfered blowtorch and blasting helmet, and went to work welding the nails sticking from his makeshift wall with the metal siding of the fence.

"They're not just monsters, you know," Solomon yelled over the roaring flame, nearly clipping his fingernail with the dull edge of the hammer.

Chuck killed the fire and flipped up the helmet from his face. "If they're trying to kill us, that makes them monsters." He smacked the blast shield back down over his face, but his welding was again interrupted.

"This isn't going to hold, you know. I'm not a carpenter, but look, they can slice or bite right through those chains. They'll rip right out what you're welding there. It'll only take them minutes to push these boards aside." Solomon dropped the hammer in the dirt, his nail only half-submerged in its wooden destination.

"We're not trying to stop them. We're trying to trick them," replied a muffled echo in Chuck's heat-resistant visor.

Liliana heard another jolting yelp from down the stairs in the generator room as she put the finishing touches on her med barrack. When it was finished, she felt light, nearly naked, no longer carrying a clinic's worth of first aid on her person as she had for those previous five days. Various medical supplies, a half-empty bottle of Höhler whiskey, scissors, tweezers, a quarter roll of adhesive tape, and a single bar of soap lined up in a roll-top dresser by the bed closest to the hatch leading up to the guard tower. Liliana eyed the hatch for some time, picturing all the scenarios that might befall it. She imagined tripping and breaking her legs, lying stranded, the last survivor of the attack, blood seeping in down the walls through the cracks of the trapdoor frame. She thought of herself, with her shattered knees in her hands swaying back and forth, and the Luger pistol in her pocket.

Cledwyn screamed again, followed by a set of indistinguishable curse words and a small circular dance. Liliana came down with bandages to see the small burn marks on the tips of his work gloves.

"These wires are older than condoms in the Pope's wallet. Jesus, that hurts!"

Liliana put her bandages away and shook her head. "I didn't take you for religious Mr. King," she proposed.

"Forgive me for sayin', lass, but I didn't take you for a doctor."

Liliana laughed and turned back up the stairs, but Cledwyn grabbed her by the wrist and spun her around into the corner of the generator room. She pulled her pistol and edged back on the worktable she'd landed on, taking careful aim.

"And I've never seen a lecture hall stiff take so quick to a boomer."

"What do you want, King?"

"I want to know who you really are, Ms. Ferreira, at least before this island—or you—kills me. You're not some researcher come to find the missing link. That's not the look of discovery I've seen in your eye."

Liliana slowly slipped her hand back into her pocket and tossed a black leather wallet at Cledwyn, who bent down to rifle through it. He picked out a card, laminated in green with a blue starry orb in the center. It read *Liliana Ferreira, Professor de Genética e Antropologia, Instituto de Biociência, Universidade de São Paulo.* Behind it he found a similar second card marked *Instituto Butantan, São Paulo.*

"Where's your other card?" King demanded, dropping her wallet and IDs at his feet. "It's not in here."

"What other card?" she asked, extending her hand, subtracting that much distance between King and what might be an expelled bullet from her gun.

"You know the one. It reads ABI. *Agência Brasileira de Inteligência,*" he pronounced in his poorly forged Portuguese.

"You think I am a spy?" she asked with a chuckle. Liliana put away her Luger. "If I was a spy, I'd shoot you."

"Would you?" asked King.

Liliana stared into his eyes. She raised her weapon again, this time to point at King's razor-sharp smile.

"The power is back. Do the fences work?"

"They'll work."

"Do the spotlights work?"

"They'll work."

"Then I guess we don't need you anymore, do we?"

Liliana smiled as Cledwyn's grin dropped sharply. Then she put the gun back into her pocket and hopped off the workbench. "Come. We've wasted enough time."

Chapter XIX

Chuck dumped his remaining dried boar and canned rations on the ground next to the charred remains of their now two-day-old fire in the center of the compound.

"No rotisserie gourmet tonight?" asked Solomon, still limping but now on his own, carrying what wood planks remained from the wagon to the fire pit.

"Eat up while you can and don't stray far," said the Texan, passing Cledwyn and walking nervously ahead of Liliana on their way from the bunker.

"Where are you going?" asked Liliana.

"Eat up," he repeated and disappeared into the generator room.

"What's up his ass?" asked King, plopping down in the chair he'd planted the night of the boar hunt.

"'Defensive operations and logistics', he called it," answered Solomon. He could see tension in Liliana's face. The twinge in her brow, the tightness in her jaw, the way she'd spaced her steps to maintain distance behind King as they'd approached. Solomon changed the topic. "Salty crap or saltier crap?"

He tossed King a helping of each, sat back in the dirt, and peeled back the fold on a can of sardines. Before he could reach for his fork, Solomon felt a twinge in his chest, a burning sensation over the sides of his lungs. He wrenched his neck backward and bellowed a great cough, dropping the can beside him so as not to spit up blood into his lunch. Instead he launched it into the ashy remains of dripped boar guts and jungle timber. Solomon sighed, reached into his pocket, and followed the blood spit with a flaming match that slowly re-sparked the planks and brush he'd pulled into the pit.

"Doc, if you had to, with your training and experience, what would you say it is, that Haze?" asked King.

181

"I'd say it's fear. The kind of weapon a coward uses to kill old people and kids from behind locked doors."

"Will it kill us?" Cledwyn asked, scratching the same spot under his ribs as Solomon.

"Yes. Eventually. You're not a smoker, are you, Mr. King?"

"Not anymore I'm not," he said, pulling his hand from his jacket and examining the silver insignia on its collar. He rubbed his fingers under it and found the stitching coming loose. Solomon was halfway finished with his fish when the little *double S*'s flung into the fire before him.

After the meal, Solomon found himself holding the hands-free and massaging it with the tips of his fingers. Liliana watched him questioningly, half of her expecting him to call the voice, the other half ready and happy to see the little plastic thing melting and bubbling in the fire. Before either could look up at the tower, just barely in view over the chirping jungle canopy, the device began to speak in its now intimate static hiss.

"The last supper?" asked the voice chiming from Solomon's hand.

He felt like closing his fist on it with all his might to see if it would bleed from the speaker if he held it tightly enough. "What do you want?" Solomon responded, not missing a beat.

"You're the one with the quizzical look Mr. Solomon."

"If we survive this attack and make it up there, are you going to show yourself? Come out of hiding?"

"When the vault is open and secure and you bring me what I want from it, you'll get what you're after."

"That's not what I asked," Solomon retorted.

"Yes it is," followed the voice.

Solomon tried another tactic. "You were right about the Volksklausur. They are just people. That's what you have us fighting. People, not beasts. People. Just better. Just freer."

There was a pause. Cledwyn chewed his last piece of sausage and kicked the can into the fire. Liliana sat looking up at the tower. Neither had anything more to add.

"You've talked to them, Mr. Solomon?"

"Yes, I have."

"Then you know it is not I who pit you against them. They pit themselves against anyone they find. We are living ghosts to them. Nazis, intruders. We are their monsters. They will attack you without guilt or remorse. All you need is a pinch of their blood, a fraction of their genius."

"And to survive," Solomon shot back. "Did you forget that? That we need to survive?"

"Surviving is your business. The blood is mine." *Click.*

Chapter XX

"On your feet, soldiers," Chuck demanded, marching out from the bunker. He lugged something large wrapped in a sheet over his shoulder toward them. Solomon squinted, quickly wiped off his glasses, and seconded his first impression. As the sergeant neared, his party indeed rose in alarm if not to attention.

"Jesus, Chuck, what are you doing with Dr. Jung?"

Chuck flipped the body over his shoulder and laid it out on the ground by the dimming fire.

Solomon looked away, preparing himself for another premature purge of the ration he'd just finished.

"Oh, wow. Where did you find these?" asked Liliana.

Solomon turned back around. Lying atop the white bed sheet was not the decomposing cadaver of Martin Jung, but an armament to raise the hairs along Solomon's neck. Rifles, machine guns, a belt of stick grenades, and several cardboard boxes filled with ammunition. Chuck reached down and picked up a rather large assault weapon.

"Seek, you said you wanted guns. You've got guns. This is the StG forty-four, the first assault rifle ever to see mass production."

He tossed it to Cledwyn, who ran his hands over the stock, finding another silver double *S* to match those he'd thrown in the camp fire.

"Feel the weight," the drill sergeant continued. "That's about ten pounds. The magazine will make it eleven. She fires about five hundred rounds in a minute if you hold the trigger down, so don't, because we only have one hundred twenty rounds in four clips of thirty. Be prepared for a kick. She recoils hard but will spray an area twice as long as this camp."

Chuck reached down and picked up another weapon, this time a smaller machine pistol, and pushed it into the hands of Liliana, picking up another identical version for himself.

"This is the MP forty sub-machine gun. It weighs about nine pounds, but it's more evenly distributed than on the forty-four. Do you feel it?"

Liliana held the gun under her arm like a soldier, stiffening her grip and planting her feet straight out in a rigid firing stance. She nodded.

"Good. The recoil isn't as bad, but it won't fire as fast or as far. It doesn't shoot the same round either."

He held up one of the cardboard boxes from the bottom of the sheet wrapping. Solomon watched Liliana and Cledwyn surveying their individual weapons with anxiety.

"It fires this round here," Chuck continued. "This is the nine off nineteen millimeter cartridge that fits your sidearm there. If one of these breaks, misfires, jams, you lose it, if it falls off the tower, it explodes in your hand—whatever—you switch weapons and salvage ammo. The MP's got a blowback to it too, but stuff it under your arm like that and you'll be fine. Just point and tap on the trigger there, on and off like a light switch. You power on, you power off, they die. Good?"

She nodded again.

"Good. Solomon," he announced, picking up one of the cartons of ammo and another Luger. He walked over and handed Solomon the carton and extracted the clip from his machine pistol. "You're on ammo duty. When one of us runs dry, you have another weapon loaded and ready to go. This will all happen quick. We need their blood, not their lives. As soon as we're sure we've spilled some, we're falling back to the barracks. Oh, and Solomon, here."

As he stuffed the Luger into Solomon's pants pocket, glancing down at the absence of his sacrificed leather belt, Chuck whispered in his companion's ear.

"Try not to shoot your dick off."

Chuck turned back to the sheet and picked up a long pipe with a small cylinder on the end.

"These are potato mashers. There's a small cord still inside each one of them that you pull here in the bottom. These are volatile, and I

186

don't trust them for long out in the sun, so we'll use them once and all at the same time. Don't touch them unless I say. If just one of these goes off by accident, those of us who aren't riddled in the face with shards will be blown into bits before the real fighting even starts."

He carefully placed the grenades back down on the sheet with the others and paced back and forth with his machine pistol holstered over his shoulder.

"When your clip runs dry, Solomon will be on check with another. You grab that one and keep firing. We'll all be close by. There's not much space up there to get lost, so you'll have to worry more about bumping into your neighbor or crossing friendly fire than you will yelling for a reload. Now's the hard part. I will be teaching you how to use all these weapons in what little time we have left. Fortunately, they don't look like they've seen action, so there's no wear on the springs or bolts. Unfortunately, they're old. Very old. Forty-four is nineteen forty-four, forty is nineteen forty, and so on. These guns are antiques; they're older than you and the sad wretches that gave birth to you."

Solomon reared back his head. "How do you know they work at all?"

Chuck held his weapon in the air and fired off a burst, showering Solomon's feet in shell casings.

"I've field-stripped every one of them myself," he explained. "They're serviceable. Nazis know guns."

Solomon kicked the burning shells away from the smoldered campfire.

"Now, we don't have the time or the manpower to displace more searchlights to the northeast guard tower, so Solomon, you will be on spotlight duty as well. One light will hit the front gate. The other one will need to be manned at your discretion, understand?"

Solomon nodded.

"Good. If you would, take the rest of this down to the gate. Be very careful. The rest of you follow me to the practice range."

Solomon did as he was told, wrapped the sheet back up, and very slowly dragged it back to the makeshift wooden tent they'd propped up against the chain-link gate. He could feel and hear something coming lose from the package, so he stopped and rewrapped. Inside he spotted three grenades, one moldy box of shells, and his tin carton of lighter fluid. He towed it along extra slowly the rest of the way.

Stowing the goods against the wall he'd hammered down, Solomon slowly walked backward as if not to wake the sleeping stockpile. Further along the gate he spotted Cledwyn's welder's mask. As he bent down to pick it up, a crackle lit out and detonated in his ears. He dropped the mask and then himself on the ground, falling over his feet in panic, staring over at the gate. It was exactly as he'd just left it. Solomon exhaled deeply to the sounds of the second crackle, light arms fire blasting a couple dozen meters away. He blew make-believe smoke from his mouth over and over again and could only think of one word. *Shell-shocked.*

Cledwyn leaned back and tapped on the trigger of his assault rifle, feeling its iron parts rattling in his loose grip. His finger slipped, and he held on for five seconds of full auto, expelling the remainder of his clip first into the dirt a few feet in front of him and then the base of the target with most of his rounds flying overhead into the jungle canopy, shredding leaves like diced salad. Chuck walked over sternly, grabbed the weapon, shouldered it, and stuck the lighter machine pistol in Cledwyn's hands. Cledwyn smiled gratefully.

"This is a distance of ten meters. From the top of the guard tower to ground level is twenty meters. Train your eyes along the small bump in the sight aperture. That little notch should hover over your target from this distance. No, no, no, look."

Chuck holstered the StG in the pocket of his elbow and torso, resting his arm over its stock and holding it up to his neck, sighted down the barrel. "This is how you want to hold it. Don't put your face too close or the recoil will take out your front teeth. Hold it tightly, and make sure you're actually looking down the sights. Don't hold it at your hip. Don't fire it in only one hand. Grab it by the little handle here and the magazine here. Good."

The Texan approached Liliana, who tucked her weapon away just as he'd instructed, and placed her feet apart at just the right bi-pod firing stance.

"Good. Perfect. Okay, raise the weapon, spot your target down range, and you know it might hurt at first but just—"

Liliana tapped on the trigger and spurted a short line of bullets up the torso and over the face of the practice dummy directly across from her.

"Wow. Um. Good. Now try the pistol."

Liliana slid the MP by its strap-around behind her and pulled the Luger from her pocket, holding it out straight with both hands. Without hesitating she popped off several rounds and watched the facial features on the dummy to her left, adjacent to Cledwyn, fall to the dirt.

"All the professors at your university spend so much time at the gun range?" King sneered.

Solomon walked over to them with his hands over his ears.

"Solomon! Solomon!" Chuck yelled. "It's going to get a lot louder than this."

Chuck drilled the team for an hour from varying ranges. Once the dummies fell to pieces, he was satisfied enough to take them up in the tower to practice shooting at empty cans of sardines he threw out into the jungle. He urged them not to fire on the heap of brush and branches he'd made around the base of the tower. Solomon began to gain comfort with the sounds of crackling small-arms fire and picked up the basics of chamber operation and loading the weapons of his allies. The spotlight, while proven rusty and unsteady, could be plied with enough force to swing in a general arc around the woodland side of the tower, from where Chuck assured him the Volksklausur would be attacking. The other light shined directly across the camp on the gate, untouched from the last time it had illuminated an angry horde bursting down its walls.

After they had expelled a third of their ammunition stock, Chuck dismissed his squad to rest in the barracks. It was four in the afternoon. They'd remounted their bunks in the concrete tower but this time had no mind or patience for small talk. Cledwyn's snores kept Solomon up thinking. He took out his Kindle.

March 18th 2020, 1900 hours

It's done. Will hit the printers tomorrow morning. Here's a copy/paste:

Washington D.C, – This October will mark the nineteenth year of Operation Enduring Freedom, the U.S Military's official designation for the war in and occupation of the Islamic Republic of Afghanistan. As the third time table for withdrawal meets with debate in the House and Senate later this month, a new revelation comes to light regarding the sanctity and intent of the operation.

This week the Post reports evidence of War Crimes committed by members of the American Armed forces in both Kabul, the capital of Afghanistan and center for U.S operations, and the detention camp at Guantanamo Bay Naval Base in Cuba. A former dissolved program entitled Operation: Firelight has been uncovered by Post reporters to have been revived in both locations illegally and against the orders of Secretary of Defense Alvarez, who signed the order to terminate the program in 2018.

Operation: Firelight as it exists today, however, functions completely independently from the judicial system and persists on a revenue stream misappropriated from defense spending currently being overseen by General Jules Tripp of the Joint Chiefs of Staff. Post reporters are in possession of email correspondence between General Tripp and Lt. Colonel Americo Salazar, operational head of the splinter group running Firelight, confirming this abuse of funds which go to the inhumane abuse and treatment of inmates as well as abducted Afghan non-combatants. Classified documents also in the possession of Post reporters highlight the transference of inmates from holdings in Cuba to the Operation's center in Kabul by Colonel Salazar. There, they along with numerous women, children, and other members of the civilian populace have endured unlawful abuse as defined by both the Geneva Protocol and the Geneva Convention.

Lt. Colonel Americo Oliver Salazar, a clinical psychologist, pathologist, and former Chief of Bio-Medical Operations for the Central Intelligence Agency in Langley, Virginia, remains on the government payroll officially as a member of the military tribunal commission in Guantanamo Bay. Salazar is one of six members tasked with the responsibility of determining sentencing for persons convicted as unlawful combatants.

Colonel Salazar is a Panamanian-American, son of the late Dr. John D.

Salazar, former U.S. liaison in Panama from 1966 to 1968, and Alondra Narcisa de Lupe Salazar, a Panamanian National. He is fifty-three years old and divorced. His driver's license is registered in Nevada. Salazar has served in the military for twenty-two years since obtaining his two doctorates from the University of California School of Medicine at Irvine, first as a clinical psychologist researching the effects of fallout radiation on the brain and then as a field technician working as consultant to NATO. He was in his fourth tour of Afghanistan before relocating to Guantanamo Bay Detention Center, where his official post lies, in February of last year.

Sources prove that Salazar and others under his direct command have murdered, to date, at least sixteen civilians and seven inmates convicted as unlawful combatants within the confines of Operation: Firelight. In addition, they have subjected as many as thirty others to grueling and unlawful experiments of wanton science, forcing the victims to submit to the testing of various weaponized biological agents, poisons, and viruses. Originally intended to dispose of chemical weapons supposedly being transported to the Taliban by terrorist elements in Indonesia but found unproven and undocumented, Operation: Firelight has since gone rogue, hiding in plain sight until being uncovered by Post reporters late last year.

Findings in the reports of the operation point to graver death tolls, possibly compiled over a length of five years leading up to the revival of Firelight. Whether the operation has received approval or recognition from the other members of the Joint Chiefs of Staff and/or ranking members of the Department of Defense remains to be seen, but evidence incriminating both General Tripp and Colonel Salazar has been provided by Post reporters to the U.S Attorney General's office late yesterday. In total, the misappropriated funding to Firelight is in excess of seventy million dollars.

Finally, inside reports have discovered the location of a mass grave associated with personnel under the Colonel's command. The site is explained by the Department of Defense to be a preemptive radioactive waste dump for the disposal of harmful materials never discovered by the original proponents of Operation: Firelight, and is located in a dried waterbed forty miles East of Kabul outside the small town of Anargay. The grave accounts for the bodies of over fifty persons. They have yet to be identified.

   — *Stephen Solomon, The Washington Post*

191

As soon as the first of these has come off the press, we'll send over the evidence to the Attorney General. It's been over a year of research and my entire career as a journalist, this story. I'm glad it's finally over.

June 30ᵗʰ 2025, 1600 hours

This is wrong. All of it. We've now collected three of the four Vorkämpfer DNA samples. The fourth lay in the pumping, very real, very human veins of the creations, the victims of the other three. Metzger was a monster, total and complete. However, he designed the Volksklausur, his isolated peoples, his drones, using himself as the model. This is why I cannot stand for what we are about to do. Biologically, genetically, in the very root and core of what science tells us is our existence, the very nature and being of what I dare not say is our souls, these people are Metzger. They are the enemy. But there's so much more there. They're innocents, slaves. They are the greatest of contradictions, masters by nature, slaves by nurture. And we're out to spill their blood tonight.

Chuck seems to give this no heed. He is a soldier through and through. He's armed us, trained us, fortified the camp, and set the trap in motion in preparation for their attack tonight. The camp. In the camp of all places! The cradle of their indoctrination. They are a few dozen men of my own age, trapped on this island as I am, hunted by the Nazis, and we've picked the very place of their first captivity to shoot them, blow them up, to fight them from unfair vantage points with cruel surprise. Now they are the attackers, coming to bash down the gates and drive us from the island, from their homes as we are the abominations, the minority of armed and unwanted house guests.

It's been six days since we were ambushed here and in all that time I've not had to compromise my principles. But in this... Chuck says they're not Jews, not my people. He's right. They're certainly not Jews. Their blood is of the utmost corruption. But I have spoken to them and found no evil to fight, no darkness to be unearthed. My chapter on them will not read "race of flesh-eating monsters," nor will it read "men of the future." Here's the title sentence: *Ultimate tragedy befalls mankind.*

I don't think anything in the vault could be worth the agony of lying here and waiting for them to come. I turn over and see Lily sleeping soundly and wonder how? She told me it was a small mercy the German children were killed along with the others. That death spared the world another generation of hate and fear and when I think about it, it sounds crazy. The Volksklausur are eight feet tall, super humans, petrifying to behold, much less engage in armed combat, but they are not the next generation of hate and fear. Maybe she's right about the children. Maybe they would have grown just like their parents. But that same hate and fear drove them to find this camp, and the rest is history. The Volksklausur are not the killing machines the Nazis intended them to be. There has to be a way to reach them, to break the hold Jung implanted in their brains. With free will, with freedom, imagine what they can tell us.

I won't get a wink of sleep tonight. I've been given the military drill. Load, lock, and watch the bullets fly into the night. And pray. Pray to what? What kind of god would allow these men to be made here, under these purposes? What kind of god would drive us to fight them now? The god of the Voice. I hope the Volksklausur come down on him and rip him limb from limb. They are not the enemy. If evil remains on this island to be fought, it's up in the tower of the Kapitalzukunft, watching us even now. He'll see the attack. He'll eye it closely, watching his little puppets like a boy with a magnifying glass, shining it indiscriminately at the ants and termites battling below. Providence bodes permanence. Foreknowledge keeps you alive. He knew everything.

Well, soon the deed will be done, you sick son of a bitch. Blood will be spilled, maybe on both sides, and then I'll come for him. This is right. I am in the right. He ambushed me; I'll ambush him. I don't know how, but as soon I find a way to deactivate this pill, I'm shoving it right down his throat.

It'll be over soon.

Dad

Chapter XXI

Solomon felt a hand pat him on the hip, so he put away the tablet and rolled over on the bed. Chuck's smiling, dirty brown face shone in the lamp light.

"It's seven. Mud time."

Chuck held out the canteen of sludge he'd collected from the freshwater swamp on the trail to the Volksklausur cove.

"Really?" Solomon replied, sitting upright against the headboard.

"Oh yeah. We're gonna get dirty, Seek. All of us."

Chuck climbed up on Solomon's bunk to wake Cledwyn next and pointed down the hall. Solomon found Liliana already missing and the bathroom door closed.

"They'll be blinded by the muzzle flashes," Chuck reassured his companion, "and the mud will help hide the smell of your sweat too." He patted Solomon on the back and climbed up through the hatch in the roof to the guard tower.

Solomon stood by the window, the light from the room reflecting in its dusky glass frame. He placed his glasses on the nightstand and unbuttoned his shirt. Hesitantly, he pulled his formerly white, dirt and blood-stained undershirt over his head and closed his eyes, imagining he'd see the bare, freckled pale skin he'd had since high school upon opening them. When he creaked his eyelids apart, he did so with a sigh, running his hands over the growing reddish-blue blotch spreading outward from the center point of his ribs like a rose blooming from his lungs. Solomon popped off the top of the mud flask and dunked his fingers in. He slid out a tablespoon of muck and applied it gingerly to the skin over his aching chest cavity. He bit his lip, less from pain than from the cold of the slime he slathered on himself. Solomon sniffed his fingers but found little to the odor at all, much less one stronger than his own. He longed for a shower.

When he'd just about covered his stomach, shoulders, arms, and hands in slick camouflage, Solomon heard Liliana call his name from behind. The bathroom door was slightly ajar.

"Mr. Solomon? Er, Mr. Solomon? Could you come here?" He reached for his shirt on the bed but put it back down. Upon approaching the bathroom door he knocked. "Yes, Ms. Ferreira?"

"Mr. King and Mr. Polanski are not with you, are they?"

"No, they are not," Solomon replied, shrugging to himself.

"Then could you come in here please? I cannot…reach all around."

Solomon pushed the door in slowly. Liliana stood with her back to him in front of the mirror, her hands over her bare breasts but still clothed from the waist down. Her long black hair dropped down around her neck, running over her hands. Solomon could see the awkward hesitation in her face through the mirror. She did not turn around, and he froze for a moment, staring at the black brassiere she'd dropped on the tank of the toilet.

"I see you've already started yourself," she said, brandishing a small smirk in the mirror's reflection.

Solomon jested, feigning covering his torso with his hands as she had done. When he pulled his hands back down, he saw the mud did not come up with them.

"The flask is there on the toilet seat. Could you… Would you please…"

"Get your back?"

"Yes."

"Of course. If you cover mine."

Liliana turned her neck to see Solomon out of the corner of her eye and nodded, turning back around to watch him pour out a handful of the sludge onto his fingers. Standing shirtless behind her in the bathroom with mud on his fingers, Solomon felt a chill running down his muck-covered arms. Softly, he pushed a fingernail of the stuff across Liliana's tanned brown skin in a downward arch, and then another, painting her back and shoulder blades with his fingertips like a brush.

196

"Thank you," she muttered. Solomon looked up from the tiny imperfections along her spine and saw her smiling at him in the mirror. He smiled back.

"Now it's like a real vacation, huh?" he cracked. "Sunny beaches, cool breezes, a hike in the jungle? Then a little digging in the sand, some cave diving, and finally a nice, pleasant mud bath to end the day."

He could feel her chuckling in the vibrations of her skin. "You do find a way to make things seem much better than they are, Mr. Solomon."

He smirked. "You've got to stop calling me that," he replied. "The only one who calls me that around here is that god-damned voice. Please. It's Stephen."

"Well. Thank you. Stephen. You do look nice without your glasses."

He chuckled again. "To say nothing of the mud, huh? I think this might be a good look for me, really. The mud covers up all the scarring," he said, painting the last bare patches of Liliana's lower back.

His fingers slid across her skin and around her waist without him even moving them. She had turned and found him stationary with his eyes on her uncovered naval. Without thinking, he wiped the rest of the mud on his fingers around it, caressing the skin of her sensitive but defined abdomen. With his hands dry he stood back. Liliana covered her nipples with the cups of her hands, her arms folded underneath them. He noticed first her expression, bare and frightened. She looked down on herself and he followed. There on her chest, emerging like an overflow from the crevice of her breasts lay the mark, the blue and red deep bruising that he himself bore. Solomon felt himself grasping his own chest again.

Liliana turned her head to peek at the mirror and found he had covered her back completely, as asked. She tried to feign a smile. "If you'll turn around, I'll do yours."

Solomon did so without a word and dropped the flask back on the toilet seat. He ducked his head when he heard Liliana reaching over for her bra, and squirmed at first when he felt the stale, crusty mush being pushed along the backs of his shoulders by warm, soft hands.

After they had covered one another and parted to finish their legs and re-clothe, Liliana and Solomon met a completely nude Cledwyn, body covered in muck, face painted in the shapes horns on his cheeks and forehead, in the hallway. He held his bucket in his left hand and a dirty old mop in his right. "We're all gettin' dirty, right?" he asked.

Solomon nodded speechlessly.

"You wanna borrow my mop?"

"Ummm...a mop for what?" the doctor asked, hiding a chuckle as she backed slowly away from the naked Welshman.

"For your backs, of course. Gotta cover up every inch. How else you gonna get back there?"

Solomon was taken aback by the sound of Liliana's quaint giggle.

Chuck popped open the hatch. "All right, troops. It's time."

Cledwyn reached for his pants and neglected his shirt. Solomon felt his feet freeze up as if nailed to the concrete floor of the bunker. Liliana grabbed the gun on her bed and moved up behind him, edging him forward. They let Cledwyn climb the ladder first, his bare, muddy back wrapped in the leather strap of his machine pistol. Liliana slipped her hand under Solomon's and ran her fingers back and forth against the darkened lines of his palm. He looked backed at her and nodded.

With the sun retreating to the west, Chuck lit an old lantern they'd pilfered from the villa. He laid out each defender's station, spaced out by only a meter at most, in a semi-circle facing out into the jungle. On the inside of the tower, a desk once accompanied by a chair since burned for firewood played host to the remaining arsenal of San Magnus Concentration Camp, two replacement machine pistols and ammo left from their hastened training. Solomon was stationed at the spotlight on the ledge closest to the desk. The Texan ran them through one last fingers-off-the-triggers drill to test their reaction times. He counted off.

"One!" Liliana and Cledwyn rested the muzzles of their guns on the top rung of the guardhouse. Solomon struggled to swing the unlit spotlight back and forth along the fringes of the jungle.

"Two!"

Solomon pulled the spotlight down to the base of the tower and ran to the desk. Cledwyn and Liliana pulled back and dropped their weapons to the second rung of the guardrail, looking down the sights to follow the invisible line of the spotlight. Solomon came running out with their replacement weapons and three magazine sticks. He could feel the mud between his legs chafing and half-hoped his profuse sweating would wipe it away. He slid Chuck the big clip and dropped the two MP's by Cledwyn's and Liliana's feet, swapping them for the still unfired originals. Chuck watched intently as Solomon swapped out the full clips of their guns for two replacement clips. Then he gave the thumbs-up.

"Three!" Cledwyn and Liliana shuffled down the walkway and pointed their guns at the front gate of the camp, still propped up by wooden reinforcement. Chuck stepped forward, swung his Mauser rifle around, loaded a small strip of red-tipped rounds, and fired an imaginary one at the gate. Solomon ran back to the guardhouse, and by the time he heard the final count of "four" had swapped out three more clips of his compatriots' ammo.

"Okay," Chuck said, exhaling deeply into the night air. He hovered the lantern over his watch. "It's almost nine." He looked up, and his team looked back at him, resting against the rails with their weapons holstered. Cledwyn pounded his bare chest with his free hand and painted a long smile with his fingertip in the mud on his face. Liliana nodded heartily. Solomon, though slow and shaking, raised his hand and gave his friend back the thumbs-up.

"Well then. Let's fire 'em up."

Solomon covered his face and flipped the switch on his and the other spotlight. They awoke slowly but without sparks, first dimly, before penetrating deep into the night. He flipped them upward in stray directions as if to spot a squadron of heavy bombers coming to strafe the camp from the face of the island. Solomon stood back against the guardhouse and rested his head.

The party waited. And they waited. The air turned cool enough to catch Solomon's raspy breathing, and it looked as if he blew smoke from the fire raging in his lungs. Solomon chuckled a little to himself at the sight of the Welshman, his legs swinging over the side of the tower, sucking from an invisible cigar and puffing long, slow drags out into the dark. In his boredom, King clanged the end of his weapon with the side of the railing, sending a sharp-pitched *gong* down the metal on all sides.

Gong. Gong. GONG. Chuck joined in, tapping the butt of his assault rifle against the rail and then Liliana and soon Solomon, rattling an ammo clip in unison with the others. *GONG. GONG.* Solomon found himself bobbing his head to the rhythm, slow vibrations running up his spine. All together the bang became a church bell ringing out from the guard tower belfry over the camp, the jungle, and the darkness.

Liliana tapped her feet to the sound and banged louder on the rail. She looked over at Cledwyn.

"Yes. Yes. Yes," he chanted, a barefoot, warpaint-covered madman aching for battle.

"Yes. Yes. Yes," followed Chuck, keeping the rhythm of the beating along with that of the shouting, intensifying, growing louder.

"Let's go, let's go!" Liliana screamed out into the night. The guard tower erupted into a screaming frenzy. Rage-filled oaths and rambling curse words in broken English, Welsh, and Portuguese were thrown out like the first shots of the battle. Solomon found himself enthralled, the blood in his veins coursing with intense purpose, a feeling that took him back to the flying carnage on the Kandahar Ghazini highway so many years before. He gazed over at Liliana, screaming out at the jungle just as loudly and as brashly as the others.

"Come on. We're waiting! We're gonna get you, you sons of bitches. We're gonna fucking kill you!"

"What, are you scared? I'm gonna kill every one of you fucking Nazi freaks!"

Cledwyn let out with a burst of fire into the tree line. It was thirteen minutes past nine. The shouting stopped. Solomon rushed to move the spotlight. Something scurried under them. A pack of Volksklausur slipped out from the jungle on all fours, claws in the dirt, eyes on the tower. Liliana fired next. Solomon swiveled the spotlight around and caught them off guard. Bursts of auto fire split and tossed the dirt up in the air around the zig-zagging Volksklausur. Chuck pressed back on his trigger. The party reformed.

"One!"

They rested their muzzles on the rail they'd been slamming and continued firing thirty, forty meters out, shredding the tall green trees and ripping leaves from limb with scattered rounds. Solomon spotted one of them in the open and pushed hard with his shoulder against the searchlight, tracking it as it dove from eruptive small-arms fire back into the jungle.

One of the Volksklausur leaped from the jungle's edge and clamped itself on the gate, but it was sent flying back into the dark by a stream of sparks and a few thousand volts of violence.

Solomon could see Cledwyn's lips moving between flashes of fire and heard his manic laughter like a man possessed and drenched in bloodlust.

Another Volksklausur leaped from the jungle and tried to tear at the walls, slicing at the charged fence and moaning. The stench of burned flesh quickly rose and battled among the ruckus with the smell of smoking gunpowder.

"Two!" Chuck yelled, signaling to Solomon. The party dropped to their second position and fired down at the horde of Volksklausur now risking life and limb to tear down the fence in electrified agony. Solomon pulled the spotlight down on them, sending them slinking back with their hands and claws over their eyes. Liliana ripped the last few rounds of her mag into the side and shoulder of one of them, sending it squealing into the jungle.

"I've hit one! Let's pull back!" she yelled, getting to her feet.

Chuck ran to her and yelled between Cledwyn's deafening bursts, "Switch mags! We're not pulling back until I say!"

Solomon protested but swapped out their weapons regardless, screaming, "If she's hit them, she's hit them!"

"Get back to your post soldier!" Chuck shouted in Solomon's face, pushing him down on the deck. Chuck turned his attention back to the attack and threw the old lantern down at the base of the structure, lighting the mass of timber and lighter fluid beneath them. Solomon picked himself up just in time to hear the sergeant yell, "Three!"

Cledwyn and Liliana shuffled down the line and took knees overlooking the gate fifty meters out from them. The searchlight, placid in its stare at the fortified entrance, did not stop the Volksklausur from pounding it down. They gathered, abandoning the climb up the tower for the ease of the front door.

The firing ceased. Cledwyn looked anxiously at Chuck, who held out his open hand. They could hear the Volksklausur's rustling turn to rattling and then banging as they tore at the melted metal with their claws and fangs. Chuck dropped his assault rifle and shouldered the scoped Mauser. From his pocket he took out the strip of red-tipped tracer rounds and lodged them hard into the chamber, slamming it shut with the bolt action. He leaned over the rail and stared down the scope at the gate. Solomon looked back and forth between them—Chuck and the gate, Chuck and the gate, back and forth—waiting for the shot to ring out. The Volksklausur broke through. The wrapped knotted bicycle chain flew in pieces over the wall of the camp like a disgraced flag.

Chuck could see their arms and legs flaying to push aside the obstruction he'd laid out in their path. A long, gray arm wrapped around the top of the wooden frame. Chuck exhaled and fired, recoil spitting back in his face. Cledwyn stared on, dazed, and Solomon dropped his head as the gate exploded in a mass of shrapnel and the crackling of fireworks. They watched as the arm, cut from the elbow, flew through the air like a projectile toward them.

"Four!"

The party displaced, running their hands along the rails to find their way back to the hatch of the barracks bunker. Liliana went first, grabbing Cledwyn, desperate to continue the fight, and pulled him down after her. Solomon picked up from the rear, huddling a few final clips under his shivering arms and diving for the small hole. He looked back. The Volksklausur were in the compound. He froze when a solemn Volksklausur hand reached over the guardrail and slashed the struts of the spotlight, sending it crashing down into the flames at the base of the tower. Chuck threw Solomon down the hatch face-forward and raised his rifle, popping another round into the creature's chest. It shrugged off the round and was joined by three more Volksklausur climbing up the guardrails.

Solomon flipped over on his ass and landed hard on the floor. He was quickly pulled aside by Cledwyn and Liliana, who scrambled to get his last few ammo clips. Chuck jumped down last to the sight of loaded weapons pointed at him, and slammed down the rigid metal lock on the hatch. Cledwyn and Liliana lowered their sights and backed away into the corner. Solomon took to the window just in time to spot the Volksklausur swinging wildly with their free hands, bashing and tearing down the remaining spotlight, throwing it, beaten and lifeless, into the jungle. With the lights out, the next thing he saw was his own reflection in the glass. His pale skin reemerged in lines running down from his eyes. Solomon rubbed the space on his cheeks, and mud crackled on his fingers. He never realized he'd been crying and reached over to the nightstand to put his glasses back on.

A pounding came from the ceiling, first on the concrete, then on the hatch. The party raised their weapons again.

"They have to come down that hole one by one. It's a kill zone," Chuck said calmly, putting his hands over their shoulders. Then the banging reached around, behind them. Beneath them.

"They can't be…" Solomon whispered to himself. He looked down at Cledwyn, whose legs sprawled out under him, gun tucked in his armpit, sweat pouring down his face, washing the battle paint from his thin pecks. He was breathing so heavily that the blood on his lips was still wet. Liliana was spitting blood too. Solomon hadn't noticed that either.

"The generator," Cledwyn muttered. He tried to get to his feet, but Chuck nudged him back down.

"Watch the hatch," he said, dropping the Mauser and taking the StG back in his hands and ran down the hall to the stairs. The room fell quiet.

Dazed, Liliana asked, "Is anyone hurt?"

Cledwyn shook his head. Solomon felt around for a wound or a stray bullet but could find nothing other than his ankle and lungs paining him. Another rattling came from the hatch above. Solomon inched forward on his toes, holding the Luger and shaking violently. He could see the tiny cracks widening in the trapdoor frame where the room light peeked out into the dark and was quickly quashed by a large, gray foot. Its bolts started to sway and come loose. Solomon backtracked and fell between Liliana and Cledwyn with his pistol arm outstretched.

Heavy breathing and fast footsteps echoed from the stairs. The three quickly drew their guns on the figure emerging from the hall. Chuck, fatigued, planted one hand on the wall and drew them forward with the other.

"Come. They're breaking through...the generator door. I can't believe it... We can't stay here. We'll be trapped. The lab."

"If we hide in the lab, they'll have us cornered!" yelled King.

"If we stay here, they'll hit us on two sides. There's no choice," said Liliana, helping to wretch Solomon to his feet and then Cledwyn. They raced down the stairs with the dim bunker light guiding their path to the basement. On the generator floor Solomon paused to look at the bulky iron door and the puncture marks being bashed into it. Chuck and Liliana dragged them down the last flight of stairs and into the air-locked laboratory, locking the reinforced translucent door behind them with a hiss. They kicked aside the shards of broken glass that littered the laboratory floor and made themselves places to collapse. Solomon dropped in the corner and found himself staring at the back of the deceased Martin Jung's bald head.

"Try to slow your breathing," Liliana muttered. "The air is sparse."

The party lay in a mass on the floor, Cledwyn against the wall, Chuck in the middle with his weapon drawn on the glass door just a meter and a corner away from Solomon, who sat silently beside Liliana. Solomon's eyes traced the room from the doctor to the soldier and then the thief. *These are the people I'm going to die with.*

Chuck expelled his clip and checked it over, laying it and his rifle out in front of him. He checked his watch. It was thirty-two after nine. "How many clips?"

Liliana held up one. Cledwyn held up one. Solomon dangled his lowly handgun. Chuck looked down at his own weapons. *Thirty rounds auto, three rounds bolt action.* He swayed his head at first and then dropped it back against the wall.

Liliana emptied her pack out in front of her by the machine pistol. She had two syringes of morphine. *Not enough to kill myself.* She looked over at Cledwyn, now shivering in the relatively warm, compressed air of the laboratory.

He swayed back and forth with his hands stretched forward on his toes. *Going to bite it without so much as a shirt on my back.*

Solomon's eyes slipped back in his head. They could hear the sounds of banging from above. Then silence. Then running. They took up arms again and pointed them out into the hall, a couple meters beyond where the light in the lab could reach no farther. The laboratory luminance flickered and died, draping the room in the dull crimson hue of the emergency lighting.

"Hold your fire until they come through that glass."

A pair of hands slipped into the red light from the black, and a tall, metal face, King's blow-torch helmet atop the shoulders of a lengthy muscled torso. Solomon instantly spotted the scar running down its chest and dropped his head into the corner between the wall and an empty cabinet. His eyes ran up and down the wall and the back of Dr. Jung's head. He felt nauseous. As they began bashing their way through the double thick layers of glass, he felt himself slipping away, flying off to someplace else, someplace safe and inviting. His old house with his girls and his wife. A winter morning with the sun beating on mounds of crisp, white snow. A snowman standing guard of the open front door. The girls ran down the stairs to greet him in as he crossed into the foyer. He could see the smiles on their faces and patted them on each head. His beautiful wife came up behind them and kissed him on the lips. The Luger fell out of his hand and plopped beside the slush meting on the oriental rug. He could smell chicken-and-vegetable soup broiling in a Crock Pot in the kitchen. Hiroto sat at the end of his long dining room table, grinning, that cunning ol' dog. Solomon felt comforted as he sat and helped himself to a fine meal with fine company.

The Volksklausur had smashed the first pane of glass and now screeched their claws down the edges of the second. Cledwyn shook violently, his weapon shivering in both hands, his finger waving back and forth on the trigger. Chuck sat firm and loaded and unloaded his weapon again and again, slamming the clip home harder every time. Looking over, Liliana noticed Solomon hallucinating, his hands outstretched as if reaching to coddle the corpse of Martin Jung before him.

"Solomon! Stephen!" she yelled at him, shaking him from the daze.

He looked back around. There was no house. His wife and kids were gone. His eyes drifted back to the cadaver in front of him. He gave a brief thought to prayer and decided to pass. *Martin Jung said a prayer. It didn't help him.*

The Volksklausur were almost through. Their claws punctured and scraped the paint off the laboratory wall. Liliana raised her gun in helpless protest. Solomon felt another cough bellowing inside him. He leaned forward to let it out, spitting another teaspoon of blood on the glass-covered floor by Jung's feet. Solomon spotted something on his neck. There was gold in the man's collar. A gold chain. Right in front of him. It wasn't a cross. *Martin Jung wasn't praying. He was blowing a whistle. The whistle!*

As the Volksklausur tore through the door and flayed forward to scattered gunfire, Solomon reached inside Dr. Jung's coat and grabbed the necklace whistle and blew and blew and blew. The gunfire stopped. Cledwyn had dropped his gun and rolled into a ball. Chuck lay sprawled out with his gun to his head, and Liliana curled into a corner by the cabinet. The Volksklausur stood, unmoving. Solomon looked up. The blast helmet stood there in the doorway looking down at him, tilting its head yet again. He couldn't see its eyes through the tinted frame, but he could feel its gaze. They stared at one another for what seemed an eternity. No one said a word or dared even to exhale through the mouth. Then the Volksklausur turned to the others behind him, saying something in German too fast for Solomon to get out his translator.

"Die Jagd ist vorbei."

Chapter XXII

It was two minutes past ten. The party clung closely to their weapons, pointing them at the hulking figure in the iron blast helmet as it bent down over Solomon in the corner. Its hand hovered over the body of Martin Jung, only now beginning the long-awaited steps of decomposition. Solomon tried hard to see through the visor, to catch a glimpse of the Volksklausur's eyes, looking for a blink if not a tear. It poked at the torn and bloodied lab coat of its master, nudging at the corpse's hands still pierced by a hundred small shards of glass. Solomon thought he could hear its breathing alleviate upon resting its hand over the dead man's crown.

Cledwyn broke the silence. "It's wearing my torch helmet," he complained softly, machine pistol held outright, shaking as if caught in a strong breeze.

"It's overcome the handicap," Liliana responded under her breath. "And just in time, Solomon…"

The Volksklausur leader turned its head to the journalist next, a sweaty little man, his heart beating too fast for his blood-soaked lungs to catch up. The masked figure rose, hunching to avoid collision with the laboratory ceiling.

"Was sind ihre bestellungen?" it asked through the slit under its visor. Solomon rummaged through his pack for the Kindle. Running his fingers over its screen, careful not to cut himself on the cracked glass, he translated. *What are your orders?*

"My orders, my orders…" Seek repeated to himself, drawing the stare of his fellow companions. He typed something onto the monitor. Liliana eyed his finger movements intently.

"Have them escort us," Liliana whispered. "We don't know what's in that fortress."

Still typing, Solomon replied, "No. I will not be another master."

"Oh, for Christ's sake!" moaned Chuck, getting to his feet, his weapon holstered. "Let me do it."

As the Texan approached the Volksklausur turned sharply to face him, holding out its razor sharp claws above his head, ready to slice into the blue-veined skin around his jugular.

"I'd sit back down if I were you, Chuck ol' buddy," Solomon said, clicking the *speak* key on his tablet.

"Sie sind frei ."

The Volksklausur leader looked back to Solomon and tilted its head once more. Pushing himself up, Solomon continued to type and stood in the Volksklausur's shadow.

"Haben Sie einen Namen?" asked the tablet's monotone voice.

He stood there for some time, eying the scar running from the golem's hip to its shoulder, waiting patiently for its response. He almost thought to reach out and touch it, but a glance from Liliana dissuaded him.

"Vierunddreißig ," it replied slowly, its hiss draining out under the sides of the visor.

"Well number Thirty-Four—" Solomon smiled, holding out the rusted old tin whistle. "—this is yours now." Slowly, he reached out, taking the Volksklausur leader by the hand and plopped the whistle, chain and all, in its massive gray palm.

"Are you sure that's the best idea, Seek?" asked Polanski.

"It's the best I can think of." Solomon shrugged and looked into the slit of the metal visor for a response.

"For us or for your conscience?"

"They're the same thing."

And then they left, stepping over broken panes of glass and trashed furniture, ducking under the low ceiling and walking back out through the gaping hole they'd torn in the generator room door. Liliana followed them out, dragging her weapon behind her. They marched in a two-line formation through the camp and out, beyond where the emergency lights were dim, into the jungle. Solomon came up behind, putting a hand on Liliana's waist. She eased her grip on the machine pistol and dropped the gun in the dirt at her feet and her head backward on Solomon's shoulder.

"Where are they going?"

"Home, I guess."

"Oh," she replied, taking a deep breath. "Lucky monsters."

Solomon smirked. "Come on. Let's head back upstairs. Get some of that mud off you." They stood together alone in the dark. He wiped his finger along the curves under her eyes.

"Wait," she said, reaching for the Kindle in Solomon's pack. He released it without contestation but followed close behind her as she shined it at her feet and trod lightly into the camp. Her steps were timid, and he could hardly fathom this was the same woman who had been shouting and gunning just minutes earlier. A few meters from the gate, she stopped and knelt to pick something from the darkness. Solomon moved to rewrap his arm around her waist but froze when she turned to him, holding a long, gray and bloodied forearm in both hands. She looked up and nodded, walking past him to the bunker. Solomon stood there for a while, until the light from his tablet had disappeared. He sniffed. Burnt, crisp flesh. Gunpowder and smoke. Frayed metal like electrical fire. He turned and shuffled back to the bunker in the dark.

That night, Solomon slept late into the morning until Chuck walked over and grasped him by the ankle. His eyes opened slowly, as if from a long coma, and met with Chuck's unflinching stare. With a long yawn Solomon tried to prop himself up against the headboard but found he could not break Chuck's hold.

"I don't see how Hiroto could stand you," Solomon sighed.

"He appreciated my frank realism."

"Doubtful," Solomon protested.

"We're going in today, Seek. We're finishing this. Grab your stuff." Chuck let go of Solomon's ankle.

Solomon found himself bringing up the rear. Cledwyn and Liliana had already packed and sat waiting on the remaining sticks of furniture around the burned-out campfire in the center of the compound. The barracks were stripped. Weapons lay scattered and stranded throughout the bunker. The closet was rummaged through, and the food and medicinal supplies had been taken. Solomon noticed he was the only one who'd bothered to make his bed.

Before their final trek out of the camp, following in the footprints of the behemoths who'd attacked them the night before, Cledwyn pulled Solomon to the side and let the others pass.

"Thank you, my friend," he said, extending his hand. Solomon shook it without any questions. His jacket was stained in blood, and Seek found it was impossible to discern whether it was his or the Volksklausur's. Chuck came up behind them.

"Today's the day, lady and gentlemen. Six billion dollars and freedom. Let's not waste time sitting around eating salted pork."

"It's the first today," said Solomon, staring up at the rising sun. "The start of a whole other week."

"So it is," Chuck muttered, leading the march out. Solomon picked up the rear and watched his companions step carefully over the burned shrapnel and dried blood spilled over the front gate. He found the torn metal rods they'd melted together. The fortified nail endings stuck slantwise like horns over his head as he slipped through the gap and back into the jungle. Without their weapons, a wheelbarrow stuffed with parts and supplies, tension, or fear, they double-timed it through the small path, deviating from where the Volksklausur's tracks led back toward the swamp and the cove.

They didn't stop by Albert Vogel's house, nor the general store, the first generator room, the plaza, or anywhere else in the Villa Vienna or Villa Roma on their walk north up Karl Braun. Solomon peeled his eyes away from the sun and the trees along the beach in the distance just long enough to see that they'd passed the welcome sign. A few times on the walk he hesitated to catch up to Liliana and wrap his arm around her, to kiss her. *It could be the last chance*, he thought. Every time he walked close enough, however, he caught sight of the huge, fractured ulna bone sticking out from its skin and medical bag wrapping, swaying back and forth on her hip.

Up on the ridge to the goliath fortress door sat Vogel's old jeep, dilapidated and smote. Cledwyn patted her trunk cab as they approached the bio-med lock.

"Well, Doctor, do your magic," Chuck said, resting his hand on the massive iron bulkhead.

"I don't know if I'm ready for this vacation to end." Cledwyn laughed and slammed shut the broken engine block cover.

"I think I know what you mean," said Solomon. "Maybe I just don't know if I'm ready to be a billionaire."

"So you're finally looking on the bright side, aye, Solomon?"

"Oh, I think the bright side, Cledwyn," he continued, wrapping his arm around the Welshman's shoulder, "is enough just to get this damn bomb out of my neck".

"I second that," said Liliana, taking the limb from her bag.

"I feel like we should be celebrating with something. As a team, you know? I'm buying rounds for everyone when we get off this rock," Cledwyn gaffed.

The terminal extended the small-finger pricker after some fiddling, and Liliana struggled, pushing the thick appendage into its human-sized receptacle.

The machine stood idle for some time afterward, gathering the party around it. Its screen lay black as they inched forward on their toes, grabbing the backs of each others' shoulders and waiting for that flashing white font. It made a click sound and then a rattle as if it were spitting cubes of ice. The screen scrambled in a display of red light and then stopped. A single dot. Blinking. Solomon almost fell over on top of the doctor.

"Willkommen, Dr. Metzger. Wo sind die Ärzte Ebersbach und Jung?"

A great, long smiled wrapped around Liliana's face when she turned around. She quickly entered the other samples, Dr. Jung's pinky finger and the pointed rib of Dr. Ebersbach. The machine took a scrape of each and concluded in great white lettering, "Willkommen, Vorkämpfer. Die Zukunft ist dein."

"Yes, yes!" Cledwyn shouted, jumping up and down. They all quickly shook hands and hugged one another as the great gates slowly unbolted and shook as they slid outward. Solomon and Liliana's embrace proved to be the longest before they were interrupted by the

Welshman, who kissed them both on the lips many times over. With the crack in the frontier large enough, he slipped inside, his hollering and leaping echoing outward. The rest of the party followed.

They were taken aback at first to find that the Kapitalzukunft was lit, small fluorescent bulbs in bright white casings lined in rows along the white-painted walls and floors. Rather than holding out his tablet to light their way, Solomon found himself covering his eyes with it and squinting through his glasses in pain. The island, bathed in the light of the sun, seemed dark in comparison. It took some time for his eyes to adjust. They had stepped into a great hall, a two-story-high space with twin curved staircases draped in purple and bright red carpeting. A huge chandelier hung low from the ceiling, sparkling in brilliance. A dark mahogany counter lay out between the stairs, longing for the touch of a host or warm receptionist to welcome in their new guests. Along the sides of the hall sat rows of leather couches and chairs under golden-framed portraits of highbrow men in brown German uniforms. As the door slowly closed behind them, Seek took a second look. This reception area, this hotel lobby, was littered with bodies from the new world, men in black armor, their hands outstretched toward modern weapons, their blood staining the colorfully sequenced Old World carpeting.

"I can't stop it!" Cledwyn yelled, meddling with the terminal on the other side of the wall. "Solomon, what does this say?"

In red lettering flashed the words *Tür ist privilegiert*, and Cledwyn found he could do nothing to change them or to keep the massive door they'd anguished so long to open from creeping closed behind them. He ran to it and looked back, flinching to and fro with the sunlight slowly dying in the crack before him. It bolted shut. Cledwyn ran back to the console.

"It won't open! It won't respond!" King found himself the only party concerned.

"It's not going to," said Solomon. "Of course not. That's why he couldn't just let us in. That's why we went through all this shit!" Solomon kicked over a chair laying closest to the exit. "I was right all along." He stared at Chuck.

Cledwyn ran over and grabbed Seek by the collar. "Right about what?"

"You don't know? It won't open from the inside. He's been trapped in here the whole time. We're not just his heist men. We're his rescuers."

Chapter XXIII

"**It's much worse**," Liliana muttered, staring at the blinking red display on the door terminal. "If he's been trapped in here the whole time, who knocked us out? Who tied us up?"

She looked around the great hall and counted seven corpses lining its floors and corners, some with the mosaic of bullet holes painted into the walls around them. Then she looked at her companions, at Solomon, whose arms were grappled by Cledwyn. Solomon stared her deep in the eyes. Their lips quivered.

Seek reversed Cledwyn's hold tightly around the man's collar. "Why did you do it, King?"

Cledwyn glared at Solomon with rage. As Chuck neared him from behind, the thief threw a hook into Solomon's ribs, broke his grasp, and took off, bolting across the hall. Chuck raced after him, reaching for the empty spot in his belt the Luger had once occupied, and as King leaped behind the visitor's counter on the far end, Chuck scrambled for cover under a display table beside a broken vase and bloodied body. Liliana and Solomon ducked and darted toward leather sofas on opposite sides of the room. Chuck rummaged through the body's belongings and found a Glock sidearm. He retracted its clip but found it vacant. Liliana propped up the sofa as a barrier and Solomon, watching her every movement from afar, followed suit.

In that moment, Cledwyn re-emerged from behind the counter, lifting a loaded HK 550 over his head. Chuck, seeing his flank exposed to the fully armed Welshman, stuck the empty pistol in his belt and took off toward another body slunk over a fort of chairs and end tables at the bottom of the left staircase. Cledwyn frantically opened up on his friend, drawing a line of bullets in the floor before Chuck's feet. The Texan rolled over and crawled into the makeshift furniture barricade and pulled the body hanging over toward him.

"Jesus fuck, King, why are you shooting at me?!"

King's voice cracked. "Why'd you run?"

"So you wouldn't shoot me!"

Solomon quivered behind his couch, holding Polanski's puny Luger pistol in his grip. "Maybe I was wrong. Maybe there was someone else on the island!" he yelled over his cover.

"Bullshit you think that, Solomon! If there was someone else, why did you run behind that futon?" Cledwyn retorted, safe behind the lobby register.

Okay, okay. Think, Stephen, think. Seek remembered his training and expelled his clip. Eight rounds. He peeked over the leather cushions. On the far end hunched Chuck, his bald head creeping over a coffee table that had been sprayed with bullets. To his right, closer to Solomon, was Cledwyn, parked with a machine cannon over the counter, cowering in front of a massive black-and-white map of San Magus Island. To the left, in the corner, Solomon thought he could spot Liliana's ponytail sticking out from behind an upended lounge seat. In the middle, among and around them lay the rotting corpses of a half-dozen, well-armed and armored elite special operatives. *It's just like he said.*

"We can't just shoot each other!" Solomon shouted out. "We have to work together."

"Why? Because the voice said? He also said my part was done. I got us in here, so now I'm expendable, right?" Cledwyn shot back indiscriminately, his weapon rat-tat-tatting on the marble counter top.

"You ran first!" Chuck yelled. "And shot first too. That doesn't paint a pretty picture."

"Why, you son of a bitch!" King let out another burst of bullets in Chuck's direction, littering his coffee table and chairs with holes, cushion stuffing flying in the air.

"I'm empty, Solomon," Chuck continued between bursts of received fire. "Do you still have my Luger, buddy?"

Solomon clutched to it even harder. "Yes."

"So it was both of you then!" screamed King, letting lose a spread of fire in Solomon's direction. "You try to pin this on me and now

216

you're trying to kill me. After all, it was you two who came for me at the tower."

"I was there too, King," shouted Liliana.

"Yeah, and who came to get you, Doctor? It was these two gents!"

"You're the one with the gun, Cledwyn," said Solomon. "You're the one that wants the money. It only makes sense if it's you who sold us out."

"I was trapped in a bloody tin can, you asshole. You're the only one the voice said was still needed in here. I fixed the generators, Lily got the fingers, Chuck took down those beastly things…"

"I took down the Volksklausur, King," Solomon yelled back, a particular rage in his tone.

"And how did you know how to do that?"

"I… I figured it out."

"Bollocks. You accuse me, so it's gotta be you! You knew about the whistle, you have the receiver, you found us all, so it's you! That helpless writer routine's not foolin' me anymore. We're useless to you now, so you're trying to trick us into killing each other."

Cledwyn fired off another burst of rounds in Solomon's direction, spraying the wall behind him, bringing down a river of splinters and paint chips.

"I know it's not Solomon," Chuck yelled. "I know him. He is a writer for the *Post*. He has children and Hiroto. He cannot be the traitor."

"And who's to say I don't have children of my own? Who's to say I don't have family? We know you don't. What about you, Doctor, hiding so quietly back there with your pistol? Maybe you're not a Brazilian spy. Maybe you work for him!" Cledwyn shouted, firing wide in her direction.

Liliana kept quiet.

"Solomon, how far can you throw? Can you throw me the Luger clip from there?" asked the sergeant.

"See, see, see…you two are in cahoots against me. You're trying to kill me!" Cledwyn yelled, firing off another large spread of bullets at both Solomon and Chuck.

"What if I need it?"

"Are you really going to shoot this limey fuck?"

"You bastards, shut up, shut up, shut up!" King screamed rancorously, firing straight up at the ceiling.

Solomon dislodged his clip.

"Don't do it, Stephen!" yelled Liliana, finally breaking her silence. "What if it's him? What if it was Chuck? What do you remember from the day you got here?"

"What are you talking about? It's King. He was the first to run," shouted Chuck.

"It's not me!"

"Chuck has kept us alive all this time, Lily," Solomon reasoned. *Trust your training, not your instincts.* "What if it's you?"

"You don't mean that, Stephen," Liliana responded, raising her weapon.

"It wouldn't be the first time I was taken in by a beautiful woman." Solomon arched back to give himself space and called out to Chuck, tossing the small nine-millimeter clip across the room to his friend. Cledwyn let out with another burst of fire as if to deflect the little metal magazine. It landed a few meters from the center display table where the Texan had first taken cover.

"Stop conspiring! It's not me. I was tied up," Cledwyn pleaded. "I have the bomb in my neck!"

"We all have the bombs in our necks," Chuck shouted back, inching to the corner of his furnished emplacement, closest to the Luger clip. "We were all tied up."

Solomon exhaled and felt another coughing attack coming up. He wrapped his hands around his neck and arched backward to fight it. With a sour look, he swallowed, sending a pinch of his own blood back down inside.

"Stop your fuckin' coughing, Solomon! "King shouted. "I don't want to hear another bloody... bloody cough. I'm on my fucking vacation." Cledwyn let loose another volley of rounds in Solomon's direction.

"I wasn't tied up. I woke up in the clock tower," Seek moaned, ducking the barrage. "The voice said to go get you all. And I did. The voice said to find the bodies. And I did. It told me to fight the children, and I did."

Solomon dropped the empty pistol on the carpet and took out the hands-free receiver. He clicked it on and off, but there was no answer.

"But if I had known he was waiting here for me, I'd never have come to this island."

Cledwyn brandished his machine gun. Liliana peered from her cover, pistol in hand. Chuck lay with his legs out, ready to bolt for the ammo clip at first chance. Solomon turned and put his back against the upturned sofa, facing the corner of the hall. He gazed up at the spray of bullets in the wall above, a litter of pockmarks above him like the star-filled, night sky over San Magnus. He tapped his head against the back of the couch, took off his glasses, and wiped them down with his sleeve. Seek sighed deeply, gazing at his reflection in the small, thin frames. He put them back on, handles latched tightly over his ears, and stood.

Everyone gazed over at the corner where the unarmed Solomon walked around the safety of his fortification and strolled casually with his hands up, surrendered, to the center of the hall.

"What are you doing, buddy?" asked Chuck.

"I'm not hiding anymore." Solomon shouted for Cledwyn's attention. The Welshman redirected the end of his weapon to Solomon and steadied himself behind the counter.

"I'm the only one of us without a gun, King. And I knew about the treasure before we got here. I knew about the Nazis too. I came here to find them both. I haven't done anything for the voice that you haven't done. My conscience is just as ruined as yours. For fuck's sake, I don't care which one of you betrayed us. All I want is to open that vault and go home. I wanna go home, King. I wanna see my daughters again. Can you believe that?" Solomon kept walking and slowly dropped his hands. "I don't care if you're behind this. Don't kill us. You want me to get that vault open, I'll do it. Just let me do my job and I'll go home. I'll just go home."

Solomon hung his head and stood there for a moment, watching

Cledwyn's expression out of the corner of his eye. He waited for the man to put the weapon down on the countertop, to back up, to itch his nose or shed a tear, to change his stance in any way. Cledwyn stood unmoved, his hand shivering over the trigger guard. They stood their ground and stared at one another, Seek with his empty hands pointing outward at his hips, King gripping the stock of his rifle tightly. Solomon took a deep breath. As the Welshman began his reply, Solomon sprang to the table a few feet away and kicked the ammo clip over to Chuck. King flinched at first but let burst a round of fire at Solomon, who took it straight in the chest, his arms flailing with the force, legs giving out, and fell in on himself, shattering the flower vase as his back hit the floor.

"Stephen!" Liliana yelled from behind cover, firing off her clip wildly in Cledwyn's direction.

King ducked behind his counter just long enough for Chuck to dive on the clip tumbling across the carpet toward him. Exposed on the floor, he flicked out a round with the back of his thumb and pushed it into the top of the Glock's open breech. He pulled back on the slide and released, gathering himself in a one-knee position on the floor.

"It's not me!" King shrieked, coming back over the top to shoot at Lily.

Chuck took aim and fired. His eighty-year-old, black-encased iron slug zipped across the hall into Cledwyn's neck, passing through and splitting in tiny pieces as it exited out through the back of his head. A small splatter of red sprayed against the map of San Magnus behind him, staining its beaches with blood. Cledwyn dropped the rifle and grasped his neck, keeling over and collapsing in a heap behind the visitor's counter.

Chuck flicked another round into the breech and racked it before raising and pointing his gun over the counter. Liliana fell over her cover and scrambled over to Solomon, who lay motionless on his back by the toppled display table. Chuck doubled back to Solomon for a moment, looking down at Liliana, who dropped her pistol to the side and took Solomon's head in her hands, resting him up against her legs.

The sergeant turned and checked on King, who was bleeding out and gurgling in the cramped space behind the counter, his legs thrashing about, pushing dry snow angels in the carpeting, followed closely by a sea of blood that seeped into its fibers. He struggled to speak, his lungs filling up far faster now than ever before.

"It... It's not...me."

Chuck stood over him and watched as he squirmed from side to side, hopelessly trying to plug the leaks in his own clavicle with the tips of his fingers. The sergeant took the resting Parabellum clip out of King's pocket and walked over to clamp King's thrashing legs down to the floor with his boots. He gingerly swapped out the six remaining rounds from the old pistol mag into the new and slammed it shut. Chuck held the weapon out, smiling as if reacquainted with an old friend.

"I know," he whispered. Chuck trained his aim and fired.

Act III:

Long Live the King

Chapter XXIV

Solomon lay on the rug in the great hall of the Kapitalzukunft, squinting up at the sparkling brilliance of an antique chandelier dangling above him. His glasses had fogged up with the moisture of heavy breathing, and the shimmering crystals looked like icicles hanging from his old porch in a thick North American blizzard. He slowly remembered he was alive, an unavoidable fact accompanied by extraordinary pain. Solomon grabbed the carpet on either side of him with his hands and crawled them along like spiders, separated from his body, walking on all five fingers and kicking over bladed fragments of blue porcelain. When a prick stabbed the tips of his fingers, he dropped his head to one side and saw that he'd grasped a thorny bouquet of four-petaled white roses. A small drop of blood bubbled over his index finer as he opened his hand and slid his arm up to his chest. *Thorns on fake roses. Why would anyone put thorns on fake roses?* That was when he heard them yelling.

"Sit... I said...down!"

"They're coming...hours. You...up now...gets worse."

The ringing screech intensified as they argued. Solomon tried to plug his ears with his bleeding fingers. Then he felt his head tilt forward, suspended off the floor, and a hand pressing down on his heart. It was a small hand covered in dirt with small strips of skin peeling off along the knuckles. It was a woman's hand. Liliana sat with his head propped on her knees and her other hand under his chin as she yelled at Chuck. Chuck. Solomon tried squinting again, now at the tall, blurry man standing over his feet, pointing a gun just over his head. Licking the sides of his teeth and sorely swallowing the bitter taste of iron, Solomon coughed over his words.

"Chuck? Did you shoot me, buddy?"

"No, but he's going to," said the soft voice through the ringing behind him.

"It's a good...that vest...after all. King...to kill you."

"He was trying to kill you!" shouted Liliana.

She lifted Solomon's glasses over his head and wiped them down with her free hand, lowering her lips to his ears.

"Stephen, are you okay?"

Solomon tried to answer but couldn't compete with the threatening figure before him.

"He's fine...than I can...you, Doctor."

"You kill me...death penalty...let us live. I'll...don't beat you when you're in handcuffs."

Chuck bellowed out laughter that, under the strain of tinnitus, sounded to Solomon like a motor backfiring.

"If there was a team...them with you. You're not CIA. Salazar picked you personally... Wouldn't have made a mistake like that."

Solomon tried to hold out his hands as if to grab Chuck by the throat while lying collapsed in a heap on the floor. He shook his head from side to side before Liliana steadied him and put his glasses back on. Chuck's face came clearly into focus, and Solomon could see the grin he'd seen at the bar in Mar Del Sur, the smile he'd flashed hunting in the jungle and joking over tins of sardines by the campfire. A razor-sharp grin, as fast and deadly as the pistol he held trained between the eyes of the woman holding Solomon in her lap. The pitch in his eardrums began to cool. Seek worked his tongue around the edges of his jaw and moved it side to side, slowly regaining control of his facial muscles.

"Salazar? He's here?" Solomon squeaked.

"He's the voice," Liliana answered. "We've tracked him to this island. We've known for months."

"There's no *we*, you stupid bitch. You can drop the act. You're pretty street-smart for an egghead, but you aren't fooling me."

Solomon rolled his head backward. Above him, Liliana's stern expression turned to welcome upon meeting with the wounded man's eyes, wide and black like a dog's under a veterinarian's light.

"You knew the whole time?" whispered Solomon.

226

Liliana bit her lip and bowed her head begrudgingly. "I'm sorry I pulled a gun on you in the cellar," she explained. "I had no way of knowing who you were."

Solomon let out a strained cough and looked back over at Chuck. "When we came ashore, you hit me over the head? You stuck this thing in my neck?"

"And I've kept you alive all this time since," Chuck replied.

"And Hiroto? You killed him, didn't you?"

"It doesn't matter anymore."

"Yes, it fucking matters, Chuck!" Solomon yelled, arching forward and coughing blood onto his legs. "Oh, God," he squealed, grabbing at his side. "Shit, shit, fuck," he whimpered, clutching the spot just below his ribs. "I'm shot. Oh, fuck, I'm shot."

Liliana slid over on her knees to the wound and ripped off his white shirt. The black flak jacket was riddled in bullet holes, but when she pushed him, hollering, forward, the flattened rounds fell scattered from the vest and bounced between the bloodstains on his legs. Trying to release his tension on the spot and see the entry hole, Liliana grabbed him by the sides and pried her fingers under the vest.

"It's no good. I have to take this off."

"No," Chuck replied.

"What do you mean *no*? Stephen's shot. I need to get the—"

"I said no," Chuck demanded, inching forward with his pistol in hand. "That's the liver. He doesn't have much time left. We're not going to waste it lying here. Get him on his feet."

"He'll be dead in hours if we don't get this off!"

"And you'll be dead in seconds if you try."

Solomon reached out with his crimson-spattered hand and dropped it on Liliana's shoulder, drawing her attention from the hopelessness of shouting at a loaded gun. He shook his head slowly from side to side and motioned to stand. "If he's one of Salazar's men, he'll kill us without a second thought."

"That's right," Chuck said, his weapon tracing Liliana's forehead as she struggled alone to bring Solomon, still clutching the gut wound, to his feet. "And drop that bag, Doctor. I don't want you coming at me with a pair of scissors the minute I turn my back."

Liliana did as she was told, dropping her medical pack on the floor by the placid roses.

"Good. That's good. Now you keep living for me, all right, Solomon?" Chuck sneered, picking the hands-free receiver from Solomon's pants pocket.

"The rest of the men," he continued, pointing the device around the room at the corpses scattered about, "made a mistake. The biggest mistake. They disobeyed an order. These men served under me in war. They stormed a federal prison with me to rescue the Colonel. They left the service, their families, their country, all the things they were fighting for, to do this. They were the absolute best. But when they got here, I ordered them forward and they refused. Don't make the same mistake."

Chuck sat up on the countertop behind him and gave a quick glance at the body of Cledwyn King. The Texan let out a high-pitched whistle.

"Let's go. On your feet! You see, these men refused to go where you're going next. They knew why we came here. It was forward or nothing, because nothing is more important than this. They betrayed the cause."

"Betrayed? Funny." Solomon gaffed, propping his weight against Liliana. "Live and learn, huh, big buddy?"

"That's right. I'd have thought you'd learn something by now, Solomon. Something about chasing 'war criminals.' The first time put you away. The second time's going to put you down."

Chuck grinned again down the sight of his pistol and held the hands-free to his mouth, clicking the button.

"Colonel, Captain Foster reporting. King is eliminated. We've breached the fortress and are proceeding to the suite on schedule."

A pause. No response.

"Colonel?"

"Rapunzel, Rapunzel, come down from your tower," Solomon chuckled, holding his side in pain.

Chuck redirected his aim.

"The colonel is a brilliant man. A visionary!"

"Ha!" Solomon interrupted, helped along by Liliana to the bottom of the unblocked staircase. "A man? You have to have a conscience to be a man. He's disqualified."

Chuck leaped off the counter and walked up the stairs in front of Solomon, back-tracking and holding the gun inches from Solomon's face.

"What kind of idealist are you? One without the guts to stand up for what you spiel. You talk a big talk about all the untapped potential in people. You say it's wasted, undiscovered, because no one cares about the big picture. You have no idea who you're fighting against. The colonel is the pioneer you're looking for. He's making the changes, the advances. He's making America what it used to be, the best and the brightest, the frontier. It's the people like you, the hypocrites who don't want it and can't see it that hold us all back. He'll force it on a nation that fights him, and the nation will thank him for it."

Chuck put down the hands-free and reached around his back for the small knife he'd clipped from the butcher's shop. Holding out his gun arm still pointed at Solomon's temple, he raised the blade to his bicep and slowly ran the blunt, rusted edge across his skin, releasing a small spring of blood that trickled down from the knife and onto the carpet. His arm shivered and he bit his lower lip hard, but his aim remained straight as he tossed the knife over their heads, down the stairway. Solomon and Liliana stood motionless halfway up the incline and stared in bewilderment. As Chuck's grin began to grow, his long, open cut began to close slowly from the ends as if pulled into a vacuum slithering in his veins. His skin absorbed the wound until only a scar like a long wavy gray snake remained.

Chuck unwrapped his free hand to expose the healed wound he'd sustained the first night on the island. "We're going to be welcomed back as heroes."

Seek stared at the scars. Genetic modification, growth hormones, synthetic limbs... He had no idea. Liliana reached her arm under him to touch the closed wound, but Chuck pulled it away. "Americans only," he said.

"Operation Firelight," Solomon whispered. "This is what he was after? This is why he murdered all those people?"

"There are a lot of people on the planet." Chuck shrugged. "Most of them think nothing of the casualty report. Those numbers are too small for them. They only see politics. Do you know how many of us have died out there? For what? For sand? This isn't sand. We're going to save countless lives. None of the people we killed made a difference in this world. But this will," he concluded, looking down at his arm. "And you're about to be a part of it, whether you like it or not."

"A robbery?" snapped Liliana.

"No, not robbery!" Chuck yelled. "You think this is about money? King was a fool. We don't care about the casket. It's the knowledge, the secrets, the work that was done here, undisturbed by pathetic glory-hunting hypocrites like 'Seek' Solomon, self-described idiot crusader."

Solomon smiled, pushing forward and running his free hand over the staircase railing. Liliana, with her arm around his waist, guided him up the royal purple carpeting. Down on the floor behind the lobby counter, Solomon spotted Cledwyn's bled-out body, motionless, his hands clamped and glued to the holes in his neck by the stick of dried blood. Solomon's smile turned sour.

"You said something too, Chuck. About monsters. Monsters are the things that try to kill us. You're the monster, Chuck. You're trying to kill us."

Chapter XXV

Liliana propped Solomon against the wall at the top of the stairs. Although he was delirious and winded, his eyes never strayed far from the pistol their former compatriot held over them. "You knew those bullets would fit that gun before we even got here, didn't you?" Solomon asked.

"That's right," Chuck replied. "The nine millimeter Parabellum. The Germans shot them then, and we shoot them now. Our weapons, space shuttles, computers—they're all Nazi plunder. Soon alternative genetics will be too."

Solomon exhaled faster.

"It must have been real hard for you," Liliana interrupted, "pretending to care whether we lived or died."

"Nope." Chuck smiled. "It's in the training."

Solomon motioned to move on, and Liliana scooped her shoulder under his armpit to push him along the walls. Chuck led them from the rear as they crossed the east wing hallway, another pure, white design lined with crystal light fixtures and the occasional crookedly hung Prussian family portrait.

"Where are we going?" Solomon asked. "And where are we?"

"This is the second floor. It's a hotel, don't you see? We're dug into the mountain. There are hundreds of feet of rock between us and the surface, and beneath that about a yard of concrete and steel. Perfectly secluded, completely impenetrable."

Solomon peered into the opened rooms as they passed, but most lay barren and empty. It had been a different sight in the villas, far closer to the beaches, than in the fortress where the only bodies they'd found were American and filled with bullets rather than toxic fumes. Halfway down the wing, Solomon stopped and fell against the wall under a painted snarly likeness of a young Hermann Göring, dressed in a studded leather flight jacket. Across the hall, Solomon spotted a spiral staircase with metal rigging.

"Does that go to the tower?" he asked, nudging his head in its direction.

"You're wasting what little time you have lying there and asking questions, Solomon."

"I agree," Liliana whispered in his ear. "Please, we must hurry."

"'That where Salazar's hiding?" Solomon continued.

"He's not hiding. He's trapped." Chuck spat back.

"Like a rat." Solomon smiled. "Please, Chuck ol' buddy. I'm dying. Can't we go up and pay him a visit? He must be lonely."

"You see those things there?" Chuck pointed with his gun up at a small, black circular protrusion hanging down from the ceiling. "Those are cameras. He can see you now. He can see your last movements. Now let's not disappoint."

Chuck grabbed Solomon from the floor and pushed him up against the wall, throwing Liliana beside him.

"Would you just let me die?" Solomon pleaded. "I'm done. What do you still need me for?"

"The password, Solomon, the password!" Chuck shouted, shaking the man violently from his catharsis. "It's someplace in Metzger's villa, there, at the end of the hall."

Solomon peered down the walkway to the closed double doors. Three petrified bottles of milk rested on the carpet beside them.

"It's filled with the Haze, so thick that five minutes in there will kill you. That's five minutes in the room or five seconds out here in the hall," Chuck demanded, backing up and aiming his weapon at Solomon's squinting left eye.

"Come, I'll carry you in there," Liliana said, dragging him down the hall past the spiral staircase.

"Uh-uh, Doctor," Chuck scoffed, holding out his arm across their path and resting his gun on it, pointed at Liliana. "You're not going in there only to come out slashing a rusty old letter opener. This is why Solomon's here. That room? That's Solomon's room. If he's not out in time, then you're next."

232

"And if she's not out in time?"

"I go back to the coast and pick out a few more undesirables."

Chuck held Liliana back but let Solomon slip by, his feet slantwise, holding himself up against the faded and peeling white wall like a crutch. He went on alone, clutching at his ribs, bobbing his head to avoid the gold-colored frames along the albescent corridor. Liliana stood still with her back to the wall with Chuck's gun still pointed at her head. They watched Solomon creep along to the engraved wooden door standing defiantly at the end of the hall. When he reached it, he turned on his good foot and looked back. Liliana smiled at him, wiped her eyes, and turned to look at her armed captor. Solomon turned the door handle. A puff of violet fog slipped through the open crack of the door and flooded up through a ventilation duct behind the closest black bulb security camera. Wasting little time, Solomon took a deep breath, held it, and scurried inside, closing the door behind him.

In the room his vision quickly failed him. With one arm held out to find his way, he freed the other from his hip and covered his face with the inside of his elbow. He searched around in the thick haze and grasped at empty air. He pushed forward, but something nabbed his foot and he tripped, falling arms first on the carpet. The force of the fall pulled his breath out beneath him, and he couldn't help but let a lungful of the Haze slip through his nose. Solomon felt his insides collapsing as if caught in a fiery singularity. He rolled over on his back and grasped at the floor around him, found the wooden leg of a chair or coffee table and pulled himself over it, his organs sucking into a hole burning through his chest.

Solomon flayed about, looking for a window. As he scurried forward, away from the door, he spotted something reflecting at him through the gas. He raced over to it, dragging his bad foot along and dove, bracing his head to crash through to the cool, salty island air. Throwing his whole force into the glass, Solomon fell right through it, toppling over the mirror desk and opening a cut in his forehead. The searing pain gnawed at his insides, and Solomon flailed about on the broken desk, feeling pinpricks from broken glass over his arms and hands and the premature grip of death wrapped around his trachea.

Then a second pull, this time from without. He could feel his lungs fighting on two fronts as he breathed the toxic fumes and then again as they were blown out from his nostrils. Looking around, he made out the ceiling and then the walls, the lines on the desk and then the floor, the toppled lamp he'd tripped on, and the door. The Haze was being sucked not just from his lungs as he exhaled but from the room, through the fan in the ventilation duct opposite the hallway.

Solomon propped himself up with vigor as the room emptied of poison. He breathed deeply and coughed coarsely, spitting nearly an ounce of blood as the euphoria of oxygen took over. Taking stake of where he was, Solomon wiped his bloody hands down on his pants and moved fast. Furniture but no beds. A sofa and a mirror. A single ebony orb stared down at him from the center space on the ceiling. He'd fumbled through open doors into the living room. Dragging himself along, Solomon staggered into the adjoining room and then the next until he froze solid at the sight of the back bedroom. It was littered in neatly ordered clutter—work benches, tools, odd contraptions large and small. His attention turned to the lone skeletons lying peacefully in three separate single beds, each tucked in under a wrap of bedsheets and blankets. Solomon waved his hand over the bodies to make sure he wasn't hallucinating. Their bony arms crossed over their bodies and met, each at the waist, as if they were praying. Of their faces, he could see only the tops of their skulls and the slits of their eyes over their molded, stench-ridden covers.

Solomon circled back to the previous room and opened the last door to the master bedroom. There he found among the silk-sheeted master bed, vintage mahogany armoire, and classic wood-paneled Wurlitzer jukebox, a fourth skeleton—a much smaller skeleton huddled in a pile over itself and hanging off the chair in front of an engraved black salon desk. As he approached he noticed something shiny in the rubble of bones, something brass. Peering around the skeleton's ribcage, Solomon noticed a wooden handle.

He glanced at his watch and moved quickly, rummaging through the drawers of the desk, careful not to disturb the remains propped up yet half-collapsed in the seat beside him. He threw combs, brushes, hand mirrors, perfume bottles crashing to the floor. He quickly ran through and put aside a photo album, rummaging through tweezers, lipsticks, makeup palettes . Solomon slammed his fists down on the desk and dropped his head in his lap. He took a deep breath. When he came back up, there, sitting snugly between his fists, was a leather-bound notebook with unlined yellow paper.

July 1ˢᵗ 2025, 1250 hours

I have to make this fast. Girls, if this is my last message, I want to say that I love you very much. I hope you've taken something from this log, some piece of me that no one else could have, a reminder or a purpose or... something worth a damn. I hope you don't hate me. You know all of this has been for you. If I don't make it out of here alive, know that both your mother and I have only ever had your best interests at heart. Only she fought the fight at home when I went abroad. Maybe she was the smart one after all.

Salazar was right about one thing; I remember it now. It was at his trial, his court marshal. I'd caught parts of it from the playback after getting out. He said our position in the world is based on knowledge and that when we lose that edge we endanger ourselves. Providence bodes permanence. It seems so clear now. I've been tricked here. I didn't learn all the facts. I was blinded by my ambitions. Knowledge would have saved me. So I want you to do me a favor. Read. Read and watch and learn all that you can every second of the day, every day for the rest of your lives. Learning is what makes you great. It's what keeps us alive, curiosity and drive. Never be afraid to learn too much. I've done that now and I've no regrets.

Okay.

I've found the last journal. It's not Metzger's. Well, it's not Gerhardt's. It's his wife's; it's Mathtilda's. Inside the jacket is inscribed, *To Milly, my greatest treasure, mother of my children.* Her cursive is hard to read in places, which makes the photocopied translation sound a little funny, and the pages themselves are torn and stained, but I've made out what Salazar was unable to find. It reads more like a log than a journal. In the first few pages she explains that her husband gave her the diary right after she had given birth to their three boys. She says that Metzger, that is Gerhardt, promised "never to read or reiterate anything [she] writes in the book," and because of this she dedicated the first few sections to herself instead of her children.

Over and over she repeats herself, reliving the "golden years of beautiful Germany" where she was a performer, singer, and dancer. The organ next to me must have been something she convinced him to have shipped over along with the plundered Polish Royal casket, of which she makes no mention. In fact, almost nothing of the island besides "the feeling of ultimate enclosure" she gets from the fortress is written with any detail. Likewise, the first thing I did after scanning the notebook was run a control + F for the keywords *password* and *pass-code*. It's mentioned only once. We'll get to that.

The further in the book she writes, the fewer of her entries involve some bombed-out Teutonic country-hall or meeting with the Propaganda minister over cocktails in Berlin, and the more they begin to cover her interest, if not frustration, in her three boys. She says they are "spezielle berührte" or specially touched. She then goes on to say that her husband describes them as "autistic psychopaths" and said that he attended a lecture before the war in Vienna held by Hans Asperger, of all people, and that "the boys all displayed similar oddities. They wouldn't play with their toys, only arranging them in certain orders."

Triplets with Asperger's syndrome. What are the odds of that happening to a Nazi geneticist? Milly continues to write, less often but more detailed, sort of like a researcher. She sounds like what I imagine her husband would, who, she says, spends his time examining the kids when he's not in the lab, probing their social development, taking blood samples, and documenting their repetitive behaviors. When they turn nine she catches them playing with one of those damnable Lugers. "[She] moved to take it from them, but Gerhardt stopped [her] claiming they were in the advanced stages of 'higher learning.'" She writes about her horror at the sight of her three children dismantling the handgun and putting it back together, each of them holding their own individual pieces. By the end she says she "took the gun away and fired it up at the ceiling in their bedroom." It worked. She popped a hole in their tiling.

But the sound, she writes, "terrified the boys, and they cowered beside their beds." They had no idea what the gun did or what it was for, but they immediately knew how it worked and how it could be broken down and reassembled.

This goes on and on, so I'm scanning quickly over the pages. At eleven they dissemble the geothermal generator under the Kapitalzukunft and improve output. At thirteen they help design his vault. The night-vision goggles, their computers, their genetics equipment... Milly explains that it all came from or "through" her three small boys. "Geniuses," she says, "gentle geniuses with blonde hair and blue eyes." Gerhardt calls them "God's gift." It doesn't appear that she has any clue about his other children, his own "gifts." The Vorkämpfer hid the program from everyone, even their own wives. Milly writes, in section after section, about her reinforced belief in the Nazi ideal. Her pride in her children and their abilities seems to come from her love of purity, and she talks about them as if they were her reward for leaving the home country and staying loyal to her husband who, she writes, is the "pinnacle of the German people" with her sons being "their future."

This goes on for some time. In nineteen eighty-four, her sons where thirty-five years old. She, her husband, and the rest of the original fugitives are now in their seventies or eighties. Gerhardt has left the triplets in the engineering lab located someplace in the fortress basement. Milly is upstairs in her room. She writes that she readied a bath but slipped on the floor and hurt her leg. The boys have built for her a calling device, a pager ten years before there were pagers. When she calls them, they come marching up to her room and bring her to bed. But there is a smell to them. She's never smelled it before. She demands they take her down to the basement facility to where the smell comes from. They could hardly argue with her, and she says they carried her down to the basement. It's hard to make out exactly what she found, partly because she starts writing frantically at this point and also because her descriptions don't translate well or sound like things that make any sense. She finds things. Lots of things. Including the vault.

Then she writes that she stood outside the vault with her sons before guessing the password. It's all there. The Volksklausur, the tests, the terror. Her sons explain with "horrific enthusiasm" how they aided their father in his work. The last page is little more than scribbles. *Betrayal* is repeated six times. *Traitor* is written twice. *Monster* is even used to describe her Nazi husband, not for his crimes in Belzic, his murder of the Jews, undesirables, and developmentally challenged (like her sons), but for the mixing of races and the spawn of something "unholy." In the end she becomes religious. She makes a decision. As I walk around I can see how she carried it out. The bullet hole in her children's bedroom ceiling tile is still there. So are their bodies. They weren't shot, not like the Vogel girls. It looks like they were muffled with a pillow or blanket, one by one. They trusted their mother. Thirty-something-year-old savants, lying in their beds, each one letting the next be strangled to death by their mother.

In hindsight I know now that Metzger released the Haze on his own people just moments later. I imagine there's a correlation. The boys had names. They're written at the top of their headrests, engraved in gold lettering. These god-damned Nazis and their gold. Their bones are black and brittle, but their names are gilded. *Jan. Jens. Jonas.* Those are the names of the three unknowing boys who pioneered this hellscape. The "engineering department," as Martin Jung called them. Three boys, three names, three words in the password. My part in this heist has come to an end.

Salazar. He knew I'd come. I was the perfect patsy. Someone needs to brave the poisonous fumes. Someone needs to go on the suicide mission. His own men refused. Who would do something so stupid just to read some long-dead fascist's diary? Predictability is something I can't deny. He knew I'd come at the chance of finding another war criminal, a fugitive from justice. He dangled those words on my hook, and I couldn't stand not biting. He got two busybody little birds with one stone, Hiroto and me, revenge against the two men who exposed him in the first place. I was his ace in the hole the whole time. He's all but beaten us now.

Out in the hall Chuck waits on me with a gun in his hand. An assassin and Liliana, a government spook, waiting out there for me to crack the code to a Nazi safe and relieve it of its billions of dollars worth of stolen treasure. Trinkets, jewels and art taken by one family from another. But that's not the real treasure of this place. It's just another lure that brings poor men like Cledwyn King to a place of evil. I could no more leave this island with that bullion than I could a can of tuna. It's all tainted. That choice, however, doesn't look like mine to make. Before this place takes my life, I hope to see the real treasure one more time. It's you. It's always been you.

Chapter XXVI

As he approached the double doors leading from the suite to the hall, Solomon stared up at the little blackened camera box above. After some time, he feigned to hold his breath and venturing back, grasping the wound on his hip, toward his awaiting captor. Outside the room, Solomon exhaled deeply and inched down the side of the wall until Liliana came running to him and took his arm over her shoulder. He tried to whisper something in her ear, but Chuck closed the gap between them too quickly.

"Do you have it?" he said, his aim still, as steadily placed on Liliana as ever.

"I have it," Solomon moaned. He pulled out a small, ripped piece of paper from Mathtilda's journal, dropped it into his mouth, and swallowed it whole.

Chuck paused, and with a confused expression replied, "Okay, then. Move out."

"Move out? That's it? You're not going to beat it out of me?"

"You want to see what's in that vault more than I do. You still have time."

Solomon sighed, getting to his feet.

"What did you find in there?" Liliana asked, shuffling him back down the hall.

"Another suicide. The first one I think."

"Was it Metzger?" Chuck asked, pushing them forward with the muzzle of his pistol.

Solomon turned his neck to face the question, his body still being pushed along like luggage. "Nope. Still haven't seen him yet."

"He must be in the vault then. Come on. Pick it up."

"Why don't you point that thing at me, ol' friend? Give the back of Lily's head a break."

241

"If I wasn't worried about you in the jungle with my pistol, I'm sure as shit not worried about you now. You were in there for more than five minutes. You needn't worry about my gun. I don't need to shoot you. Either the Haze or that wound will kill you. You can't tell me you don't want to see what's in the vault before you die."

Solomon pulled Liliana back, making space for another large hack of crimson stain on the carpeting.

"I'd rather die here than rot in a federal prison the rest of my life," he murmured, wiping his mouth dry.

"Ha. I'm not doing either."

"Chuck, think for a second. You're a fugitive of justice, you and Salazar. You're not getting away. You can't sell anything you take from here. No one will buy it. The whole world is looking for you both and the treasure. There's nowhere to turn."

Chuck scoffed. "I'm constantly surprised by how little you know, Solomon. It's amazing you found us at all. My name isn't Chuck. And we're not alone. But you will be soon."

They continued down the hall of open, empty suites until they crossed over the lobby stairs. The west wing hallway was the same as the east with white-plastered walls. Just as before, the staring eyes of a dozen Nazi warmongers seared holes through their portraits at the sight of a lone Jew being carried along the corners of their fortress by a brown-skinned woman doctor. At the end of the corridor, however, the double doors were steel rather than oak, and it took a heavy kick from Chuck to push them apart. Inside, there was no Haze—no floating, purple hazard—only a long concrete ramp leading down into darkness. Chuck reached over the guardrail and pulled an old industrial tin-coated flashlight from a bucket. He held it out with his left arm and crossed his weapon hand over it.

"You've been here before?" Solomon asked.

"And I've seen what you're about to see. I'll be the first non-Nazi to step foot in that vault."

"You're joking, right?" Solomon laughed, grabbing his side. "Non-Nazi? You're more Nazi than any of the bodies we've found so far."

"You haven't found them all."

With the light, they could see their surrounding was not unlike the caves the Volksklausur had made their home. There were no tiled ceilings, no wallpaper designs or Old World portraits, just the cold, gray, man-made ramp and an array of smooth granite and low-hanging limestone above their heads, keeping them hidden from the surface. Solomon grasped the metal railing as they slowly shuffled down but slipped in places where the water from the stalactites had dripped and moistened his grip around the shedding, brown iron rail.

The gradual incline widened along with the overhead, opening into a gargantuan space before them as they neared the base, nearly two stories down from the western hallway. Solomon tapped the rail with his big knuckle and listened closely as the echo vibrated along the walls and dropped into a hole underneath them. Chuck's handheld torch shone on a cage of metal at the bottom of the slope. A massive iron-grated elevator, as big as any two-car garage, hung suspended over a blackened pit by huge metal rods and a man-sized set of pulleys sticking out from the rock face. Solomon turned around to face Chuck, who ordered him to open and step into the cage. Liliana dropped him softly in a corner inside and worked to get the lift operating. Reaching his hand through the bars, Solomon could almost touch the sides of the cave, where drips of water ran down and dropped into the black without a sound.

"You think I could have a drink, ol' buddy?" Solomon asked when Chuck entered behind them, slamming and locking the lift shut.

Chuck sent them slowly down with a button-activated winch. As the cables squeaked along the ride, he unclasped his canteen from his belt and threw it over to Liliana. She knelt beside Solomon and held it to his lips. When he'd had enough, Seek shook his head back and forth. Liliana placed her forehead on his and looked down at the blood stains on his lips.

"Stay alive, Stephen. I will get us out of this," she whispered. She could feel him shivering in her touch.

He held out his left hand and cupped her wrist. "Don't you dare," he whispered back, pointing up at the small black dome covering on the top of the elevator, staring them down.

The elevator clanked when it came to a stop. Solomon had tried counting seconds as they descended and guessed that they were now at least five stories under the surface. For all he knew, they were under the island itself, surrounded on all sides by the crashing waves of the Atlantic. Chuck pushed him out of the cage on his hands and knees and marshaled Liliana over to collect him as he closed the lift behind them. Solomon looked up from the cold, wet, granite floor. The space was cramped by comparison and not without manmade intrusions. With Liliana helping him to his feet, Solomon could hardly believe his eyes. Around them stood row upon row of cages in a wide, open darkness, a cave, a camp underground, a hell below the Earth. They continued on, scraping their feet on the granite floor and staring at the chain-link holding cells illuminated by Chuck's roaming flashlight. Although the room's odor struck him hard in the gut, dizzying his senses, Solomon could not spot a single body in any of the cages, animal, human, or otherwise.

In the center of the gap, they found a long concrete lair barred by a tall steel gate with an open hanging lock. Solomon pushed it aside and looked in at the rusted spring cots, ancient-looking machines, IV stands, bowls of dripping, murky water, and layers of torn and stained sheets within. Liliana slipped Solomon onto a chair beside an uneven metal desk and walked over to one of the beds while Solomon examined its contents. No weapons. Not even so much as a pen. But one thing did stick out to him. In a bin beside the desk lay a bundle of black metal shackles. "Oh, God," he heard coming from Liliana's direction.

"This is an Elektrocardiogram machine. And these..." she said turning to a tall device covered in knobs. "These are incubators." She ran over to a cabinet in the corner across from where they'd come in and swung its doors wide open. Solomon could see objects flying over her head in the dark. A set of syringes and clamps crashed on the rock near his feet. Chuck ran over, pistol out and up.

"I guess it's time," Captain Foster murmured under his breath.

Liliana turned around with a scalpel in her hand. "This is a hospital, Solomon," she screamed. "For pregnant women!"

"Why would they have their children down here?" he asked, trying to push himself off the chair.

Chuck took a step back from Liliana but continued his steady aim at the center of her face.

"No, don't you understand? These women gave birth to those monsters here! This is his laboratory."

"That's enough!" Chuck demanded. "It doesn't matter anymore. They're all dead."

Liliana, gasping at air, continued in hysteria. "Chuck, don't you see what he's done? He's—"

"Yes, I know! They were incubators. He put himself inside and made his science. They were undesirables, no one's. Their loss is our future."

Solomon shuffled toward Chuck, who stood with his back to the man, pistol still drawn at Liliana. Spotting the wounded man limping over to him, Chuck said, "Well then, I guess you can walk on your own. There's no more need for you then, Doctor."

"Where are all the mothers, you monster?" Liliana shouted, charging at Chuck with the scalpel in her hand. He didn't hesitate. Chuck inched back on the trigger with the sight over her left cheek but was hit from behind just as the shot rang out. Solomon, with his arms out to receive him, checked the big Texan at the waist and plowed through him, knocking him to the ground. Liliana fell, blood pouring out through the hole in her left shoulder. Chuck tried to pull the gun, but Solomon's hands went around his neck, his weak bloodstained fingers pushing into the little blue pill in the captain's throat.

Solomon drew Mathtilda's fatal brass letter opener from his sleeve and slammed it down hard on Chuck's gun hand, piercing through his palm and sending the pistol skidding under a bare metal cot. Chuck didn't scream but threw all his weight against Solomon to push him down on the floor beside him. He rolled over with the blade still stuck through his hand. Desperately grasping, Solomon tried to puncture the skin around the little blue device in Chuck's neck with his nails. With a little pinch of blood drawing down from his neck, the bigger man bit his lower lip and expelled a bloody chuckle.

"Mine's fake, Solomon!"

Chuck batted Solomon's arms away and pulled the letter opener through his own palm, letting out a bellowing scream that echoed all along the walls of the dank cave infirmary. He tossed the blade behind him and smothered Solomon's face in the blood running out from his opened fist. Solomon lay helpless, pinned to the cold granite, running red with his attacker's fluids. His eyes stared unflinchingly at Chuck's punctured hand and watched in horror as the wound slowly closed around the skin as if pulled inward by torque until only a small mark remained. Chuck looked over his knuckles and grinned his souring grin, then with both hands, he grabbed the little man's throat, squeezing until Solomon could feel the pill along his jugular push into the skin between his attacker's fingers.

"You can shoot me, stab me, and scratch me, Solomon. Salazar's serum pumps through my veins. Not training, not instinct will save you from me." Chuck laughed, crushing Solomon's windpipe.

Solomon squealed something the captain couldn't quite make out. He looked over at Solomon's side and retracted one of his bulging arms to check the bullet wound under the man's jacket. His hand came back dry, empty of blood, and enraged, he beat Solomon over the face with it.

"You weren't shot, were you, you tricky fuck? Oh, I am so looking forward to watching the last breath creep from your insides."

Solomon mouthed with his lips but couldn't sneak a syllable through Chuck's grasp.

"Still trying to talk your way out of everything, huh? Talk, talk, talk. It's no good, Solomon. Even if you die now, we'll still get the password!"

His grip tightened. Solomon's eyes rolled back in his head.

"There are only three words I want to hear out of you. Tell me what it is, and I'll let go. You can lay shackled to a bed and die on your own time while I scour the vault. Don't, and I'll kill you now. We'll get someone else, someone more cooperative, but I can promise you, we'll kill both your little girls if you don't say those words right now."

Chuck reached over with one hand and pulled out a pair of

shackles from the bin beside the desk. He dangled the cuffs over Solomon's face. "Now tell me the words I want to hear!"

Chuck lessened his grip around Solomon's throat. With what little strength remained within him, Solomon lifted his head off the floor, spitting up a pinch of blood with each syllable.

"Goodbye... big... buddy."

A hollow-point round exploded in bits out of the side of Chuck's face, taking out his left eye and splattering Solomon with mucus, blood, and brain tissue. The Glock's crackling echo deafened him, and he lay there in a trance for some time, grasping and itching at the burn around his throat, staring down at the flowing river of blood that emptied over his chest from the top of Chuck's skull. When his strength built, he pushed the body off and scurried around the floor, ears ringing, fingers sliding through unseen liquid, to grab the flashlight. He pointed it in the direction of the shot to see Liliana, blue-faced and breathing heavy, lying sideways with her cheek on the floor, pistol in her hands. Her chest beat rapidly, and in the light her wide pupils tightened. Solomon pulled himself along by the cracks in the rocky granite floor and collapsed beside her, their faces just inches apart. They lay there for a moment as their spastic exhaling synchronized. Solomon blinked and then let out a painful little chuckle. Liliana looked at him as if insulted.

"Lily, I think you need a doctor," he said, his gut shaking.

Chapter XXVII

Solomon pushed himself up and propped Liliana against a steel bed frame. Staring as if seeing a ghost, she watched him wrap a long brown bandage over her shoulder and under her armpit. The round had splintered inside her and penetrated the tendons along her upper arm. Solomon found a half-drained bottle of scotch in the desk beside the shackles and poured it over her wound, drawing her grateful ire. There was little he could do but try to stop the bleeding.

"Find a sink," she seethed in pain. Solomon circled around to one of the enclosures on the opposite wall and fidgeted with the nozzles on each industrial water bath, but none came back with more than a spit of paste-like, cruddy discharge. In his haste he ran back to a medical cabinet and grabbed a bag full of instruments, then dropped it on the bed she lay rested up against. He took out a small pair of pliers and held them to his eyes, examining them closely.

"Don't... Don't bother. It's too dark, and that's not sterile. Besides...I don't trust you wiggling those things around inside me."

Solomon smiled and dropped the little tweezers on the cot.

"Your bag. Your med bag. It's up in the lobby."

"Do you remember Martin Jung's log?" she interceded. "The one about night hunts with the children?"

Solomon slunk down on the floor beside her and put his hand on her thigh.

"Yes, I remember."

"These are what they hunted. Their own mothers."

"Yeah," Solomon sighed.

"And all of the bones in the cenotes by the beach."

"And all the bones, yes. They must have seen the Nazis pile them there. They just...continued the tradition," Solomon finished.

Liliana sighed. "So much evil. Do you think he was bluffing about your family?"

Solomon exhaled and looked over at her wound. A small line of blood trickled down over the knot he'd tied around her shoulder.

"Their men are dead. Then there was Chuck, and Salazar is trapped in here. I think we're the only ones in danger."

Solomon tried to straighten the bandages as Liliana struggled and wiggled about in pain.

"We could really use his good knots right now. The fucker." He looked over at Chuck's body. The blood and mucus membrane drained from the gaping hole in his head down into the cracks of the granite like a steady brook seeking refuge. Liliana's leg shook pitifully under his palm as she held back her laughter.

"I don't suppose he'll grow that back," she said.

"We're really up against something else. I had no idea what Salazar was really up to with Firelight. That's why I need to know," he said sternly, looking her in the eye. "What are you really?" Solomon gave up redressing her wound.

Liliana took a deep breath and pulled tight on Solomon's knot.

"I was not lying when I told you my grandmother raised us on her own. My mother, she grew up very beautiful. When she was young, she married a rich business man from the capital. I rarely ever saw him. He was always traveling. But he was my father."

Solomon listened closely, expecting the worst.

"They had me and my two brothers. Papai wanted to hand them the business, and it was my place to stay at home and help my mother. I didn't want to. I read a lot. I went to the library every day. I wanted to go to university. I wanted to be a scientist. My father, he refused and would pay for none of it. I applied anyway. But when they said I wouldn't receive any scholarships because my family was rich, I felt defeated. There was nothing I could do. Science was my dream since I was a little girl. All I ever wanted to do was learn."

"Why are you telling me this?" Solomon slipped in between her breaths.

Liliana dropped her head and tightened the grip of her bandage wrap, biting her lip as another pinch of blood seeped onto her clothes.

"Then one day a man approached me. We had all heard of such men before, pessoas desprezível, pimps, despicable men. This one was an American, and he offered me money, enough to pay an entire semester if I went to his hotel room that night. So I did. When I got there, I was expecting to be raped. I had prepared myself for it. Instead he asked me to sit in a chair and listen. He was an American agent and said that he knew all about my problems, that I was a smart girl and that the Presidente dos Estados Unidos wanted to pay for my schooling. In return all he asked was for me to meet him in his room twice a month and tell him about my professors. I only found out later that he was looking for collaborators in the country. By the end of the semester, two of my professors had been fired, and I never heard from them again. I felt terrible. When they asked again and told me they would pay for my doutorado and sponsor my fellowship, I said yes. They paid me. They questioned me. They trained me. I'm with them, Stephen. I'm CIA."

He arched back against his metal cot and blew air from his mouth like a smoking gun.

"But you're a real doctor? And all that trouble with your tenure?"

Liliana grinned through the pain. "Stupid. I am missing three years of research quota. All my time I'm not in the classroom, I'm spying on my colleagues, making reports, talking to your government. I don't have time for field work. I wanted so long to study science, to contribute, and I've sold it all away. A secret kept so well, not even Salazar found out. It's funny."

"Why is that funny?" Solomon asked, disturbed.

"They had asked me to keep watch for him. They thought he might flee to South America and hide in one of our universities. When he reached out to me, I showed them, and they knew immediately it was him. But his message made no sense. I was to come to an island that didn't exist. I didn't come alone. No doubt the agents who came with me are buried someplace in the jungle. They were dressed as researchers. They were so good that even after that bastard there killed them, he still didn't know who we were."

"But he got the jump on us anyway."

251

"Yes, well," Liliana said, cupping her wound as she pressed herself back and up onto the cot. She picked up the pistol lying on its springs and discharged the clip, checking its capacity. "And now I am going to wait here and get the jump on the other one when he comes down."

"What, are you nuts?" Solomon gaffed. "You're shot up! And he has the detonator for these *things* in our necks."

"You go into the vault," she said, undaunted, "and I will wait here in the dark. He won't know to kill us, and before he crosses here—" She drew an imaginary line with her finger across the floor. "—he'll be dead".

"No, no, that's not the smart play," spat Solomon. "The elevator is rigged with a camera. There's no way of telling if there are more along the walls of this cave out there in the dark. At the very least he knows we're down here. He'll be wary of a trap."

"And if I go back up," she said, feeling over the hole in her shoulder, "he'll know he has you alone down here."

"It doesn't matter!" Solomon yelled. "You could die. You're bleeding bad. You have to go back up and get that bag. The suite at the end of the hall has a mirror. There's no Haze in that room anymore. I want you to go. Go and patch yourself up."

"I haven't finished the job yet, Solomon."

"Yes, you have," he responded, leaning in with the flashlight between them, pointing up at the cave ceiling. He brought his hand to her chin and scratched off an illuminated bloodstain from her cheek. "Your job wasn't to kill Salazar. Your job was to save me."

Liliana put her open hand on his wrist and inched forward on the cot in the dank, odorous laboratory cave, her lips closing the gap with his.

"Thank you, by the way, for saving me," he whispered.

"You're welcome." She pressed her mouth slantwise against his, sucking in his lower lip, caught like a meaty morsel between her teeth.

"Hmm, you taste like lung, Mr. 'Seek' Solomon," she moaned in between kisses.

"Nah, you just think that 'cause you're in shock, Ms. Ferreira."

Liliana wrapped her arms around his waist as they kissed.

252

Solomon fought the urge to place his hand on her shoulder. He closed his eyes and imagined her as she'd stood naked in front of the mirror of the camp barracks, the imprinted lines running down her back from where her bra had pulled too hard against her skin, the curvature of her hips and the smoothness of her tiny navel. When he'd opened his eyes he saw her staring into his, her face covered in dirt and blood, only wiped away by the stain of sweat dropping from her brow and rolling down her nose and across her cheeks. He kissed her even harder.

"If—you—want me—to leave for—the bag—you're doing a—bad job of—convincing me."

Solomon pulled away with a great big grin on his face. "Sorry. I've been in prison for a while."

He moved in to kiss her again, but she pulled back, tilting her head, and put her hand over his mouth.

"Right," said Solomon, getting back to his feet. He looked around the room and spotted an IV stand beside a bed on the far side of the enclosure. "Is there really a team coming?" he asked. "Or was that just talk?"

Liliana sat on the edge of the metal cot, tapping her feet wildly on the floor, massaging her wounded right arm and mouthing the word *wow* as soon as Solomon had turned his back. "They should get here soon."

"God, I hope they bring sandwiches."

"But it's no good if they can't get into the fortress."

"Where are the…DNA fingers?" Solomon asked, nauseated.

Liliana dropped her head back and sighed. "In the bag."

"Fuck," Solomon exclaimed, pulling the rivets in the stand apart and slipping out the top rod. "Should have put a sign on the door."

"Forget about the door and the team, Stephen. I'll take him out myself," she said, hissing in pain as she struggled to lift her gun arm.

Solomon wheeled the half-length IV stand over to her and propped it under her.

"No. I want you to promise me you won't approach him. Promise me." Solomon put his hands on Liliana's knees and stared her straight in the face, shaking his head back and forth.

"I know him, and I know how to get him. You saved my life. Let me save yours."

Liliana sighed and looked down at her lap. She took his hands in hers and ran her fingers down the lines of his palms.

"I—" she stuttered. "I think my bandages are coming loose."

Solomon smirked, sitting up on the bed behind her and putting the final tugs on her bandages.

"Salazar is mine to handle."

"Then at least take this," she replied, shoving Chuck's Glock over her shoulder at him.

"I'm not going to shoot him."

"You're so sure?"

Solomon knelt behind her on the cot for a moment and let his eyes wander. He looked down at Chuck's body for the last time and took Liliana's wrist in his hand. She felt a cold metal chain dangling down her arm. Solomon took her pistol in his other hand. He stared at the two objects. Both black. Both cold. The first, old, rusted, and burnt-smelling iron shackles. He thought long about how they'd been used by Metzger and the others, chaining the poor working women of the coastal villages, women like he'd seen serving drinks at the Vista de Balcarce social club, women like Liliana's widowed grandmother, and his own grandmother. In the other open palm he balanced the pistol, daring not to close his fingers around its lightweight, glossed grip. It was the weapon Salazar's men had brought with them to the island. The weapon Chuck had pulled on him. When she turned around, Liliana saw Solomon leaning over behind her, holding the shackles out in both hands as if cuffed. The handgun sat on the cot by her hip.

"Take the gun," he said. "If Salazar comes for you on his way to me, it'll be your last bargaining chip."

Solomon helped Liliana to her feet and with his makeshift wheeled crutch, walked with her to the elevator shaft they had descended from. She felt along his fingers as he closed and locked the gate. Grasping to the door for stability, she grinned and kissed him through the metal links. Solomon pulled away very slowly, savoring the taste for as long as his mouth, still battling the taste of iron from his lungs, would harbor it.

"Wait. The vault."

"You're afraid I'm going to sneak all the treasure out from under your nose?" Solomon scoffed.

"At the camp, you asked me what I would do with the research when we found it, and I told you I didn't know."

"And now?" Solomon replied, his hand over hers through the space in the bars.

"I still don't know. But I'm not the one going into the vault. What are you going to do down there? What are you really hoping to find?"

Solomon opened his mouth but answered with only a sigh. He licked his lips and bit on the edge of his tongue, still looking Liliana in her big, green eyes. Then he shrugged, holding out the electric panel and pressed hard on the little red button, sending the shaft steadily upward with a solemn creek. His eyes traced Liliana rising above him, her lips quivering for a reply until finally the light of her eyes disappeared into the black of the cave, and all he could make out were the dangling chains clinging against the sides of the dripping granite walls.

Then it came to him. Solomon ducked his head into the gap and shouted up at the clanking cage as it escaped above. "Providence!"

Chapter XXVIII

Solomon stood like an ant in front of the fifteen-foot-tall, stainless steel and reinforced concrete vault door that blocked his way. The behemoth obstruction was surrounded on all sides by massive slabs of the inner cave wall, laced in row upon row of carbon steel rebar. There would be no digging or blasting through. He held the hands-free device, covered in dry, splattered blood, in his right hand and gripped the bulky antique flashlight in his left with his pack, containing his tablet and the rusted black shackles hanging from its opened flap, wrapped over his back. He eyed the bolts and rods protruding along the edges of the great metallic ellipse and sighed deeply, thinking about home and his dear friend Hiroto. Putting his open palm to the door, he found it freezing to the touch as if guarding a glacier within. Gazing upward around its walls, his eyes stopped on another familiar sight, a small black dome sticking out from the side of the cave wall just above the vault door, wiring embedded into the rock itself.

Solomon stared into the camera for some time, cleaning his glasses and pushing his shirt into his trousers, and approached the small tin terminal extending from the fixture beside the vault. Gently dusting off its screen, he woke the terminal, which extended its keyboard much the same way as the door of the Kapitalzukunft had. Flashing in white lettering and above three distinct space marks read the word *Paßwort*. Solomon placed his fingers on the keypad without hesitation, entering the words *Jan*, *Jens*, and *Jonas*. He tapped the enter key and took a step back. The machine flickered for a moment before the tallied letters displaying a bright light show of characters and numerals until finally going black. *Willkommen Vater*, it blinked again in white before retracting the keyboard. The gigantic vault door creaked as its bolts shot back from the massive rotary piston chamber surrounding the steel bulkhead. When the last of the bolts had fallen, the door slowly revolved like a colossal six-ton gear, rolling to its side with a heavy hiss, spouting cold air through its cracks.

Solomon wiped down his glasses of the icy mist. When he opened his eyes, the vault door stood open, standing astride the huge gap in the rock face. He raised his flashlight and pointed it inside, strafing the walls of the steely interior. With the vault exposed, its frozen draft overtook him, and Solomon found himself shaking and tugging at the ends of his sleeves. He looked back for a moment at the rows of man-sized cages along the sides of the cave before pushing forward into the gap.

Walking along the walls of the subterranean tundra, Solomon quickly ran his hands up and down his body for warmth. Sheets of ice lathered the rock face, dripping little puddles of water on his feet as he passed. His heavy breaths stuck in the air like flies in a web, and he pulled tighter on the ends of his threads, shivering as he went. The path curved away from the vault door, left and then right, a cramped, frozen arctic path like a snake trying to shake him off its trail. Near the end of the path was darkness, guarded by another camera staring down at him from the ceiling. It spoke.

"Tell me, what have you come here for?" echoed a heavy-toned gloom from on high.

Solomon, startled, took a step back and looked up, exhaling deeply into his frigid, bare hands.

"For you, Salazar. I've come for you," he shouted up at the little dark bubble.

"Salazar?" it replied. "You mean the robber? He cannot see you in here."

Perplexed, Solomon continued forward in the black, his footsteps drawing a new clanking sound as he trod through the frost. He zigzagged the flashlight over his path, revealing concrete flooring covered in metal grating.

"You're an American?" the voice boomed again. "An American who's come for another American, only to be betrayed by a yet another? The world has changed little, then. Are you the only ones left? Is the planet your America now?"

258

Stepping into the clearing, Solomon found his flashlight useless as a blindingly bright light flashed in the chasm. He dropped the torch on the floor and fought to cover his eyes. Desperate to see, to gaze upon the discovery that had nearly claimed his life so many times, Solomon strained to peer through the cracks between his fingers. The vault was a laboratory, ten times the size of any he'd yet uncovered, and was littered in foreign apparatuses, indistinguishable by their age and the blankets of ice and frost that had grown over them. Even the grating at his feet lay dotted in tiny snowflakes. In the center space lay a metal platform suspended above the cave bed with rows of metal stairs on all sides. Solomon squinted but saw no more watchful black lenses. He wiped down his glasses to make out the tall, rectangular shape standing upright in the middle of the chasm.

"What do you mean? What are you talking about?" he said, searching for life or movement in the room.

"Americans only ever care about Americans. This is why I've allowed you here."

"Allowed me?" Solomon replied, creeping slowly into the space toward the towering shape. Through the mist he could make out petrified wood and gold handles on its sides. "You pumped the Haze out of the suite? Not Salazar? Who are you?"

"Who am I?" the voice bellowed. "Hubris of your kind! He has discovered my secret island, survived the wrath of my children, broken into my impenetrable fortress and unlocked my deepest sanctum, and he knows not who I am? He mistakes me for a thief in my own house!"

Solomon froze, his boots digging together in the frost-covered concrete as the shape rose upon high, suspended on metal struts, and turned solemnly to face him. As it neared he could see its unmistakable engravings, the rich hue in its borders and the strength in its robotic pallbearers. Inside he saw not stacks of gold, silver cutlery, gems, and treasure but a corpse wrapped in robes and cut away at the waist, just a torso, frozen and alone. A frayed white beard hung half a meter from its chin, and its face lay burdened with frost burns where the skin had long since peeled away. It lay upright in the coffin, bare and withered, its arms latched behind or missing all together. It shook the standing hairs on Solomon's arms when it spoke with stentorian ferocity.

"Has the world no longer a harbor in which to rest my name?" it said, a jagged tongue reaching around to lick the freeze-dried cracks along its shriveled lips.

"Metzger?" Solomon muttered, pulling his hands away from his mouth. He stepped a little closer and spotted latches, tubes, and grapples along the inside of the casket, puncturing through its faded velvet walls and holding the body in place. "There's no way. You can't be alive. Salazar said there was no way you could be alive."

"And what does a thief know of science that he has to come and steal it?"

Solomon couldn't look away. His feet propelled him closer, up the steps of the metal incline on which the casket stood. He stared at the face, more composed and alive than Vogel's or Martin Jung's, not complacent or embalmed in the rage of a thousand chemicals. The scar, the long curved stab he'd seen displayed with such pride in the pictures online, ran from its wrinkled neckline to the patches of frost-simmered skin on its cheek. As he eyed the ancient wound carved into the face of the "Butcher of Belzic" with such vigor and rebellion over eighty years before, Solomon could make out a movement in its brow. Metzger winked at him.

"I have introduced myself…" Metzger continued, his lips barely parting, in a voice Solomon found bland and absent of Austrian accent or dialect. "It is only polite to return in kind."

Solomon shook his head. Responding on pure instinct, his eyes were unflinching in their stare.

"My name is Seek Solomon. I'm a journalist from the United States."

"Seek Solomon? What an odd name for an American. What is it you 'seek,' Mr. Solomon? Have you come to take your robber from my island? I'd say I was quite thankful were it not for the explosive in your neck."

Solomon slid his hand back along his neckline, warming the skin along the lump in his throat as if just reminded of its danger. He looked down at his hands, riddled in little droplets of his own dried blood.

"No. No, I came here for you, Gerhardt. For you and the rest of the Vorkämpfer."

"Having a hard time making up your mind as to which? The American or me? No matter. How are my pioneer compatriots? I admit it has been decades since we've spoken."

"They're all dead. And their families. From your virus or your creatures. Or themselves."

"Oh, it's not a virus," Metzger gloated. "They're much deadlier than that."

"They?"

"Synthesized micro-organisms. Like tiny little lice, they feed and feed until there's nothing of your bronchiole remaining. The little beasts were Ebersbach's creation. Ironic, if they killed him. It's the gas they're secreted in at which one should marvel. Completely self-sustaining, nutrition-filled and dense enough for them to become airborne. They can live for nearly a century on V12. The V stands for vitamin."

"Vitamins, V12, micro-organisms... The fuck? It's a plague! And you're proud?"

"Wouldn't you be? I'm a scientist. You're a journalist. I'm certain you've felt pride in your work. What do you report on?"

"War Criminals."

Solomon, still shaking from cold, blood loss, and now the shock of witnessing a dead man speak, slid his pack around his shoulder and retrieved the black shackles. He dangled them ever so slowly back and forth at knee level.

"Are those for me?" Metzger asked sardonically.

"Something tells me you'll die if I try to put them on you."

"One of us would. Do you really think I am without defenses here?"

Solomon just stood for a moment, staring at the pale gray complexion on the man in the casket.

"Where are the Polish jewels?"

"That's not the question you want to ask me."

261

Solomon sighed. "What's wrong with you? Why have you done this? All of it?"

Metzger's coffin rattled as its robotic struts walked to the side of the platform to reveal a large, torn, frosty leather sofa behind it. Solomon cautiously ascended the top of the stairs and approached, keeping an eye on the broken and shriveled body of Dr. Metzger. At the top of the platform the journalist found yet another skeleton, the last skeleton, lying on the floor beside the couch. It was a massive frame of bones, still mostly intact, with a skull like he'd never seen before. It had massive eye slits on either side of its face and wide, low-hanging fangs from the top of its jaw.

"Her name was Hera," Metzger said. "My only daughter. You want to know what became of the jewels? They're here, in her marrow, her DNA, in the walls of this place. Gone. Spent. For the sake of the species."

"So what's left?" Solomon demanded. "The secrets of your research, packed away in those snow-covered contraptions?"

"No, packed away here, within me, safe from the likes of you and your friend."

"From me? He's after your work, not me." Solomon yelled at the casket. "I... I'm not sure..."

"You're not sure what to do now that you've found me...right where you wanted to put me? In my coffin?"

Solomon looked away rather than respond. He bent down next to the skeleton and found two pairs of chains, like the links he carried in his pack, extending from steel grips in the platform and wrapped tightly around the creature's skeletal ankles.

"She was the reason. The beginning of a new humanity," Metzger explained. "A rebirth of our species. My second chance."

"Your wife found her that day, didn't she? Chained here, waiting for you," Solomon replied, sensing an ocean of sorrow beneath the sunken eyelids of Metzger, the animate cadaver suspended before him. "She saw all the empty beds and cages and this, the 'final product'?"

"That's right. Milly... She was the most beautiful flower in all Europe. But a flower is just a flower, conceited and without purpose.

Her pride was in her skin, her race, in the ambitions of a dead man, another flower. She was too stubborn. We must pick the flowers, Mr. Solomon. They are pretty little weeds and accomplish nothing. We must pry them from the Earth."

"She was just a Nazi, Doctor. And so were you."

"Yes, that's right. But am I now? You've been close enough to my creations to steal their genetic code, which means you've either talked to them or you've spilled their blood. Either way, you know how truly intelligent they are and how futile it is to oppose them."

"They're vampires. Nighttime only. Stolen from mothers you had them murder!"

"Yes, I know!" The body shook. Solomon realized it wasn't Metzger who boomed so loudly, but the speakers lying around the lab, brought to life by the small microphone resting on the inside of the casket. There was no way of knowing what other tricks lay buried in its twisted, royal purple covers.

"But next time," Metzger continued, "I will correct this. The cornea layering, the thickness in the lens. I know how it's to be done. I only ne—"

"There's no next time for you, monster!" Solomon yelled, point-blank in his face. "You've lived far longer than you deserve. Far longer than what's right. Far longer than the hundreds, thousands of your victims and of your victims' children."

Metzger's casket pulled back on the platform to allow the most amount of space between the two men.

"You're a Jew, yes, Mr. Solomon?"

"Yes, that's right. I am. My grandparents were at Dachau. My grandparents and the grandparents of a million others who haven't forgotten your name."

"But I was not at Dachau, Mr. Solomon. Nor Auschwitz nor Majdanek. Nor the camps of your nation where they sent the Redmen first and then the Filipino, the Japanese, and eventually the German. Have there been no more of these camps in your world since I left it? What kind of man is your Salazar?"

"Like you. He buries his guilt in rhetoric and numbers. But my nation does not support his kind. He is on the run, like you, and we do not…murder…"

"No? Well, neither do you find results. You've been so complacent that one of your own has broken your precious rules and been forced to find me, the last of the Reich's scientists not stolen away by the Americans or the Soviets."

"The Soviet Union is long gone," Solomon retorted, rubbing his arms and hands, feeling the crisp, icy cool fighting his elevated heart rate.

"Then it's only a matter of time before the American Union does the same."

"Forget about politics. What is so wrong with *people* that you've tried so long to replace us?"

Metzger made a grunting sound at first, which sent a chill up Solomon's spine and a gag in his throat. He fought hard not to spit up blood in the presence of the man, the thing, responsible for it.

"You already know the answer to that question. You've seen what people do. What I've done. You've done those things to get this far. I've seen you," the doctor said. "Murder, trickery, lies. And this on the world scale. Our species has not evolved to meet our demands. We are not moral. We do not look out for one another. We kill for scraps and ideas while the planet shrinks around us. When we run out of land to live on, will we develop gills? The world is so preoccupied with what remains to be burned that no one thinks to stop and invent a new kind of flame. And worst, our genes are unnecessary. The most dominant and impressive traits in our code have long been turned off. They cannot so simply be turned back on. Our species will not survive what's to come."

"And what's that?" Solomon asked, inching forward.

"Nothing. Apathy. We lack a challenge. We lack a purpose. All frontiers have been exhausted, first exploration, then politics. There is nothing left. Soon there will be no grain of sand without a body, no drop of water without an arid tongue. The fight will continue but for hunger, for thirst, not for flags. Humans as they are will not travel space. They will not colonize and make the next great discoveries. They will not escape Earth. They are not the future."

"What do you know about the future of humanity? You've been trapped down here for forty years, and you know nothing of humanity!"

"Has it really changed so much? I was sixty-seven years old when your Armstrong and Aldrin took their first steps on our moon. I watched it from this very room. I am one hundred and twenty-three years old. How much further have you gotten? Have the cancers been cured? My children are immune. Has the threat of nuclear weapons been eliminated? My children have no need of them. Have the finite sources of energy been replaced? Have all the camps, the Belzics of our past, been closed? I believe I can do better. No flags. No committees. No wars. No bickering or dissent. Only consensus. Only achievement. Only science. I will make a new humanity, tune the planet into a new frequency. Did you not wonder why your little device won't work in my fortress?"

Solomon dug his hand into his pocket and pulled out the hands-free receiver, looking down to see it slowly accumulating frost in his open hand.

"The Volksklausur, my children, they can see the waves that surround us. Their violet is ultraviolet, their red is infrared. They can see the radiation we release into the air, the radio waves we bounce off the surface all over the globe. And so can I. I've tampered with your connection. I've kept your thief trapped beyond a wall of my V12 toxin. I am holding all the answers. No matter how much you may hate me, Mr. Solomon, I'm the only chance you have of escaping this island alive."

Chapter XXIX

"Why should I make a deal with you?" Solomon snapped.

"Because you're not stupid, Mr. Solomon, despite your incessant drive for rhetorical questions. The explosive in your neck. Did you think your Salazar brought it *to* my island? He found them in my lab, where you found those shackles. They're one of the Vorkämpfer's many achievements. Frequency, you see. I became fascinated with frequencies, seeing them through Hera's beautiful eyes, bending them to my will."

"You're not an engineer," replied Solomon. "You're a geneticist. These aren't your inventions," he continued, massaging the spot on his throat with his freezing fingertips. "Like the night-vision goggles. Or this chamber, your labs, your equipment, your computers. They're your sons' inventions."

Metzger didn't respond. Solomon searched the emptiness of his eyes for a response but could find no emotion, no movement, no response. Only silence.

"Your murdered sons," he continued. "Killed by a harmless, pretty little flower."

The casket rose again and rotated away from Solomon. He could hear gears at work and on the wall across from him he saw a light flicker and fill a ten-meter-wide screen protruding from the cave interior. Through its feed came the blur of the ceiling-mounted cameras, a dozen or so small boxes displaying the lifelessness of the Kapitalzukunft, from its lobby riddled with bodies to the dank elevator cage which had brought him below. Solomon trod down the steps past Metzger and took a closer look. There, on the top right corner of the screen, he saw a man, old and feeble, pulling fungus from a box full of dirt in the center of a small, cluttered space. He was tall, hunched over the little garden and pulling with all his might. Almost none of his hair remained, but the face was undeniable. It was the face Solomon had seen on the inside of his eyelids night after night for two years. As the feed came through in black and white, he wondered if Salazar had truly become so pale, the desert sun of the east having forgotten him like so many grains of sand whisked away by the wind.

"She is not just a harmless little flower," Metzger's monotone pitch spoke from behind him. Solomon turned. Metzger stared at a plot on the bottom of the screen. In it, a dark-haired woman sat at in front of a mirror. Bloody rags and shell fragments lay on the desk in front of her, where she worked with a needle and string in her hand, stitching up a wound in her right shoulder. A pile of bones lay riddled on the carpet by the bed behind her.

"She is not a part of my plans. Should I release the toxin back into the room?"

"What is it you want, Doctor?"

"I want what you want, Mr. Solomon. Redemption and a second chance."

Solomon stared down at Liliana through the view screen, watching the lines in her face crumple up with every passing of the needle through her flesh. He sighed.

"You're beyond redemption," he said, fighting the urge to reach out and touch the glass.

"Then one more death won't trouble my conscience."

Solomon turned. "What must I do?"

"Unplug me."

"Unplug you?" Solomon said, charging back up the platform. "Kill you? What kind of trick is that?"

"It's not a trick. This body is only a vessel, one without time in its favor. It is nourished and frozen by my machines, but they will not last forever. Everything decays in time. My body is dying, but I may live. As you said, I've been trapped down here for forty years, away from people, away from the world. In all that time, I've studied. I've listened to the frequencies. Our minds are little more than frequencies, Mr. Solomon. The firing of our synapses and pulsing of electricity through our brains is a song, a choreographed wave that I can transmit to any beacon I desire. I will become this, escape this body, leave this cave, this island that's been my prison for far too long. You see, as long as this station remains active, as long as my body lives, I am trapped. I am trapped just as you are trapped. Free us. All you have to do is kill a monster. I cannot do it myself."

"And if I do, you'll transmit from here and escape? To where? The whole world will become your Belzic."

"And if you do not, you will freeze to death down here or bleed to death up there. Do this. It is the only way. Do this and I will deactivate your fuse and unlock all the doors between here and the surface."

"What of Salazar?"

"He has shut down the tower and cannot be touched but it matters none. He has less time to live up there picking mushrooms than I do down here in this coffin."

"Let him out. Deactivate the fuse. Turn off the Haze. I'm taking him back to the States."

"You will release me?"

Solomon paused. He strode back to the monitor and gazed at the thin, weak old man gnawing on the edges of a raw, dirt-covered fungi, and then down to the pain-stricken woman rolling new bandages over her tightly sewn wound. He felt another cough bellowing up inside him and could not fight it through the cold. A mouthful of blood erupted from him, steaming on the floor beside the screen. He reached out his hand to the glass to balance himself, spitting out a long, sticky strand of red-coated saliva as it froze immediately, leaving a crimson stain on the white granite floor. Solomon picked himself back up. His hand slid down the glass pane, leaving a long streak of blood over Liliana's face in the screen.

"Yes," he muttered, turning back to the platform. As he looked up at Metzger's face, he felt a small vibration in his neck, just as he had in the plaza so many nights and days before. Then it stopped. Solomon grabbed at the lump, feeling no change in density and took off running to a tall, ice-covered machine in a corner of the chamber. He brushed aside the frost with his hands and turned his neck to face its clear, icy reflection. The bomb remained, with his veins around it still drawing a bright hue, but the tiny blue light in the center, the little insignia of his doom, had dissipated and shone no more. Solomon ran back over to the monitor and wiped his blood down from Liliana's screen. She, too, itched at the lump in her neck and held it to the mirror, staring at the empty spot where the light had poured through.

"We had a deal," murmured the voice through the chasm. "The door, the vents... All will power down once this terminal is deactivated."

Solomon nodded and walked back up the platform. "Where are you going to go?"

"Away. And far."

"You know I'll find you."

"I'll expect you to look but how will you search for something you cannot see? Do not expect to succeed."

"How can you accomplish something you cannot understand? I'll find you long before you know that word, *humanity*."

Solomon looked down at the thick, winding cord running along and down the steps of the platform from the base of the Polish Royal Casket. He propped his foot over it, just a few inches from the port where it ran through and powered Metzger's life-support machines.

"Your sons," Solomon continued. "You loved them very much."

"Yes," Metzger responded with a solemn hiss.

"Why did you release the toxin? Why did you kill all those people, your friends, your countrymen?"

"Do you have children, Mr. Solomon?"

"Yes, I do."

"When you've lost your children, Mr. Solomon, perhaps you'll understand."

Solomon stared into the man's face. Metzger's black, round eyes dropped into the pits of skin under them, looking down at the cord under Solomon's feet. He did as he promised. Bending down and grasping the frozen metal end of the wires, he pulled hard and ripped them from the casket. As they came undone, a great blue flash of light spit forth from the casket. Solomon could feel the electric shock reverberate through his fingers. A sonic pop echoed throughout the cave and vanished. Solomon looked up. What little expression in the face of Gerhardt Metzger had remained, now fled as his vessel gave in to the long, unrelenting pull of death. Solomon eyed the body, the lining of the grave up close and the engraving on its insides. He took out his tablet to translate. It read, as expected, *Polish mementos assembled, 1800 by Izabela Czartoryska*. He had indeed found the stolen treasure of San Magnus Island.

Turning and plopping down on the flaky sofa cushion, Solomon rubbed the hands-free in the palm of his hand and watched the fog of his breath squeeze through his teeth and float up to the cave ceiling. He clasped the receiver to his ear and pressed *call*.

"We're here. I have the password, and we're at the vault. Are you coming down?"

Solomon looked over at the big screen still displaying its numerous camera feeds. In the top right corner, the old man sitting at the window, looking through a small telescope down on the island, raised his head and looked over at a small HAM radio set on the table beside him. His walk was stunted and languid, and when he reached for the transceiver, he fumbled with it in anticipation.

"What's taken so long?" snapped the high-pitched voice scrambler.

"There was a problem. Liliana and King turned on us. We had to kill them both. It's just the two of us now."

Solomon watched from his relaxed position on the frozen sofa as the old man turned, transceiver in hand, and stared at him through the black glass of the tower security feed. The lines on his face ran deep, and his eyes opened wildly as if piercing the screen to see Solomon sitting in the bottom of the vault and looking back at him. Salazar smiled as though he expected something grand and held the device up to his mouth.

"Not for long," he said, dropping the transceiver and letting it swing behind him and drag along the floor, his desperate stare still cemented to the camera lens.

Solomon smiled and took the hands-free off his ear, pressing it to his lips as if forced. "What do you... Chuck, buddy, what are you... No!" he shouted into the receiver, following his enacted squeals with a little heavy gurgling. He dropped the device on the metal platform and, with a great, wide grin, quickly stomped it to pieces.

In the feed, Salazar scrambled to pick the transceiver back up off the floor, arching and holding his back in pain as he did so. "Captain, captain. Come in, Captain Foster." He waited for a moment and then threw the radio over, lurching over to a hatch in the floor. Solomon watched closely as Salazar upturned the hatch gingerly, ducking to the side in preparation of an influx cloud of toxin rising from within. But the air was clean. Salazar looked down the shaft, and Solomon could see his scrawny torso inhaling deeply.

As the Colonel reached down and grabbed onto a rail, followed closely by his legs in precarious descent, Solomon redirected his attention down to the skeleton chained to the platform. He bent forward on the floor over it, looking into the eye holes along the sides of its skull, the small slits of the nose and ears, the pointed cranium and collapsed jawline. It was human, certainly, but a new kind of human. He reached around and pulled one of its arms around from under the sofa, running his finger down the length of its massive, claw-like fingernails.

Chapter XXX

Salazar pulled the tiny detonator from his pocket as he descended from the final rung of his climb into the east wing of the Kapitalzukunft. Squinting heartily to adjust his eyes, he looked about and tried to remember the scenery he hadn't seen in nearly a year. He looked down the hallway behind him toward the double doors leading to Metzger's suite and regained his bearings, starting his trek down the opposite direction. Without giving much of a look to the lobby floor below, he continued to push his feeble legs as fast as they'd take him down the west wing, down into the great darkness of the chasm toward the cage elevator. At the top of the ramp he reached around and pulled the last of the flashlights from the bin along the side, shifting his feet gently down the walk and grasping hard onto the wet metal handrails.

Frantically searching with his electric torch over the cave walls, checking for dangers, he finally made his way to the elevator shaft, waiting for him at the top of the flight. Nodding and smiling at the convenience, he stepped in and lowered himself into the depths where the stench of the human cages grew beneath. With anxiety and delight he paced back and forth in the shaft, running his worn and wrinkled fingers over the bars like a caged animal until it finally halted at the bottom of the gap. Detonator still tight in hand, he passed through the morose maternity ward, careful to spot for traps or an ambush around every corner, shining his light at the crevasses and under beds until he deemed it safe to continue. The massive vault door, that stainless steel beast he'd seen in countless dreams, lay ajar, rolled aside from the icy gap into which he stood and stared. He rolled his hands over his arms and chest.

The chill came as a surprise, and at the precipice of the opened sepulcher Salazar stood frozen, daring not to continue on. He shined the flashlight along the inner walls, a cramped space compared to the outer cave, running with icicles and drips of cold water. Salazar licked his lips at the sight and found new motivation to delve inside.

"Captain?" he called out, his natural weak and raspy voice echoing along the halls of the vault. "Captain?" He received no reply. Looking back around, shaking the spotlight at the absence of people, he made a mad dash to a spot just inside the vault where the clear water ran most freely down the sides of the frost-riddled cave wall. He dropped the flashlight and the detonator beside him, cupped the little spring in his palms, and funneled it down into his mouth. Salazar drank and drank until his teeth stung from the cold and his stomach felt full to bursting with the clear, cool water. Exhaling with great relief, he grasped the flashlight yet again. Turning it inward to the sanctum of the vault, he spotted the shadow of two legs standing several meters away. The figure moved forward and, to Salazar's horror, revealed not the tall, muscular outline of Captain Foster, but the scrawny, shaking, limping and half-crippled Seek Solomon.

"Hello, Sally," Solomon said, a gruff insolence in his voice. "Having a nice vacation?"

Salazar scrambled with his hands on the icy floor to push himself back against the wall. Solomon, turning on his own flashlight to reveal the great, wide grin on his face, pointed the ray at the detonator lying beside his opponent's feet. Following the illuminated trail, Salazar ducked, feeling a crack run through his spine, grabbed the detonator, and then struggled on the floor to prop himself back against the wall.

"You don't look so good, Sally. Would you like me to help you?" Solomon snickered, walking closer.

"You stay back, Solomon," Salazar yelled, his finger hovering over the button. "Where's Captain Foster?"

"Around. I pulled most of him into a ditch back out through there, but you walked over some of him on your way in."

Salazar sighed deeply and ran his index finger along the side of the detonator, which was slowly accumulating a light layer of frost on its shiny metal exterior. "He was a good man. And a great American."

"That makes sense," Solomon replied sarcastically, slowly inching forward, one hand on the flashlight fixed on Salazar and the other resting soundly in his front pocket. "He said the same thing about you.

274

The question is, which one of you was more full of shit?"

Salazar held up the detonator between the two beams of light stabbing into one another. "What's back there?"

"Oh," Solomon retorted nonchalantly, continuing his stroll, "just everything you've ever wanted. Power, knowledge, weapons, riches. Death. Providence."

Salazar huffed and feigned a smile. "So you remember? Good. It's a shame, then, that you didn't bother to heed my advice." With his hand outstretched, Salazar pressed his thumb down on the detonator and ducked to shield his face against the blast. There was no sound, no explosion. When he turned around, Solomon stood, still striding forward, within a couple meters of him. Salazar tapped the button again and again but to no avail, no fireworks, no gushing volcano of blood from his captive, not the slightest impact. Dropping the detonator and then the flashlight, he held out his hands to block Solomon's shining brightness, which his eyes could no longer behold.

"Let me go through, Solomon, and we'll share in all I unlock. All the wealth that stems from my discoveries can be yours. We'll sell our work back to the military, and your little girls will live life as princesses."

"I thought you were a man of conviction, Sally. A man of vision."

"Sometimes, under the circumstances, compromises can be made. Can't they, Solomon?" he begged, shivering in the cold.

"No. No, they can't."

Salazar dropped to his knees and groveled at Solomon's feet. "Please. It's just so close. All of it. Lifetimes, nations of work— everything that we need and so much more. Wisdom. Clarity. Purpose. Forget about our past; you must think about the future! Please, Mr. Solomon, I'm begging you. I need this. I need this. This is all that's left of me. Give me this. Get out of my way!"

A clink echoed in the hall, the swing of a short chain in a long room. Looking down, Salazar spotted the pair of black shackles he was quite familiar with dangling from Solomon's open hand. With a smirk, Seek dropped them, and they landed with a clank at Salazar's feet.

"Try them on. They'll fit you well," he said, reaching back into his pocket.

"And if I don't?" Salazar snarled, building from pauperism to rage. Solomon flashed the light directly into Salazar's eyes, pushing the man back against the wall. When the colonel was on his feet and thoroughly blinded, Solomon put it away and pulled something else from his pocket—a long, sharp bone, a claw covered in blood, and held it to where he was certain Salazar would see it.

"There's room in the ditch for both of you."

Salazar tried to force a laugh but came up coughing. When he wiped his mouth with his hand, Solomon could see the small spatter of red that trickled down his thumb and stained the crisp, white granite floor. "You wouldn't. You couldn't. You're a family man. What would your girls think? You're not a killer."

"First Cledwyn," Solomon snapped. "Then the girl. Then Captain Foster. I have to say I didn't think it would be him. Or you. This will make an unbelievable story. 'Fugitive War Criminal recaptured by investigative journalist.' Or maybe you prefer the headlines read "Found Dead?"

Salazar ran his hands along the wall behind him, looking at the shaded visage of his nemesis and the very clear bloodstain on the cutting edge of the claw. Reluctantly, he reached down and grasped the cuffs, rolling his fingers over them and drawing rusted flakes under his fingernails. His breathing intensified as he slipped them over his wrists. No longer ducking from the light, Salazar's eyes blazed with hatred, his nostrils flaring, a gangly, malnourished skeleton standing not on two feet but floating to the top on an ocean of savagery. Solomon came in from the dark and clamped the chains shut, pulling Salazar's hands over his head in agony to test their restraints. Solomon brought the claw up to Salazar's exposed, pale varicose jugular. Squealing in pain, the colonel looked down at its serrated edge and the dried crimson thereon. Solomon smiled and retracted the blade, kicking Salazar out through the gap in the vault chamber door and onto the hard rock surface.

"It's my blood," he said, walking up behind his captive. "Get on your feet. I'm taking you back."

Solomon dragged and kicked Salazar over and over on the walk to the elevator and struggled to toss him inside. He pressed the lever and sent them up, watching Salazar closely for brash movements, keeping the flashlight fixed on him as he sat collapsed in the corner.

Solomon stayed his joy at watching Salazar climb back up the slippery ramp on all fours, his chains clanging on the cement. When they reached the hall, Solomon grabbed him by the back of his collar, leading him around the light fixtures and down the middle of the staircase into the lobby, making sure to avoid the guardrails. Looking up, he spotted a light he'd nearly forgotten, the sun, creeping through the opened blast door and into the lobby.

Metzger kept his promise.

At the bottom of the stairs, Liliana stood waiting for him, her pistol out and trained on Salazar. Solomon edged him down the stairs, watching as he fumbled and struggled to push aside the makeshift fortifications at the bottom of the steps. When she spotted him smiling down at her, Liliana lowered her weapon from Solomon's direction.

"He also needs a doctor."

Solomon followed Salazar down the stairs, picking him up again and tossing him against the lobby counter, then turned back to Liliana, whose weapon had remained trained on the shackled man.

"I've never actually seen him before," she said, trembling. Solomon stepped over and put his arm over her aim. She rested the weapon back in her belt and took hold of his hands.

"Are you all right?" he asked, exhausted.

"Yeah. Fine. The bullet's out. I'm fine."

Solomon nodded and stepped to the side. "Your friends are late," he scoffed. "Can you watch him?"

"Yes, of course," she said, puzzled, watching Solomon walk past her and toward the sunlight glistening through the front gate. "Where are you going?"

"It's been a week since I had a shower. I'm going for a swim," Solomon said, sliding his pack with his Kindle off and onto the floor beside the upturned table and fake four-petaled roses. He reached into his pockets and emptied them, scattering the broken hands-free receiver, a small can opener, a dried stick of boar meat, and a handful of bullets like garbage on the floor. Then he turned back. Liliana watched him intently as he walked to the counter, past her and behind Salazar, who stood silent with eyes fixed with menace.

Solomon paid him no heed, not even meeting his gaze. Instead, bending over Cledwyn's body, he pulled the last object from his pockets, a little silver coin, minted with an eagle standing over a laurel and holding the Swastika. Taking it in one hand and pulling Cledwyn's fingers from his neck to his lap, Solomon dropped the coin soundly within King's grasp. Liliana could see him mouth something to the dead man but was too far to hear just what. When he walked past her again, she stuttered.

"Is it over?"

Solomon didn't turn around. His eyes were fixed on the sun slowly dropping to the west out in front of him.

"Today it is," he muffled.

Solomon kept walking.

"What did you find?" Liliana yelled, her weapon trained on Salazar but her attention out the door, following Solomon.

"Another monster," he replied. "Another search."

Liliana turned around, contemplating his words as she stared down at the decrepit man in irons hunched against the counter between her gun sights.

Solomon stepped through the threshold of the Kapitalzukunft and trudged down the cobblestone hill of Karl Braun street toward the beach far in the distance. Feeling winded, his breathing rapid and heavy, Solomon ripped off his bloodstained and tattered shirt by the seams and tossed it on the broken-down Jeep as he limped by. He unzipped his Kevlar jacket and dropped it in the dirt. With his burdened and bruised chest to the sun, Solomon pushed on toward the white sandy beaches of San Magnus Island, and as the humming rotors of helicopters echoed overhead, he felt a great suction from within and surrendered, collapsing on the cobblestone.

August 20th, 2010, 0700 hours

The Soviet Union dissolved on this day twenty years ago. The Civil War ended on this day a hundred and fifty years ago. You were born on this day, today, and lay asleep in my arms. I've decided to dedicate this journal to you, baby Samantha, the most beautiful sight I've ever laid eyes on. This is everything I remember, everything I want to tell you, and it'll be waiting for you when you're ready for it, my little girl. My line and my blood. My legacy.

You were born with your mother's green eyes and my wrinkly dimples at five in the morning. Doctors said you couldn't wait to join us, not even for breakfast. You cried, for so long you cried, until I got you in my arms, rested you in my cradle, safe and dreaming of the future. I don't know. I guess all fathers think this. It's just a dad mentality, but when you sleep I just stare, and all I can think is how lucky I am to lead the life I've led. There isn't anything I wouldn't do to protect you, Samantha, tiny baby Samantha, my precious little girl.

Your mother says I dote on you too much, that it's possible to spoil a baby. You don't cry when I hold you, but when I put you down you wake right up, like something's wrong. That's fine, little girl, my little girl. I don't ever care to let you go. You can sleep soundly from this day on.

As of tomorrow I'm quitting the editorial desk. I've been pushed by a friend to take up something else, something braver and more noble, something necessary. Looking down at you slumbering so preciously, I know it's the right course to take. We're establishing a new desk, a renovation of the old, and will focus solely on corruption in our midst—corporate, government, military—with no retreat or stagnation in the search of truth. A world so dark cannot bear the likes of this girl so bright and beautiful. I will beat it back from you with the pen and the keystroke and without compromise. This is my promise, here for you and no other, that you will not grow up in the world of my grandmother, a little girl with no parents, hunted by monsters, thrown into cages and worked, tortured, butchered, or murdered. There will be no secret horrors. There will be no haunting dangers for you while I toil. I will seek them out. This world will be good enough for you, my beloved. This is your world.

Dad.

ABOUT THE AUTHOR

N.B. Goldzer is a third generation American, grandson of two Auschwitz survivors, and avid free-time historian. He holds a B.A in Creative Writing from Montclair State University in Montclair, NJ, is a native of Willimantic, CT and a dweller under the Wasatch Mountains of Salt Lake City with his beloved Jennifer. *Seek* is the first novel in his working trilogy (*The Suffering of Solomon*) surrounding Stephen Solomon and the secrets he unearths in the depths of San Magnus island.

www.ingramcontent.com/pod-product-compliance
Lightning Source LLC
Chambersburg PA
CBHW051249260626
47162CB00002B/680